Two Wo[rlds]
Fa[ce to Face]

"I am growing very tired of you, Dire-lord."

Brock stared through her in the Held manner of supreme indifference. "Then kill me, and put an end to your troubles, Colonel. I will tell you nothing about the godas. You waste your time."

"You persist in misunderstanding us," Falmah-Al replied. "We don't want to use the godas for war. The war is over. We will deactivate them, so they can never again be a threat to us."

"You *will* use them," Brock said flatly.

Falmah-Al smiled, her dark eyes glittering. "Very well. If you cannot bring yourself to trust us, then we must try other, less pleasant methods. Either way, Dire-lord, we shall have the godas . . ."

Ace Books by Jay D. Blakeney

THE OMCRI MATRIX
THE GODA WAR

THE GODA WAR

JAY D. BLAKENEY

ACE BOOKS, NEW YORK

This book is an Ace original edition,
and has never been previously published.

THE GODA WAR

An Ace Book/published by arrangement with
the author

PRINTING HISTORY
Ace edition/May 1989

ISBN: 0-441-28855-3

Ace Books are published by The Berkley Publishing Group,
200 Madison Avenue, New York, NY 10016.
The name ''ACE'' and the ''A'' logo are trademarks
belonging to Charter Communications, Inc.

PRINTED IN THE UNITED STATES OF AMERICA

10 9 8 7 6 5 4 3 2 1

In memory of my pal Ace . . .
Nullus amicus magis dilectus est.

THE IMPERIAL FLAGSHIP *Aruba* flamed across the twilightjade sky in a comet of coral and blue fire, a grim omen of defeat as it passed overhead in a low arc, following the sun spinning below the black horizon.

Crouched on one knee atop a sandy knoll overlooking the beleaguered capital city of Impryn, Dire-lord Brock bowed his head at this final sighting of the ship he had been aboard only minutes before. His fingers dug into the loose earth and were pricked by sharp burrs. He welcomed the pain, so tiny beneath the greater agonies. Reality . . . had he truly managed to *flick* so far? Gingerly he pressed the center of his armor corselet. His atrox had never ached like this before. He must have strained it in *flicking* all the way down to the planet surface with the suprin in tow.

He drew in a deep breath, trying to clear his nostrils of the stench of burned flesh and clothing, and winced, crossing both arms over his chest. Even the thumping of his heart, still racing from that desperate split-second escape as the bridge of the *Aruba* exploded into a fiery inferno, jolted his atrox mercilessly. He sank lower with a groan, fighting down fear of serious internal damage while he used the Disciplines to push back the pain. Had a Sedkethran ever *flicked* four hundred thousand kilomyls before? Of course the great, noncorporeal mystics could. But he was no mystic. He was only an outcast to his own people's philosophy.

A distant staccato of disruptor fire, alien to his ears, and the replying rattle of heavy strifers jerked him around. He stared down into the broad valley of the slow-winding Marupish River where the capital city of Impryn sprawled. Cannon set on wide dispersal flared green and scarlet in random flashes across the night sky, momentarily illuminating buildings and transender towers like a malfunctioning video freezing one frame after another in a disjointed pattern upon its screen. Ground jets screamed through the air, either intercepting Colonid drop bombs aimed at the city's force shields, or exploding from collision with deadly sensor missiles. A drop bomb got through the defense grids, and blue electricity crackled for hundreds of myls across the central area of Impryn. City lights abruptly went dark except at the farthest perimeters. Brock straightened to his feet, forgetting the need to stay low as he watched in despair.

Come back up, he pleaded silently, torn between his duty to tend the suprin and his desire to be down there in the beleaguered city, helping.

Power flickered back on in erratic patterns, but the central area remained dark. The palace was now defenseless unless ground shock troops could hold it.

But how could they? Beyond a few ancient fighting techniques used primarily for traditional ceremonies, elite Chaimu warriors concentrated their entire training upon space maneuvers. Primary imperial defense systems were designed to rebuff anyone foolish enough to attack a Held planet, with the Heldfleet then swooping in to finish off the attack. Chaimu considered it an insult to fight upon the ground. They thought only of space and of parsectal tactics. Yet here were the Colonids—barbaric castoffs of the old-humans. They had come blasting through every defense system with suicidal boldness and were already installed upon Darjahl Imperial, landing all sorts of armored land crawlers that were battering steady inroads through outmoded and long-unused city defense points.

Brock cast a look up at the dark sky. The stars were blanked from sight by thick clouds. The air was close and heavy from the threat of a storm. The stench of strifer discharge and nust gas rolled up from the valley, intensified by the humidity and warmth of the night. How was the Heldfleet doing up there beyond the atmosphere? Were they holding? Or had Esmir Eondal lost heart at the destruction of the suprin's own ship and ordered surrender? Did they think the suprin dead?

Reaching for his communicator, Brock found only a melted lump fused to the flank of his corselet. His charge armor had saved his life, but only just. He touched the split running between his left shoulder and chest. His left arm was burned badly, making movement difficult. But his injury was nothing in comparison to the suprin's. In his mind's eye Brock stood again on the bridge of the flagship *Aruba*, his body fired by the rush of adrenaline, every trained muscle poised to strike, every sense straining to concentrate over the distractions of orders in Battlespeak lashing back and forth, the screaming of the injured, the fear, anger, and desperation, and most of all the disbelief that this could be happening to Heldfleet's finest as ship after ship fell from formation, dragging half-severed pylons crackling with escaping radiation like birds trying piteously to fly with broken wings or with side bulkheads gaping open like burst fruit spilling out tiny crewmen bodies into the cold grave of space. Brock had been standing directly behind navigations, keeping one eye constantly upon the suprin, the other upon the tactical screens, his mind filtering all the incoming reports from various parts of the ship just as the modore was doing at his station beside the suprin, who was speaking into a separate communications link to the sub-esmirs on the upper bridge. They, in turn, were linked to Esmir Eondal's heavy cruiser on the port side.

When in the forward line the battlecruiser *Ramsa* had blown, her bridge shattering and her port engines exploding so that she careened into the next ship, there had been no choice but for the *Aruba* to move from her protected position to help plug up the gap.

Modore Istan paused in the midst of a rapid-fire chain of orders to the weapons stations and glanced at the suprin. "The Superior Life must clear the bridge. The center of the ship—"

"Fore shields, brace!" shouted someone. "R-level blast direct on in three seconds."

Brock whirled from his place, already moving toward the suprin. The *Aruba*'s only chance of survival from an R-level blast was to maneuver enough to deflect the worst of it off her flank shields. But in this formation the ships were too tightly bunched to move with sufficient independence. None could sustain such a blast, not on fore shields.

Brock could move faster than any creature alive. He could

move faster than time itself. But there were only three seconds, and it took three seconds to reach the suprin . . . .

Now, standing there upon the crest of the hill, Brock clenched his fists, feeling again the concussion of the blast that tumbled bodies into exploding instrumentation, feeling again the sharp ache as space sucked the air from his lungs, feeling the scorch of fire and his own sick despair as he was knocked back, the suprin exposed on top of him to take the brunt as the upper bridge collapsed onto the lower. A dire-lord was supposed to die for his suprin, not the other way around. He had *flicked* too late, too late, too late!

Brock coughed, and lifted a hand to rub his face as though by doing so he could erase the guilt. He had been afraid to *flick* so far, and that fear might have cost the suprin his life. Brock had learned how to live with his own people's rejection in order to serve the suprin. But how would he live with his failure to save the suprin whom he had sacrificed everything for?

The *phut-phut* of Colonid weaponry started up again, sounding much closer. He would have to alter position soon, but if he moved much farther from the city's edge he was likely to run into a nest of Colonid outbases. He bared his teeth, running a series of decisions through his mind. This was no safe place. If he could get the suprin to the underground bunkers networked beneath Impryn . . .

Another ship entered Darjahl Imperial's atmosphere, its configuration hidden in a trail of crimson and black. It roared overhead, too close, too *close*! There was a highpitched scream like that from a dying animal, and then a mighty explosion rocked the world, filling the night sky with a ball of flame, and flinging Brock flat to the ground. He lay there stunned with his face buried in the coarse sand, aching with shame. It was the end of Held, the enormous Chaimu empire that had stretched across the galaxy. How could it be happening?

"Dire-lord."

That hoarse whisper reached through the ringing in Brock's ears. He shook himself, stiffening his arms to support him as he levered up.

"Suprin?" he answered, coughing as he reinforced the Disciplines holding down the pain of his wounds. He scrambled across the sand to where the suprin lay propped up

4

within the slash of a shallow gully and reached out his hand for the suprin's jaw to put him back in a light trance.

The suprin's seared, bloody fingers caught his and held them. "No," he whispered, his agony seeping across Brock's empathy threshold. "The ship. My fleet. What . . ."

"The *Aruba* has been destroyed," said Brock, straining to draw more of the suprin's pain into himself. "I have no word concerning the rest of the battle."

"Call them!"

Brock hesitated a moment, reluctant to answer. "It is not possible. My communicator is destroyed."

The suprin's blackened face was increasingly visible as, to the north, a vast ball of flame from the crash spread toward the sky. A jut of sharply ridged nose and jaw stood out against the leaping shadows. Red gleamed faintly as the suprin's eyes moved, searching for Brock's face.

"Use your mind, dire-lord. Use whatever you have to contact the esmir!" A spasm of coughing wracked him.

Brock tightened his clasp, drawing the pain into himself as he willed the suprin to live. The life force seemed to be fading with every ragged breath, and yet the suprin fought. His fingers crooked around Brock's burned arm, causing Brock to wince sharply.

"They must know, Dire-lord. Tell them—" Another spasm shook the suprin.

Brock held onto him desperately, seeking to keep him alive by sheer willpower. How he longed now for one of his own kind, a Sedkethran healer who, with a touch, could erase the suprin's agony. Brock's mind leapt out, seeking one who might be in the city. But he encountered no spark of an answer. Sedkethrans rarely visited Darjahl Imperial; they never stayed. His own mental loneliness, so horrible an exile at first, so commonplace to him now, echoed around him.

As for obeying the suprin's order, it was impossible. The suprin was growing so weak, Brock did not dare release contact with him, and to touch another mind such as Esmir Eondal's would be to flood it with the suprin's pain. He could not do such a thing to a non-Sedkethran, certainly not in the heat of a battle.

"Nairin . . ." whispered the suprin, his voice a ghastly rattle in his throat. "My son . . ."

Brock bowed his head, grieving for the man he had served so many years with love and respect. For Suprin Utdi he had

5

defied his own heritage, his own race, and the Elder Council of Felca. He had endured a terrible exile in order to serve Utdi the Great. A Sedkethran was not permitted to love, and yet Brock had loved . . . like a son loves his father, like a servant loves his kind master. He had been both son and slave to Utdi. He had been more. He had been Utdi's shield, more relied upon than any technological marvel of protection from assassination. And that had created its own bond. Yet, in the end, at the most crucial moment he had failed the suprin. The swirled scar Brock wore on his right cheek, marking his position as bodyguard to the Held Suprin, seemed to burn anew through his flesh.

What else could he do? He was helpless. The suprin was dying, slipping away with each harsh breath. The injuries were too severe for Brock's minor empathic abilities to salvage. He could do nothing more. He wasn't a healer. He had spurned that training, revered most upon Felca, in favor of the arts of war. He had learned to kill rather than to save lives. Without the proper training, he might easily die in trying to do more.

Yet, what good was a dire-lord without a suprin to protect?

Brock concentrated, feeling the slight pain in his atrox as he started to drift, and ignored it as he lowered his own thresholds to merge with the suprin. There was the sharp flinch from feeling the suprin's terrible wounds, and Brock had to battle his own instincts of survival in order not to draw back. He went deeper into the pain and began to shake not only from those raw, bloody burns but also from the inner assaults of the suprin's system. He felt the twisting influence of *skial*, the metered drug the suprin took to elude age. Fear seized him. No Sedkethran permitted any foreign substance into his system, especially pleasure drugs, which could render his natural abilities erratic and uncontrollable. Brock did not know the techniques of protecting himself. But it was too late to draw back now. There was a shudder in his chest as though his damaged atrox could not handle the demands of healing another as well as himself.

Suddenly everything within him seemed to be draining away. Brock snapped contact, his hands thrusting him physically away from the suprin's tortured body. Brock fell to the ground, still convulsed with the suprin's pain. For a moment he knew nothing but agony flooding him in a red wash of intensity. Then his mind seemed to separate from his body,

6

and he was floating, his thoughts kicking themselves into minute fragments without cohesion.

The *skial*! What was it doing to him? The link! How could he break it? He was still too close!

He *flicked* rapidly without pattern or purpose, unable to stop himself, terrified in some distant corner of consciousness that he would rematerialize in a solid object. Time whirled about him, out of control. He felt his atrox swelling, bursting, and he seemed to be flung completely off the planet before he was snapped back like a toy on a string.

Brock opened his eyes, coming back to an awareness of reality. He was struck by how hot it had become, as though he stood in the midst of an inferno. There was a loud roaring all around him. His eyes were dazzled, unable to register anything save an intense red.

Fire! The fire from the crash. It must have spread to this knoll during the time he had been unconscious.

He blinked, lifting an arm to shield his face from the intense heat. He was dazed, unable to get his bearings. Then urgency grabbed him. He must get out!

With a cry he rolled, going over and over, and then scrambled back across sand and burrweeds to where the suprin lay slumped in the gully. The flames, fed by dry sandgrass and the low-growing scrub trees dotting the hills surrounding the city, grew higher and higher around him. Grimacing against the heat that now seemed to be peeling the flesh from his face, Brock gathered the suprin's body in his arms and stood up. In doing so, he felt again a sharp burst within his atrox, and he went cold all over inside.

"Please!" he whispered, unable to draw a breath. "Once more." And he *flicked* just as the flames reached out hungrily for their prey.

TINY RIVULETS OF consciousness seeped slowly through him. He became aware of sound far away, big booming muffled noises that shook the earth beneath him. He became aware of being cold, blissfully cold, and that coldness soothed him for it meant that he had escaped the fire.

Brock opened his eyes. He was lying on his stomach in the dark. A pebble under his right cheekbone was cutting into his flesh. He frowned and tried to move his head. It seemed to weigh five times more than usual. He dislodged the pebble, then rested for a while before he rolled over onto his right side. Each movement exhausted him. He could not remember being this weak since childhood on Felca when the magstrusi had starved him into learning the Disciplines.

Sitting up seemed impossible. He finally managed it by degrees, levering himself up onto his elbow, then gradually stiffening his arm until at last he was up, quivering with fatigue, and feeling as though a giant pair of hands had twisted him in half. At least it was cold, wonderfully cold. He reveled in the low temperature, his senses bathing in the cool damp air. He was very stiff. He must have been here a long time.

How long?

Memories came swarming back. The fire! The suprin!

Brock jerked to his feet, only to stagger, gasping and doubling over with his fists pressed to his chest. He sank down to his knees, helpless for a long while.

8

His atrox, he remembered dimly, trying to let himself float away from the pain. He had damaged it, possibly ruptured it in that last attempt to *flick* the suprin to the safety of the underground bunkers. Obviously he had made it, but where was the suprin?

As the agony faded to a bearable degree, he slowly straightened and climbed back to his feet. Putting an unsteady hand to his brow, he began to search mentally for the suprin. He found a feeble spark of response a short distance away.

It took an eternity to walk there in the darkness. Each step required all his strength and concentration. The booming, which had ceased for a while, resumed. It was louder, closer. The walls and floor shook, making him stumble. A little splatter of dust rained down upon his shoulder. He paused in the darkness, uncertain of his bearings, blind except for his higher senses.

"Dire-lord?" came the suprin's hoarse whisper. "Is that you?"

There was death in the suprin's voice. He had lived this long perhaps because of Brock's attempt to help him, but his time was ending. Brock groped his way carefully to the suprin's side and sagged to his knees with a sigh. Exhaustion washed over him, but he pushed it back as he reached out to clasp the suprin's hand.

Immense age and weariness surged across the empathy threshold. Immediately they were one, bonded by earlier pain, held together now by the strength of their own wills.

"You must not die," said Brock. "The Held cannot continue without you."

"It is time," breathed the suprin. "Help me."

"I am not a healer. My skills are—"

"Do not evade me. You know what I ask."

Brock lifted his head and let his clasp fall from the suprin's. Yes, he knew. Thoughts flew faster than words. The suprin's wish had leapt into him at the first touch. Brock closed his eyes. He had been exiled for becoming what he was now. If he did as the suprin asked, the Sedkethrans would surely kill him.

"Many of my sons tried to betray me over the years," whispered the suprin. "None of them succeeded. I have eaten much *skial* in order to live until someone worthy could follow me. Tregher is my last son."

"He betrayed you too," said Brock, feeling the suprin's grief.

"Worse!" The suprin grunted a Chaimu oath with some of his old vehemence, then fell into a violent bout of coughing. "Betrayed . . . all of us. Betrayed the throne . . . just to . . . save himself. Betrayed the . . . Held. I cannot forgive him."

"No." Brock bowed his head, his own anger swelling through him. The Held, as old and corrupt as it was, still permitted the greatest freedoms to an individual. Anyone could reach for what he wanted. No one cared if he laughed, or cried, or sang. No one sneered at emotion. No one sneered at the most remote meditations. To be Held was to be free, unfettered by prejudice and repression. Of course that freedom permitted gross injustices to occur. But were any of the evils committed as bad as those of prohibition and restriction? Brock's own race lived in the shadows of its own doubting. To feel was to be a fool. To care emotionally for anyone or anything was to be wasteful. All was hidden, folded away within layers upon layers of quiet solitude. Such restrictions had logical origins; they were designed to keep self away from patient, to make self a perfect receptor to draw out the illness without sharing or intruding upon the patient's psyche. But to force such inner denial upon all was wrong. It had to be wrong.

And the Colonids, those brawling, savage old-humans who could think of nothing save destroying the Held and all it stood for, nurtured a hatred based on ancient injustices and resentment at being flung out of the Held centuries ago. Old-humans had been too primitive, too erratic to fit comfortably within the Held. Kicking them out had not improved them, however. They had forced themselves to evolve into higher abilities out of no greater desire than revenge. And it was a blind motive. Brock had heard the spy reports. He knew of their rigid militaristic societies, of how everyone was geared from birth toward the single aim of destroying the Held. He knew of how they scorned anything which was designed for pleasure rather than utility, of how they preferred to destroy something unfamiliar rather than try to understand it. To live under their reign of terror would be as bad if not worse than to live on Felca.

Brock tightened his hand into a fist, thinking of how he had first learned to take life, to kill, not just to defend but to

10

attack. Those had been the first dark days of a life spent in shadow. He could not go back, even if he still wished.

"You cannot let the Colonids succeed, Brock," said the suprin. "I am very old. I have lived a careless life. I looked the other way at the corruption in Heldfleet. I wanted only to laugh and play, just like all my honorables. But my mistakes do not mean I loved the Held less. You think of it as I do. Keep it, Brock. Fight for it!" He sighed, his voice thinning to a faint thread. "In my place."

Brock swallowed. The air seemed to be choked from him. "I am not Chaimu," he whispered. "Who will follow me?"

The suprin's hand found his in the darkness. The blood had dried on the scar-ridged fingers, making them rough and cold. "You are Held," he whispered. "Those who are . . . Held . . . will. Brock, receive the Superior Life."

He tried to lift Brock's hand but was too weak. Brock himself placed his fingertips upon the heavy ridges of the suprin's skull. He closed his eyes, opening his mind.

Utdi's mind met his sharply. The images burned their way in: inventories of Held treasures, loving words for favored *dalmas* and children, the faces of trusted friends and of enemies, the oinrth serpent which never left Nairin Tregher's arm, the laws of the honorables, the sacred recital to Meir— supreme Chaimu deity—and last of all, the all-important codes to the goda weapons.

A sharp tug followed by the vicious sucking of a void made Brock pull back, snapping the link that had nearly pulled him down into eternity. He moved himself a pace away from the suprin's body, afraid to touch it until all vestiges of spirit and soul were truly gone, and painfully bowed himself low until his forehead touched the floor. Grief, silent and keen, filled him, but he could do nothing except crouch there. The Sedkethrans had no way to express sorrow. They could not weep at the eyes like the humans; they could not scream from the soul like the gentle Slathese; they could not wail the death chants of the Chaimu. To feel such grief was forbidden. There was no physical means of release, no way to show honor to the suprin.

No way . . . except to fulfill the request of the Superior Life.

Drawing in a deep breath, Brock raised himself up.

"I will not let the Held die with you, Utdi," he vowed. "I will *not*!"

Carefully he bent over the dead suprin, arranging the black-ened limbs according to the formal Chaimu Rites of Eternity. On his hands and knees he crawled about the floor of the unlit bunker, using his palms to scrape dust together into a small pile. This was then sprinkled over the suprin's face.

Brock paused. He must leave soon. He must find another place of safety where he could tend to his own needs of rest and healing. He must also find the sectors of Impryn still protected by Held warriors.

The muffled sounds of battle overhead vibrated through the bunker, raining more dust down upon him. Brock looked up, fearing the seepage of nust gas down to his level. It was time to go. He drew in an unsteady breath, seeking courage. His fingers unbuckled the wrist bands of the suprin's armor and took the heavy corybdium bracelet that signified ultimate power. It had been bonded to the suprin's own mental pattern; it could not be removed unless one possessed the specific code awarded upon the passage of the Superior Life. With difficulty, Brock clamped it upon his own wrist. It was too large and slid on his arm, chafing the burns. He grimaced, holding himself still until the new bonding was complete. There remained one last thing to do.

Slowly he drew the ceremonial dagger from its jeweled sheath and laid it across his palm. He could not see it there in the darkness, but he did not have to. He had seen its golden brilliance flash a thousand times uplifted in the sun or wink-ing steadily at the suprin's side. The curled hilt which fitted so perfectly into a Chaimu palm and felt so alien upon his own was studded with gwirleyes, purple jewels renowned throughout the galaxy for their incomparable brilliance and rarity. The grooved blade was fashioned from bard crystal, glittering and thin, its molecular structure so unique it re-fracted light into color spectrums revealed in no other man-ner. If swung swiftly enough through the air, the blade would sing in a piercing note capable of shattering ordinary glass. Abruptly his hand closed on it. He drew his own plain dagger from its sheath and placed it in the suprin's stiffening hand, pressing on the finger ridges to extend the vestigial claws. The ceremonial dagger went to its new place at his side. Brock got to his feet. He had performed the ritual acts. Anyone who now came upon the corpse would know at a glance that the suprinship had been properly passed on to a named successor.

The Held continued!

He swung aloft his right arm, crashing it into his aching left shoulder in a final salute to the man he honored, and left Utdi lying in the cold darkness.

COLONEL KEZI FALMAH-AL paced slowly around the circumference of the battle room, listening to Governor Nls Ton receiving his final briefing from the nine fleet commanders sitting around the vast table of black malachite. The gold and scarlet of their collar braid reflected off the table's gleaming surface.

She did not like the battle room with its broad expanse of windows. Even the floor was transparent to give the illusion of being suspended totally in space. A useless achievement, this new need growing within her culture to create illusions. All around her lay the void, a limitless black vacuum that sucked at her vision. The stars blinded her. Some glowed red like feral eyes attracted to a desert fire. Blue giants as big as coins yet millions of miles away dwarfed the little ones twinkling white or glittering yellow. There was the aqua of Darjahl Imperial's sister planet shimmering like a distant jewel, and the grey deadness of Darjahl Imperial's twin moons hanging in orbit as stony witnesses to the death of an empire. Falmah-Al grimaced, resuming her pacing. She felt as though at any moment a misstep would send her plunging forever into the black throat of space.

What am I doing here? she wondered, prowling around the room once again as Lt. Izak droned on with statistics of ground casualties and damage to city structures. *What induced me to take this godless assignment of protecting Ton?*

Until now she had been too busy to permit the questions to boil up inside her. There had been all the excitement of battle, the intense hours of planning strategy and of directing her security staff. She had been caught up in a united rush of adrenaline, eager to succeed in finally achieving the dream her people had striven toward for centuries. But now, swift upon the heels of this ultimate victory, the doubts came rushing upon her.

What insanity had driven her back into Ton's circle? What was she trying to prove? That she could ignore the past as though it had never been? The emotions remained a knife thrust under the ribs. Would she never forget? They were no longer partners, no longer lovers, no longer serving side by side as in the early days when they were both junior lieutenants assigned to death squads assaulting the out-worlds of the Held. The union was over, bitterly ended in a series of worsening quarrels that replayed endlessly in her dreams at night, words still cutting wounds that refused to heal. For a few years the solution had been to avoid him, to take brutal assignments that kept her far away from Kentra while he spiraled higher into governmental authority. She, limited by her own rage, which had sent her down this career path of assassinations and poison sniffings, had finally been offered the plum—the chance to be security chief to the governor of the conquered Darjahl Imperial. She had accepted at once, only to find out afterwards who the governor would be. Ton, who pretended they had never known each other and had never shared a life together at any time, did not dispute the appointment. Pride kept her from backing out of it. She intended to prove that she was still his match. She could do her job. *Besides*, she thought half-ruefully, *if anyone ever does stick a dagger in his back, it will be me and no one else.*

Lt. Izak's recital faltered a moment. The governor glanced up in swift annoyance. His face was stern and blocky about the jaw, the kind of face that would become fleshy and harsh in old age. Ton was famous for his leaps of judgment and insight which made him a skilled negotiator and diplomat, but those skills never extended into his personal life. He was courted and flattered but not liked. *But I loved him once*, she thought, watching him as he gestured at the sweating Izak, now hastily consulting his notes. *Gazal help me, it was so long ago.*

Clearing his throat, Izak managed to resume.

Falmah-Al's strategy, as always, was flawless. It had been

her idea to destroy the breeder planet Mabruk last year instead of letting the fleet sweep on in at that time to attack Darjahl Imperial. Other military strategists had protested, arguing that such a merciless attack against children would rouse the Chaimu into an invincible fury. She had convinced them that a race which no longer bore children from their own bodies would lose rather than gain courage from such a blow. She had borne two children of her own, both of whom had died during her own agony to give them life. She knew the difference. She had judged the honorables' reaction correctly. Spies had relayed accounts of the mourning entered by whole sections of Chaimu society. And as the fall-out from Mabruk began to filter through the atmosphere of Darjahl Imperial, the suprin himself had spoken publicly, saying, "We breathe the ashes of our own children." The Chaimu honorables, shackled by intense dynastic traditions, had fled to Darjahl Imperial for refuge, abandoning their huge estates on the mid-worlds, and bringing their treasures with them for safe-keeping in the imperial treasuries. They launched no concerted retaliation and had simply waited until now, depending upon their outmoded planetary defense systems to protect them from annihilation.

Falmah-Al had also correctly read the character of the heir to the throne, and her agents had succeeded in persuading the nairin to give Imish forces the defense keys to Darjahl Imperial in exchange for a guarantee of his safety when the capital fell. It had been these two great successes gained from her suggestions which had won her this appointment.

Governor Ton had not been permitted within range of the final battles. His ship had come in only after news of the victory had been transmitted. As chief of security on Darjahl Imperial, renamed Baz I on Imish charts, it had been her duty to oversee the mopping-up efforts of Major Millen, the half-breed mercenary who commanded the planetside assaults. She had divided the city Impryn into sectors, and her crews had swept clean the buildings chosen by the governor and his staff for their private and official use. The Chaimu honorables were reputed to enjoy intrigue, using Fet assassins as private bodyguards and countless poisons to eliminate their feud enemies. Death devices had to be searched for continuously. Throughout the city there were still nests of resistance, but most of the population was quiet, stricken with shock, and giving no trouble. She kept troops visibly armed and out on frequent patrol through the rubble-strewn streets. For the moment, control was at a satisfactory level. There was only this final meeting to go through before the Imish fleet withdrew to patrol more troublesome areas of the dead empire. One ship would remain as backup to Ton's ground troops. There was, after all, the rest of this planet to clean out.

Izak finished droning and nervously shuffled his documents.

"Colonel?" prompted the governor without looking her way. "I am sure you have a lot of ground to cover."

Inclining her head, she hid her scorn of his patronizing tone while more than one of the fleet commanders shifted restively. Her eyes stabbed at Izak, who again consulted his notes and began the series of statements she had prepared.

"Troop deployment has been spread evenly through Sectors Four through Seven. Concentration has been stepped up along city perimeters." Izak cleared his throat. "Heavy usage of nust gas has poisoned the river. Water supplies are being rationed. Approximately five thousand Chaimu honorables and their families took refuge in the palace. They are being held until appropriate labor quota requests are issued. Other races currently imprisoned have not yet been inventoried."

Falmah-Al resumed her pacing, like a sand tigress behind the backs of the fleet commanders. Her movements made them uneasy, and that's how she wanted it. She saw Ton's eyes move in her direction and felt as though she had scored a triumph. *Our bodies mature*, she thought, angered by her own emotions, *but inside we remain children.*

"What," asked the deputy of one of commanders, "about these scattered nests of resistance? Are they all being eradicated with bombings of nust gas, or are prisoners being taken for interrogation?"

Izak's eyes sought Falmah-Al's. She gave her head an imperceptible shake.

Another deputy, prompted by his commander, leaned forward. "We know the Held has doomsday weapons scattered throughout the galaxy. Those locations must be found before rebel factions can trigger them!"

"Naturally this is a priority effort," said Izak smoothly, his eyes still upon her for his cues.

"Can you even guarantee that the suprin is dead?" demanded another. "His ship was destroyed, but he may have escaped the crash."

"We are certain that—"

"Certain! How?" snorted Commander Daggio, impatiently breaking etiquette to speak for himself. "Eondal got away. The suprin did too. The Chaimu are canny bastards—"

"It has been six days since victory," said Izak, sweating now. "He would have surfaced—"

"A hope, nothing more." Daggio threw himself back in his chair.

"It will soon be substantiated by a valid report, Commander," said Ton with a frown. "Besides, we do have the heir . . . what is he called?"

Ton was looking at her as he spoke. Too experienced to fall into the trap of answering him directly at a high-level meeting, Falmah-Al snapped her fingers at Izak, who shuffled hastily through his flimsies and said, "The nairin's name is Tregher."

"Yes," said Ton in displeasure, drawling the word. "He will be the central figure of any resistance efforts. And I am sure the colonel has contingency plans concerning his future."

"It's all loose, Governor. Far too loose," said Daggio. "I don't like the situation. The fleet should stay here—"

"We are ordered out in three hours," said another commander, stung into protest. "For valid reasons. We can't hold up the entire fleet here. Sala's cruiser will be sufficient."

Falmah-Al twisted her gloves in her hands as her gaze swept away from their faces to the yellow and green lights winking in complex patterns upon the instrumentation banks forming a narrow band between windows and floor. Everything else around her was black: the metal grids supporting the glastel, the chairs, the tables, the uniforms, space itself. Only the braid of rank, the winking lights, the gleam of hooded eyes, and the stars themselves showed color. And color was truth. Tired of meetings and arguments, she could not wait to plant her feet back on the ravaged earth of Darjahl Imperial.

A soft beep in the communications module fitted unobtrusively in her ear made her step falter for a second before she resumed her slow pacing. Falmah-Al clenched her jaw so that the tightened muscles activated a response.

"Millen here," said the major. "We've found the suprin's body hidden in an underground tunnel network. Dead for several days. Barkey's examining the corpse now. There are . . . complications. Request your attention first possible opportunity."

18

She clenched her jaw in acknowledgment, holding down the excited urge to pull out her communicator and question him thoroughly.

"Right," he said. "Millen out."

She swung back to the men assembled in the battle room. The meeting was over; they were rising. The deputies snapped to attention. Falmah-Al stood quietly, deciding not to share her news just yet. The years had taught her the value of caution over a momentary grab for glory. Millen had said there were complications. She would evaluate them before she made any official statements.

The shuttle flight down to the planet's surface took two hours. Lt. Izak, his stiff collar still betraying a stain of dampness from the report presentation, sat across from her, busily shuffling flimsies before her with rapid-fire summaries of their contents. She could read as fast as he could talk; she never let him forget it.

"The cargo bays are on standby, Colonel. Your low priority interrogation equipment will be dropped as soon as you authorize this release form. Er, the palace itself has sustained some damage but the smoke is being sucked out now, and the undersecretary has submitted it might be used for better things than holding prisoners—"

"Let it burn," she broke in. "We are establishing a new order of life for the Chaimu. We will not adopt their soft ways."

Izak sighed and ripped the flimsy in half. He replaced it with two others. "There is an office building directly across from the palace which the governor wants to use for a similar purpose. However, the initial sweeping was inadequate. A junior staff deputy was injured this morning from a device attack."

"I'll send in another team to take care of that. Keep the building evacuated until it's re-guaranteed."

As Izak nodded, making a swift notation, she pressed a switch. The map screen near her seat lit softly, showing Impryn cut into arbitrary sectors and gridded already according to her specifications. She punched in an overlay of the tunnel network. The suprin had been found in Sector One. Too close to the governor's newly established headquarters. The correlation made her uneasy. How many exits and entrances to the tunnels were there? How easy was access? How easy was infiltration?

She frowned. She meant to keep a tight lid on this city and refused to be awed by its tremendous size. "This amphitheatre here." She pointed at a dot on the screen less than a radiam from the palace, governmental complexes, and the embassies where the governor and his staff were now living. "Destroy it. Shut off the other buildings directly around it. Gas them to make sure they are empty, but burn that amphitheatre first. We are not here to enjoy ourselves."

Izak ducked his head and looked at her from beneath his thin black brows. This habit made him seem both timid and sly. He was too ambitious to make his loyalty unimpeachable. Ton seemed to trust him, but she was far from being in the governor's confidence. She meant to keep a close eye on this deputy and appoint one of her own as soon as possible.

"The public buildings of Impryn are famous even to us, Colonel," he said in soft protest. "Chaimu architecture is stunning, surely a universal treasure. Wouldn't preservation be a better—"

"We are not here to preserve the sites of Chaimu atrocities!" She slammed her rank signet into the pressure sensitive corner of the flimsy authorizing her equipment to be unloaded. The mark of her crest gleamed a momentary blue against the yellowish tint of the flimsy, then faded to white. "You have your orders, Lieutenant. Anything else?"

He jumped to whisk things away and opened a second document case. She glanced out the port. They were in atmosphere, descending through fat clouds tinged with sun's gold on top and rain's black on the bottom. It did not rain on her homeworld. She turned her face away from the view.

"This," said Izak warily, "is a request for your prompt inspection of the royal prisoners collected thus far."

"How many?"

"Approximately two hundred, mostly females and children, and a collection of, er, of creatures."

She looked at him sharply. "Explain. Pets?"

"No, Colonel. Mature Chaimu males, royals but—"

"Ah!" She sucked in her breath, recalling a spy report. "The Gwilwans. Royal male Chaimu who are not in line for succession are not executed but are instead neurologically altered at birth so that they develop the physical vestiges normally bred out of their race. They are reputed to be quite colorful in appearance. I believe they are trained to hunt down and eat humans in the game arenas.'' Her eyes narrowed on Izak, who had paled. "Your precious amphitheatre, I believe. Have them killed.''

"Yes, Colonel.'' He made a notation of the order with alacrity. "Then there is yet another complaint from the nairin and his party.''

She smiled, wondering how the nairin would react to the news of his parent's death. She glanced forward, where the governor and his administrators sat in a small conference of their own. How long dared she wait before she informed Ton of the discovery?

Falmah-Al grimaced, impatient to be on the ground. "What else, Izak?''

"A request from the nairin to meet with you.''

"With me?'' Her brows shot up. "I thought he had been clamouring for Ton.''

"After several denials I am sure, Colonel, that he thinks you may be more receptive to his demands.''

"I am too busy to spare time for traitors,'' she snapped. "Let him wait. If the governor has no immediate instructions for my attention, I will be occupied in the field for the rest of the afternoon. Inform my office, please.''

A warning light from the pilot blinked on overhead. She reached for the safety restraints as Izak began filing away his documents.

The landing was featherlight on a pad cleared and marked in the rubble of a broad street carving a winding path between towering buildings. Falmah-Al closed the port shutters and drew her disruptor. On her way to the hatch, she paused to peer into the crowded cockpit.

"Perfect, Molaud,'' she said, clapping the man on the shoulder that had been blown away years ago in her service and had been replaced with metal and bionic nerve fusions. He was the only pilot she trusted. "Raw meat to your table.''

"*Alamam*, Colonel,'' he responded in the traditional way, grinning at the compliment, and handed her a head-set.

She spoke into it briefly, nodding at the affirmative answer. The outside was clear. She handed the head-set back to Molaud, lifting her thumb. He cut off the hatch lock.

The hatch sprang open with a faint hiss, and she waved the lesser staff members through first. Ton stood back, impatient but docile enough with standard procedure. His hair, silvered

21

but still thick, gleamed under the dim interior lights. His pale blue eyes watched her without expression. When she glanced back at him, however, he did not immediately fall into step behind her.

"You've received information, haven't you?" he said. "You're on the scent of something. I can tell by the way your eyes are glowing."

Falmah-Al put her back to the open hatchway, unable to suppress a grimace of impatience as she faced him. It was the first time in the entire campaign that he had made any attempt to speak to her beyond the necessary requirements, and all she wanted to do was get out and find Millen.

"My report will be on your desk soon," she said.

"Don't be so damned secretive!" he exclaimed. "I am supposed to be on top of everything here. If you're going to start undermining my position by setting up your own factions, then you can ship out with the fleet right now."

"Threats are unnecessary," she retorted, angered by his insecurities. "I am being cautious, not secretive. The suprin's death has been confirmed—"

"When? During the meeting? *Gazal*!" Ton threw his arms up in the air. "Why didn't you say something? All that those men wanted was confirmation. We could have saved ourselves an hour of arguing and speculation."

"Not while there are complications," she said. "I'm going now to check out the situation and receive Millen's full report. Until then I don't think it wise to shout the news from the rooftops."

They glared at each other for a long moment. Finally Ton snorted and dropped his eyes.

"All right. All right," he said irritably. "But I want your behavior modified, Colonel. Do you understand? We are on the same team here. There's no room for personal conflicts."

She stiffened. "I am not offering any. I am doing my job properly and efficiently. If *you* cannot trust my judgment—"

He cut her off with an oath. "This is a pointless conversation. I should have known you couldn't keep personal feelings out of your work. Get on with it, Colonel. I'll expect a full report in my office the moment you feel you can present yourself. It's about time this matter was cleared up. We need to be concentrating on finding the records that will show us where those doomsday weapons are located."

Furious, Falmah-Al opened her mouth, but managed to hold back the unwise words. What a pompous paranoid!

Unable to stay inside the shuttle with him another moment, she snapped up her disruptor to a ready position and descended the steps with him right behind her in standard protected position. But there was no problem with snipers. The area was secure. Imish troops in black unit suits, their helmet screens only lightly polarized since the sky overhead was dark with the menace of rain, ringed the shuttle and formed a gauntlet running toward a land crawler waiting nearby. A bubble shield had been fitted over the top hatch, and Imish purple and amber flags draped the sides listlessly. There was no breeze to make them flutter.

As soon as she and the governor cleared the shuttle, soldiers ran forward to enclose them and as this phalanx proceeded toward the crawler, Falmah-Al broke free to hurry ahead, already checking the route again upon her communicator. She hauled herself up the side of the crawler, gave a swift but thorough examination of the interior, eyed the energy readings supporting the bubble shield, and got herself out of the way. Ton positioned himself inside the bubble, mumbling to himself as he practiced his speech, and security outriders on stri-jets flanked the crawler as it lumbered forward for the governor's third parade through the city.

Falmah-Al caught her breath, still seething as she broke out the thumbnail-sized module from the base of her communicator, tuned it to the parade frequency, and fitted it back into her ear. The chatter was almost constant as points reported in on the crawler's progress. She took a moment to glance around at the tall silent buildings. The last fringe battles had ended three days ago. Her nostrils quivered over the lingering scents of nust gas and exploded disruptor charges. Victory! Nothing smelled sweeter.

She punched in Millen's frequency over her communicator. "Major?" she said as soon as he responded. "Falmah-Al. I'm planetside. Give me your location. I'm coming now."

"Right," said Millen over a burst of static.

Backlash in her ear module made her wince and hastily pop it out to tune it down.

"Repeat that last, Millen," she said into the communicator, refitting the module into her ear in time to hear someone say the governor's parade was going to get rained on. "I didn't catch it."

"Are you sure our little friend sitting over in Interrogation One is the real nairin?"

She went cold inside. "Explain—*gazal!*" She swore loudly, jumping as the first drops of rain hit her hard enough to sting.

"Colonel?" asked Millen sharply. "Are you—"

A deputy was waving. She ran for the land crawler indicated and scrambled up and over the side into its cramped shelter just as the heavens cracked open and sheets of water began drumming down. The operator slid past her and closed the hatch, cutting off the noise and wet. Falmah-Al bent to peer out one of the port views and frowned at the water gusting across the street and driving soldiers before it like a violent shepherd. A part of her was awed by such a display of natural wealth. Imagine water pouring from the sky.

"Colonel?" shouted Millen over the static on her communicator. "Are you all right? What's happening over there?"

Jolted out of her fascination, she jerked away from the port view and cracked her elbow painfully on the corner of an instrumentation bank.

"*Gazal-ma!*" she swore and savagely cut off Millen's alarmed questions. "It's all right, Major. Don't send down the Benshas."

"Thought you'd been ambushed," he answered more calmly.

"Rain," she snapped. "A waste of natural resources. Give me a repeat on the nairin."

"Are you sure we've got the right man?"

"Yes." She frowned, signaling for the operator to start up the land crawler. "Why? Is this your complication?"

"I think so. If I understand Chaimu customs correctly, someone else has snatched the throne."

"*What?*"

Millen's voice cut over the static, dry and slightly amused. "Looks like we've got ourselves a new suprin to contend with, Colonel."

By the time the land crawler lumbered over the debris and rubble obstructing most streets, the storm had ended. Falmah-Al climbed out warily into the warm damp air which was fresh with unfamiliar smells and found this district similar in appearance to the one the shuttle had landed in. More office and governmental buildings, some nondescript, others florid with ornamental architecture, stood about her. This area had suffered more damage. The street ahead was closed entirely where several walls had fallen, leaving skewed structures and burned-out shells.

Millen was waiting for her on the wide steps of a porticoed

building. As she emerged from the crawler, he came toward her with a wide grin. He wore the grey camouflage uniform of the mercenary auxiliary army. It was torn at the knees, ripped along one sleeve, and stiff with dried blood and mupalm stains. He had never exhibited a neat military presence. It didn't matter. He always turned in the results she wanted.

"Major Millen," she said as he halted before her and sketched a sloppy salute. "Are you sure there's a new suprin? Do we need to bring in Nairin Tregher?"

"I'm sure his reaction would be useful." Millen's eyes were as yellow and flat as a reptile's, with the same narrow pupils. Set in a wide square face above a squashed, lumpy nose and a scarred mouth, they were startling eyes, utterly cold and without expression. She suspected he was not entirely human, and although one of the Forbidden Directives commanded the Imish never to deal as brothers with those of mixed blood, Millen was too valuable an ally to investigate closely.

Those dead eyes came alive for once as Millen jerked a thumb at a subordinate who pulled out a communicator to call Interrogation One.

"There's an access point to the tunnels in this building," Millen said, nodding at the porticoed structure. "While we wait for Tregher to be delivered, you might as well look at the body."

Millen fell into step beside her as she strode forward. They trotted up the wide steps and into the gloomy interior. Portalamps had been strung up. Power was still off in the city on her orders. Outside, lightning split the sky with a sizzling crack, and she flinched.

"Nature's fireworks," said Millen, grinning at her with an impudence no one else dared. "It seems to rain several times a day on this damned bog-hole. Down this way." He turned immediately left down a short corridor that ended in a powerful fission-lock door. Through it steps led steeply down. "We've been scanning the tunnel system below the city and digging out the nests gathering there. But here below this sector which was supposed to be cleared, Alim kept getting trace readings that he never could pin down."

"An equipment malfunction?"

"No." Millen's grin widened. "We finally figured out that he was picking up a Sedkethran."

"What?" She nearly stumbled two steps from the bottom. "Impossible. What would one of those be doing here?"

"I don't know, but at least that's why we started poking around down here and found the suprin."

Falmah-Al followed Millen along a gloomy, low-ceilinged passageway to a cluster of cells. The place smelled of dampness and of something even more repugnant. Two guards were standing alertly at another fission-lock door. At Millen's gesture they moved aside.

"The entrance to the tunnels lies through here. A complicated system."

"I'm not interested in a tour, Major." Impatiently she went through the door and down another series of steep, crumbling stone steps into a dark web of damp, low-ceilinged tunnels. She gripped the butt of her disruptor, uneasy in such a hellish place.

Millen switched on a porta-lamp, and its beam stabbed the darkness back. Another beam shone in an answering signal somewhere ahead. They moved toward it, and were met by one of Millen's men.

"Any more readings, Alim?" he asked.

Alim, dark, greasy, and looking at home in this place, shook his head in the bobbing manner of the Walicas. "Some, Major. Very faint." His beady eyes moved to Falmah-Al, and he made a respectful gesture. "*Alamam*, Colonel."

She ignored him, glancing ahead through the surging shadows that seemed to leap at her and fall back with every careless shift of Millen's porta-lamp. "Where's the body?"

"Here."

They moved out of her way as she crouched by the corpse, her face puckering in distaste. It had been down here in the damp for several days. The body was swollen, the skin turned a noxious color. She gagged at the stench and tried holding her breath.

"Here, Colonel," said Alim, respectfully holding out a small filter mask designed for wear during nust spraying.

She fitted it gratefully over her face and went back to her inspection. The suprin had been an ugly creature. Taller of stature than any of her race, with heavy skeletal and muscular development, he had been horribly burned. *During the battle that destroyed his ship*, she thought in satisfaction.

"How did he escape the battle?" she asked.

Millen shook his head blankly. "His dire-lord should be somewhere around. I've heard they usually kill themselves when their suprin dies. No readings for another Chaimu though."

Alim shook his head in agreement.

Still in charge armor, the suprin lay on his back with his arms and legs folded precisely in a curious arrangement. The sharply defined nose ridges and heavy brow plates of his face were obscured by a covering of dust. In his heavy, clawed hands a plain dagger projected toward the low ceiling.

Millen pointed at the swollen left wrist where the armor had been unfastened. "His band of office is gone. Priceless corybdium, I've heard. And his ceremonial dagger is supposed to be taken only by the successor."

Falmah-Al snorted. "Simple robbery—"

"No." Millen shook his head. "I had Barkey do a rundown on customs. The bracelet has a bonding lock on it. No one could just steal it. And a thief wouldn't replace the dagger in that way. It means the successor has accepted the responsibilities of the Held."

"There is no more Held!" she said angrily. "We have ended it."

As soon as she spoke she regretted the outburst. She strode away from the corpse, tugging off the filter mask with a toss of her head.

"This means great trouble," she said in a calmer tone. "I'll have to inform the governor at once. Obviously the rebels do not realize they are beaten. Since we have the nairin imprisoned, they are using the next available figure to spearhead their resistance."

"So," said Millen heavily, rubbing the back of his neck. "We are going to have to—"

A squawk from her ear module interrupted.

"Colonel! Colonel! Trouble! The governor—"

Static crackled in her ear. Wincing, she snarled a curse and thumbed the frequency on her large communicator. "Point Six, this is Falmah-Al," she said urgently. "Respond. What is your difficulty? Respond."

There was another long burst of static. Then the voice blared out at them in raw panic. "The governor! He's gone! *Gone!* They've got him!"

FURTIVE EYES PEERED out at Brock from silent buildings as
he made his way slowly along the deserted street. The sun
was setting on the city's horizon like a vast bloody eye,
tinging the evening sky with rust and ochre. The last ruddy
slants of light filtered through the streets crisscrossing overhead. It was a very old part of Impryn. The buildings were
lower, more crooked, jammed closely together. Steam gusted
from street grids and curled about corners like fog. Walls
glistened with damp. It was hard to breathe. His lungs felt
full of water. Ever mindful of the danger of nust gas, Brock
kept his nostrils alert for that acrid smell among the myriad
odors of garbage, mold, burning *mongcense*, and private uba
distilleries. There was a sniper watching him from overhead,
positioned in the fork of an upper street girder support. Brock
walked steadily, aware of the hand cannon trained on the base
of his neck. No one could mistake him for a Colonid trooper,
and he wanted to make contact with any Heldman he could
find. But the sniper did not have a Chaimu mental pattern,
and Brock feared he must be one of the citizens, slum dwell-
ers who followed no law or allegiance but their own. After a
moment Brock turned a corner and was out of cannon range.

He had been walking for hours, moving short distances
then concealing himself in pools of shadow as one more
entity among the millions of people hiding in terror from the
black-suited Colonid troops patrolling everywhere. No one
was permitted out on the streets. Signs had been posted.
Sectors had been marked off. The patrols came through on

irregular circuits. To be out was to invite being arrested or ruthlessly shot down on the spot. Brock had witnessed both, and either fate seemed to depend upon the whim of the Colonid soldiers. Brock paused a moment to rest, then resumed walking. He could feel other eyes upon him. Their curiosity lapped at the edges of his mind. But no one sought more involvement than that as he moved deeper into the slum.

Power was on here. Intermittently he passed a spitting, half-circuited light that had been broken. Others were black. The shadows grew inky. Clammy steam blew into his face as he walked over a grid. There were service tunnels directly underfoot. Beneath them lay the shielded defense bunkers. If only he could *flick* down to them! Then he would be safe. And he would have a better chance of linking up with other warriors.

A faint scuffling noise from behind him made him melt at once into the shadows of an alley off the street. He reached up to tug at the hood of the cloak he had taken off a dead body earlier and wore now as a dirty, bloodstained cover of anonymity over his armor. For a moment there was only silence, then he heard very soft footsteps. Someone was following him.

Whoever it was had just picked up the trail. Brock closed his eyes to concentrate on the hunter. He caught no scent. He dared not drop his mental shields to risk contact. The footsteps paused again. *Trying to decide which hole I'm hiding in*, thought Brock. His concentration drifted. With an effort, he shook off his fatigue and rubbed his chest where the internal pain continued in a persistent throb. This alley deadended. There was no way out except the way he'd come in. If the follower was an idle thief, he might decide to continue on. If he was an informer for the Colonids or something worse, then . . .

I'm in no condition to fight, thought Brock. He would have to *flick*.

As alert as he was, nevertheless, the sudden rush at him from the street was a surprise. Brock had not expected such quickness. His own lightning reactions seemed frozen. To whirl, flinging his arms free of the hampering cloak to thrust the attacker aside, and to jump back was like moving while submerged in water. He gathered himself, but the attempt to *flick* brought only a terrible, debilitating stab of pain through

29

his chest that left him nauseated and dizzy. Doubling up, he staggered to one side in an attempt to elude another attack, but strong arms pinioned him and hot, fetid breath blew down his neck as his hunter tackled him, sending him crashing to the ground.

The clatter of Brock's armor upon the stone brought a grunt of surprise from his attacker. Dazed, with the wind half-knocked from him, Brock felt himself hauled back onto his feet. He was shaken violently until the cloak swung open. A fist thumped the protective surface of his corselet.

"*Merc sic-t 'a ki!*" said a husky voice in Slathese. With a hiss he drew Brock closer to the mouth of the alley where there was dim illumination from the street. "What is this?" A fingerpad traced the swirled scar upon Brock's cheekbone. "Dire-lord! You have survived. *A' chk di!*"

The slim wiry arm around Brock suddenly became protective. Throwing the hood back up over Brock's head, the Slathese looked cautiously up and down the street before hustling Brock along.

"Hurry," he whispered in Brock's ear. "We must be quick. This section is not good. Here, this way." A few steps farther along, he abruptly pulled Brock into another alley. This one was so narrow they could scarcely walk abreast and wound for a considerable distance through dingy, run-down buildings where the denizens could be heard scuttling to and from the broken windows and wired-shut doors.

The streets overhead ended, leaving them suddenly under open sky. Clouds had gathered in a black formation, hastening twilight into darkness. Wind gusted suddenly at their backs, whipping Brock's cloak between his legs. He stumbled, leaning on the Slathese more than he meant to as they hurried. He could not seem to catch his breath completely. The pain was making him dizzier with every step. He wanted to speak, to establish identification, but the effort was so difficult.

"Quiet." The Slathese whipped them around a corner and pressed himself flat to a wall slick with the blue, fuzzy growth of fungus. They stayed there a moment, the Slathese listening and Brock concentrating on holding himself together. He still could not *flick*! Was the damage permanent? Desperately he pushed the fears away, trying to find the necessary Disciplines and failing.

"Hear anything?" The Slathese cocked his head at Brock,

who could not answer. "*Merc t'*. Let's go." He released his grasp on Brock's arm and bent down, straining at something until he grunted. There was the sound of metal grating on stone. A rush of damp warm air exhaled from the earth.

Raindrops fell in a swift patter across a stack of discarded cargo boards and engine parts. Brock lifted his face to the rain, wincing as it came harder. The Slathese gestured urgently, pulling Brock ahead of him to descend the steps leading down into the tunnels. Brock groped his way slowly, feeling out each step with his feet as he supported himself by leaning on the wall. The Slathese pulled the metal grate back into place, cutting off all light, and thumped Brock's back impatiently.

"Go. Go. Can't you see in the dark? There are four more steps in front of you, then two paces forward, then turn to your right. Easy. Go. Hurry. We can't be caught here. They are scanning the tunnels too."

Brock fumbled his way through the directions and finally caught enough breath to speak. "Who are you?"

"Names later. No time to talk. Keep going. Follow the wall with your shoulder. Hurry!"

Brock turned the corner and stopped, sagging against the wall. It was slimy beneath his cheek and stank of mold. "I . . . can't."

The Slathese grabbed him by the arm and propelled him along without mercy. Brock felt himself floating in and out of consciousness. *Dangerous*, he thought in alarm, then remembered that he could not *flick*. He was trapped in this dimension, hurt, his reflexes slow and unreliable. *I must find a healer*, he thought in desperation just before he stumbled and fell to his knees despite the Slathese's attempt to catch him.

The Slathese tugged at his arm. "Get up. Dire-lord, you can't stay here. You'll endanger us all. *Akc't mut s*."

Brock lifted his head, trying to focus on the Slathese's face through the darkness. There was something he must tell him, something important. But although he tried to speak, he just faded slowly away into the mists of blissful coldness.

"You're a fool, Rho!" boomed an angry voice, jolting Brock to the edge of full awareness. "I put you out on the streets to keep your eyes and ears open, not to come dragging in more wounded. Anza can't take care of what we've got now. How far did you carry him?"

The soft reply was too far away for Brock to hear. He drifted off again, only to be brought back by the angry voice:

"I don't care if he's the dire-lord! That only means the suprin really is dead. It's the nairin we're concerned with now."

"But look, Davn," said the Slathese's husky voice, coming into range now. A slim hand patted Brock's side, moving the fold of the dirty cloak. "Look what he guards. Important—"

"The dagger! Meir preserve us."

Brock struggled to open his eyes, to turn his head just in time to see a broad-shouldered newan dragging the ceremonial dagger from the sheath at Brock's side.

"*No*!" Brock's hand gripped the newan's wrist, startling him into releasing the dagger. It slid back into the sheath, and Brock flung the newan's hand away before falling back with a gasp.

The Slathese grinned widely, revealing a wicked set of poisonous fangs, and tapped a clawtip against his narrow skull. "Not dead yet, Davn. Plenty of life. *Sic*!"

The newan grunted and frowned down at Brock. Broadshouldered but short of stature, his face was wide at the forehead and square-jawed beneath a thick golden beard. Blue eyes glared at Brock without patience. He looked tired, and there was a half-healed cut along his left cheek that would doubtless leave a scar. Brock's own gaze met his with equal intensity for a moment then faltered. The face was vaguely familiar. But he was too tired to think.

"Oh, you've seen me before, Dire-lord Brock," said the newan with a certain degree of insolence. "I'm sure you're trying to remember where. I'm Davn. Arkist."

"Arkist!" whispered Brock. "Of course . . . gunnery."

"That's right. The infallible memory of a Sedkethran. Arkist is the highest rank a new-human can hold. Only now, all of a sudden I'm in command of the forces remaining in the city. The honorables are all dead." Davn grinned without amusement. "Amazing how war levels us all. Where's the suprin?"

Brock heard someone coughing, but he couldn't see anything past Davn and the Slathese. He felt himself sliding off again and tried to hold himself together. "Dead."

"Obviously." Davn briefly touched the jeweled hilt of the ceremonial dagger with a fingertip. "What happened? And how is it that the Superior Life is ended, yet the dire-lord pledged to his protection still lives? You owe us a full report on that.''

"Let him rest, Davn,'' said the Slathese with a faint hiss of protest. "Let Anza tend him. You should rest too.''

"And you should get back out to your post,'' snarled Davn. But with a shrug he walked off.

Brock lifted a hand slightly at the Slathese. "Thank you,'' he whispered, then winced, pressing a hand against his chest as the throbbing started again.

"Anza!''

A young woman came over at once. She was also a newan, with short dark hair that hung untidily in her eyes. She wore a smock with a green medic's band around one sleeve. Her dark eyes, intelligent but glazed with the cynicism that medics achieved so soon in their careers, ranged swiftly over Brock.

She smiled slightly and made the small formal gesture of one healer to another. "Have I the dire-lord's permission?''

Bracing himself to erect shields against her touch, Brock lowered his eyes in an affirmative.

"Right,'' she said briskly to Rho. "Help me get this armor stripped off. I'll need my kit, I think. These burns look serious. The dire-lord has been neglecting himself.''

Brock allowed his consciousness to fade behind the strictest Disciplines while the sections of armor were carefully pried away from his burned flesh. He made no sound although they could not be entirely gentle, but inside he beat against the walls of Sedkethran pride which would not let him scream out his agony. His senses swam; pride made him fight that. To hang on he focused on Rho's thin ugly face with its lipless mouth and long, pointed teeth, orange deepset eyes, and pointed ears towering above his skull. The Slathese was wiry and slim, but his folded wings made his back look thick beneath the slitted tunic he wore. Anza's face was rounder, with plump cheeks like a child's, flushed pink as she worked, her dark eyes narrowed with concentration as she dressed his wounds. They helped him, but they remained distant, restrained in their care by the formality not only of his rank but also of his species. A Sedkethran permitted himself no friends. *But I would*! he thought, engulfed as always by the loneliness he could never escape.

Anza shone a narrow beam of light into his eyes, frowning. "Is there anything else the dire-lord wishes me to examine?''

He shivered with shame. The atrox . . . but he could not speak of it. The taboos, enforced from the whippings of childhood, could not be broken down.

"The dire-lord thanks you," he whispered, despising his own cowardice.

She nodded, not satisfied with her own medical instincts yet obedient to his dismissal. "Rho will bring the dire-lord some soup. It's all the food we have. And then the dire-lord should rest."

As she spoke, she moved her hand across his chest to check the bandage on his shoulder which had not yet fused to his skin. He jerked, his cry choking in his throat.

"Easy." Her hands gripped him, holding him until the spasm ended. "What is it?"

There was real concern in her face now, breaking through the mask of formality. He felt himself shaking in her grasp and knew he must break down the taboos and say something. He needed her help. A Sedkethran healer would stand aside under the condemnation and let him die. But if he asked her, she would help.

His eyes fell from hers as he struggled to find the words. "There is damage . . . inside."

Her fingers touched his lips. "I understand the taboos," she said swiftly. "It is that which is injured, isn't it? That organ which the taboos protect?"

"Yes." The pain was betrayed in his voice, but in his relief at her understanding he did not care. "Rest will help."

"What else can be done?"

He lay there, looking up at her and could not answer.

"Here is soup. *Sic t'hk*," said Rho, coming up with a bowl cradled in his long claws.

"Rho will help you sit up," said the medic. "I will let the dire-lord rest before I return. If the dire-lord will permit my dismissal, there are other injured to tend."

"Of course." Brock started to say something more, but she had already turned away.

Propped up on some rolled bundles, he drank the soup, finding the taste unspeakably foul. But his hunger overcame that, and he drained the last drop.

This was one of the larger, more modern, of the underground bunkers. It was heavily shielded and should be safe from any Colonid scanner probes. Porta-lamps provided ample illumination. There were perhaps thirty people in the bunker. Some of them were injured and lying on pallets. Anza and another medic moved among them with quiet competence. Others were sitting about or pacing, speaking among themselves in low, excited voices. Something had happened, Brock realized. Warriors ducked in and out a low doorway into a tunnel obviously connecting with the next bunker. Had there been a skirmish? Or were they just plotting their next one? Dismay rose in him. Was this small group all that remained of the ground forces?

Davn appeared in the doorway, ducking inside and standing there a moment to survey the room. He saw Brock watching him and came over, picking his way with care over the pallets.

"I'll need your help," he said without preamble.

Brock looked at him warily. "I do not understand. A few minutes ago you were accusing me—"

"That will be gone into later." Davn cut him off with a chopping gesture. "We're about to open communications with the Colonids. If you're present, that will make us look even stronger."

Brock sat erect, ignoring the throbbing which immediately resumed in his chest. "What have you done?"

Davn grinned, his teeth gleaming whitely against his beard. "We pulled it off. We have Governor Ton himself. And we're going to exchange him for the nairin."

Brock stared at him in disbelief, then anger surged through him. "Impossible! It must not be done!"

"Look—"

"No! I tell you, no! Are you mad? Tregher betrayed the Held. He gave the defense keys to Darjahl Imperial to the Colonids in exchange for his own safety. In his dying breath Suprin Utdi condemned his son." Seeing all of them staring at him, Brock swung his eyes to each face. "None of you must risk your lives further for the black one."

"Lies!" shouted Davn, red-faced. "You are the traitor. You let the Colonids kill the suprin. And now you try to discredit the nairin in an effort to distract us from your own cowardice."

"Arkist Davn!" said Rho, coming to his feet with an angered rattle of his folded wings. "This is the dire-lord whom you so accuse."

"Yes, and it is the dire-lord's place to die before his suprin," retorted Davn. There were several murmurs of assent. "And look at his arm. Look at the bracelet he wears. Look at the dagger he carries. They belong rightfully to Tregher, our new suprin. The dire-lord does not guard them for the successor, he *wears* them as though they are his own possessions. He slanders Tregher with lies. Next he will say Suprin Utdi named him as successor."

"Indeed I do wear the goda band," said Brock, scrambling to his feet. He held up his arm for them all to see although the movement aroused the burns Anza's medications had soothed. "Could I do so had Utdi himself not given it into my keeping? I served him unto death. I serve him now. Tregher has betrayed us. He was renounced by Utdi. I swear that to you on my honor as a dire-lord."

One of the other warriors, a Chaimu whose eyes were glittering a fierce red beneath his jutting brow plate, took sufficient courage from Davn's scowl to jeer: "And will a Sedkethran lead us as our suprin? A *Sedkethran*? A child would be more fierce—"

Fury exploded within Brock. Just as Davn swung out a hand at the Chaimu and said, "Take care," Brock seized the curved dagger from Rho's belt and was upon the Chaimu with reflexes none of them could match, pinning the warrior back against the wall with the blade against his throat.

"You are a fool," he said through his teeth, his eyes blazing into the startled ones of the Chaimu. "Do you truly dare challenge a dire-lord? Do you?"

The man remained silent, and Brock released him, tossing the borrowed dagger back to Rho. There was silence in the cramped room. The eyes ringed him.

Brock let out his breath loudly, refusing to let anyone see how dizzy his attack on the Chaimu had left him. "So." His gaze swung to Davn's.

But the newan stared back stubbornly. "You have made your claim," he said, breaking the quiet. "But I am free to choose. And I choose to serve Tregher. We will make the exchange at dawn. Will the dire-lord help us?"

Brock lifted his head. "Us? Do you choose for all who are here?" He moved back to his pallet and bent to unsheathe the ceremonial dagger. The bard crystal blade flashed in the light as he held it aloft. "The Superior Life was passed to me, not Tregher. Do not think of me as Sedkethran. I am a Held warrior. I have proven that. So choose. Are you going to follow Utdi's choice, or are you going to follow the man who sold you to the Colonids?''

For a moment no one spoke or moved. Then Rho moved from the ranks to stand at Brock's side. Brock expected others to join him, but no one else did. Their eyes swung uncomfortably away from Brock's.

Davn's chest swelled. ''You are answered, Dire-lord. So much for a Sedkethran's personal ambitions. So much for your accusations against Tregher. Guard that dagger well, for at dawn the trade will be made and you can then turn it over to Suprin Tregher.''

HUMILIATION, RAW AND HOT, poured over Brock. He was supposed to be sleeping, but he could not sleep. The bunker was empty except for the wounded. The others had all gone, gone to sell their allegiance to a traitor.

Only one porta-lamp glowed softly, providing a dim illumination for Anza as she woke up at periodic intervals through the night to check on her patients. He was aware of her movements, but he ignored her. His face stayed turned toward the wall. Had he been physically capable, he would have *flicked* into interstitial time and stayed there where his shame could not be witnessed.

He reached out and ran his pale, slim fingers up and down the damp wall. *And thus ended the reign of Suprin Brock*, he thought, letting his hand fall back to the pallet. *Forgive me, Utdi.*

"Dire-lord?"

Anza's soft voice startled him. Reluctantly he turned his head to look at her as she knelt by his pallet.

"I am sorry you are not able to sleep." Her dark eyes gazed at him with a hint of a frown. "We cannot spare the power for a suspensor bed."

"Understood." He hesitated a moment. "There is no danger of drifting into solid matter."

"Because of your injuries?"

He dropped his gaze in an affirmative. Normally a Sedkethran could not sleep on any solid structure because of the possibility of drifting out of sequence with reality. But how did she know so much about his culture?

"Basic emergency procedure training for variable species," she said, anticipating his question. "An injured Sedkethran must be set up on suspensors. An injured Chaimu must be inverted with the head lower than the extremities. An injured Slathese must never be placed on his back. An injured Varlax . . ." She smiled and brushed her uneven hair out of her eyes. "Need I go on? I also spent two months on Felca for an observation residency."

He blinked and looked at her with new respect. "This is rare."

"Yes, I'm well aware of how your healers look on ordinary medics as barbaric quacks who rely on guesswork, scanners, and erratic drug effects to take care of people. I think a residency is granted once every century. But I went and I learned a great deal from the magstrusi, in spite of their damned arrogance and all those stupid taboos!"

She crammed her hands into the deep pockets of her smock. Her vehemence seemed to fade as swiftly as it had appeared.

"Forgive me," she said, shaking her head. "I should not—"

"Say what you wish," he said, amused. "Your words do not insult me."

The pink of her cheeks deepened. "But you're—"

"I am a warrior, not a healer." He stared through the gloom at his hands, unable to take pride in that statement now. "But . . . I wish I could have saved him."

"Oh." Impulsively she reached out to touch his arm, and unexpected sensations of compassion flooded into him from her. "You cared for the suprin, didn't you? I mean, we all respected him but you grieve—"

"A Sedkethran does not," he snapped, the denial flying from him like the lash of a magstrusi's whip.

She drew back as though struck, and he turned his head away in shame. She had not deserved that.

"The dire-lord is weary," she said. "Have I permission to go?"

"No, I . . ." He hesitated, unable to find the words. Loneliness engulfed him. He realized that all of his pride at having escaped Felca and its harsh self-repressions was ill-founded. For although he was among the highest-ranked after royalty in the Held, that very position made him unapproachable and just as alone as he had ever been. Why didn't he stop reaching for what he could never be?

"I swore to him that I would not fail him a second time," Brock said softly, refusing to look at her as though that would hide the deep shame he was revealing. "I swore that I would not let the Colonids destroy the Held. Yet, look at me. I have one follower, and he stood at my side out of pity. If the people refuse help, what can I do?"

She made no sound. When he finally brought himself to look at her, he saw tears running down her face in long streaks. Of all those belonging to the Held, only the human species wept.

He touched her face, the paleness of his fingers almost translucent against her darker skin, and the warmth of her tears burned his fingertips.

She sat without moving, her gaze far away. "My sister was a breeder on Mabruk," she said. "She bore for the highest-ranked newans, but most of the time she worked as a tender for the Chaimu children. She loved the little ones so . . . so very much. She was good and kind and loving. She wasn't interested in wars or political philosophies. She just wanted to care for the little ones, to give them life, to bring them up, to laugh with them, hug them. Those Colonid bastards k-killed her. They just came in and blew everything to bits. They—" A sob escaped her. She buried her face in her hands.

The wrenching sounds of human sorrow were ugly. Brock watched her, grieving inside for her. He was not the only one who had lost. They had all lost. He frowned at the goda band on his wrist, thinking of what it stood for. The godas were the most horrible weapons ever created. They had never been used. The fact of their existence had almost passed into legend. No one wanted to believe that anyone would be willing to unleash such destruction. Brock drew in an unsteady breath as he rubbed the band with his fingers. The code numbers played through his mind in a horrifying litany. Did he have the right to use them? Did he have the right to force the people of the Held to accept a responsibility they no longer wanted? If they chose to accept defeat, was he not wrong to push them away from that choice? They wanted Tregher. They did not care what Tregher had done. They wanted only to cling to tradition, the last remaining piece of what had been their way of life.

Brock sighed. He could unlock the goda band from his

wrist and leave it and the dagger here on the pallet for Tregher after Davn made the exchange.

His fingers curled around the band.

"Dire-lord," said Anza through her tears. She looked up and he saw her eyes were red-rimmed and puffy. Her face was wet, and her voice shook as she said, "I wanted to stand by you earlier. I want the Held to go on as it was. I want revenge for my sister. I want Tregher to pay for betraying us. But what good would it do to resist? They've won. But you refuse to accept it just as much as Davn does. What good is fighting when there is no chance to win?"

Brock's eyes lifted to hers. "If there was a chance, a terrible chance, but nevertheless a way to defeat the Colonids would you fight? No matter what it meant? Do you want to fight for freedom, or live as a Colonid slave?"

"You're alone," she said, staring at him. Her dark eyes glistened black behind her tears. "What can you really do?"

He tapped the band on his wrist, his eyes meeting hers with a grimness that made her audibly catch her breath.

"But that's a legend. They don't really exist, do they?"

"Yes."

"But how could you? You're a Sed—" She broke off and swallowed. "You're a warrior."

"Yes. It is a terrible choice, Anza. Am I wrong?"

Her eyes widened as though she could not believe he had actually admitted doubt. And then conviction suddenly blazed upon her face.

"No," she said. "You are not wrong. And I will help you to beat them, Suprin." She reached out and traced the swirled scar on his cheek. "Shall I remove this?"

How long had that proud scar stood as a barrier between him and the life he had abandoned? Without it he would be naked, forced to fight for a place all over again.

"No one will ever believe a Sedkethran has dared reach for the throne," he said slowly. "But the entire galaxy recognizes this scar and what it stands for. I must wear it until we are free again."

She nodded and started to rise to her feet. "I'd better check on my other patients—"

"Anza," he said, aware of the present stream of time. There was not much left. "We must go before Davn returns with the nairin. Your patients will have to be abandoned. Can you, as a sworn medic, do that?"

47

She shook her head, her dark eyes like glass. "I will help you go before Davn comes back, but I can't leave my patients. And I can't leave . . . Davn."

She looked at him with raw misery. "He is very stubborn. If you could only convince him—"

"No."

"No." She sighed. "I'll find Rho for you."

Brock waited until she had ducked out of the bunker into the tunnel before he gathered himself tightly within the Disciplines, seeking the self-control necessary to ignore the pain that would come when he stood up. But his abilities, while high-scaled, had always been erratic. He had been marked for advanced training in an effort to bind his talents into usable form. He left Felca before that training was completed. Since then he had learned his own methods, grafting them onto the teachings of the magstrusi. At this moment, however, he could not seem to grasp anything. Whether it was due to exhaustion, the *skial* he had experienced with the suprin, or weakness from his injuries, he was not sure. But as he forced himself upright, clinging to the wall for support, he felt his consciousness splitting into multiple timestreams. This was a mystic talent under strict repression. Magstrus Olbin had sealed it when Brock was a child. There was not supposed to be any way to release it, yet suddenly it was freed, perhaps accidently by his efforts to maintain the Disciplines without benefit of his atrox.

He rose to his feet in the gloomy damp bunker. They had to hurry. He could worry about his mental condition later. Where were Anza and Rho? What was taking them so long?

He rose to his feet in the cavern of ice lit by a vaulted ceiling opened to the sky of Felca. Around him sighed the thousand voices of the wind through the crystal harmonies— quartz formations in precise geometric arrangement studding the walls. It was the day of Change; when he left the cavern he could never again acknowledge parents or family or home. He would be nameless, assigned a number and a barracks, both of which would rotate randomly so that he could never become familiar with or attached to a new identity or location. Other races called Change adolescence, and its duration varied. From a childhood of harsh discipline and enforced lessons softened by the kind remoteness of family, he would enter a stretch of constant testing and uncertainty until he was mature.

Brock shivered in the cold which was below comfort. He was naked, fogged by the condensation of his own breathing. He crouched back down in the center of the vast cavern, feeling very small and frightened as he listened to the ethereal voices of the wind singing in whispers about him. Fear was not permitted, he tried to remind himself and dug his fingers into the frozen slush beneath his numb feet. It was getting colder, but he could not shake off the illogical conviction that as long as he remained inside here he was safe. When he stepped outside, Change would begin. And he did not want to go. . . .

He rose to his feet in the overheated audience chamber of Held Suprin, dizzy with the heat and fumes from the incense braziers, deafened by the hissing of metal brands glowing red in the fire, and stretched with tremendous pride at having been chosen from all the candidates to replace Dire-lord Marsk, a coarse, aging Varlax who had died during mating leave on his home world. The chamber was packed with curious honorables, wide-eyed cadets in new Heldfleet uniforms, members of the court proper, skulking Fet assassins, jesters, region servants, minor officials, and the red-cloaked warriors of the suprin's notorious Death Squad. The murmuring swelled, undulating back and forth through the crowd. No Sedkethran had ever been chosen before. No Sedkethran had ever been seen shielded and armed before. A few aged honorables, dried to living husks by *skial* and puffing on noxious sift-pipes in protected corners of the chamber, nodded wisely to each other and tapped their bony nose ridges as if to say, remember the legends of antiquity when the Sedkethran Corps stood among the fiercest of the Held's auxiliaries.

But legends were only legends. Brock stood on the small dais, conscious of being the center of a thousand eyes. He was clad in the heavy charge armor of a warrior; his helmet rested on the floor between his feet. High above him the Superior Family sat in their gallery: the suprin, two of his favored *dalmas*, a selection of children, and four resplendent Gwilwans, scaled purple and vivid green, glowing in the light with their fangs bared and their eyes gleaming insanely as they stood rattling their chains about the suprin's throne. On the dais with Brock were the brazier heating the brands, two arkists with ceremonial knives held ready to strike if cowardice was shown, and the masked chief assassin of the Death Squad now drawing on his heat-proof gloves.

There must be no flinching, no sign of pain. Brock steeled himself as the brand was selected from the fire and lifted toward his face. His eyes remained locked upon the tip glowing white. He heard the hiss of the metal on fire, felt the heat upon his skin as the chief assassin aimed with care. He must not flinch, not by the slightest bit. For it would show for the rest of his life, his cowardice branded upon him in a blurred scar. He must not flinch.

"Prepare yourself," said the chief assassin, his voice muffled by mask and artifice. Identities within the Death Squad were close-guarded secrets.

"I am ready," said Brock and closed his eyes as the brand seared into his flesh. . . .

He rose to his feet, struggling against the weakness of a body grown old. Giant trees towered above him, the girth of their trunks telling their immense age. Briars and vines snaked together in a treacherous undergrowth, walling him in. There was moist warm air upon his face, and the subliminal throb of a jungle living, hunting, and dying beyond the leaping flames of the camp fire. He held out a withered hand as though to ward off what stood waiting in the darkness about him. A sound startled him and he whirled around, having to catch himself by clinging to the tree at his back. The bark was hard like metal and razor sharp. Blood ran across his hands. . . .

"*Dire-lord!*"

A voice, insistent with panic, cut across the multiple thoughts, jolting him back into the present. He blinked, disoriented, as Rho hissed urgently at him.

"Hurry! They're coming."

"Yes." Brock pulled himself together, thrusting aside the daunting implications of what was happening to him for later consideration. He lifted his head, letting his mind quest cautiously. *There*! He drew back and gestured hastily at Rho. "We have waited too long. Is there any armor?"

"*Sic*! Zamar died an hour past. He will not need his now. I'll get." Rho dashed away, pausing in the doorway to let Anza enter. He gestured impatiently at her, and she came at once to Brock.

"Can you walk?"

Insulted, he stared down at her from his full height. "I am in control," he said, grasping the sheath of the ceremonial dagger tightly in his hand. She said something else, but he ignored her. Under normal circumstances he could have maintained repression while performing several simultaneous tasks, but he felt too unstable to dare split his mind among more than one or two actions.

Getting to the exit of the bunker seemed to take an eternity. Brock again had the sensation of being submerged in deep water. His movements were slow and awkward. *Illusion*, he thought. *The atrox is warping my sense of time passage.*

Rho met them in the tunnel, the armor bundled under his long arm. His mouth was open and he was hissing steadily in the Slathese manner of exasperation.

"Too late," he said. "They are coming. Hear?"

Anza glanced worriedly at Brock. "You'd better stay here and wait for a better opportunity."

"No," said Brock fiercely. "I will not give Tregher—"

"You will not give Tregher what?" asked a silken voice out of the darkness of the tunnel stretching behind Rho.

The Slathese whirled, spitting, and Brock drew his strifer.

"Put it down!" ordered Davn, coming into view suddenly as a torch snapped on, stabbing blinding light into Brock's face. "Dire-lord! Don't be a fool!"

Others crowded into sight behind Davn, weapons aimed. Anza gave a little sigh, and Brock slowly slid the strifer back into its holster.

Emotions, he thought in sudden disgust. *I sat and pitied myself instead of getting away while I had the chance. I have been illogical and inefficient.*

"Very wise," said Davn, striding forward. "Just where do you three think you were going?"

"You were right, Arkist," said Tregher, coming up to stand beside him. The nairin was slender for a Chaimu, and his nose ridges were lightly pronounced, almost vestigial. They gave him an immature look which did not match the cunning in his eyes. Coiled about his wrist was a thin black oinrth. Its wedge-shaped head was swaying lightly from side to side. The reptilian eyes stared at Brock without blinking. It was the only weapon Tregher ever carried. Brock had seen him throw the serpent with deadly accuracy. It took only seconds for oinrth poison to kill. At the moment, Tregher looked as though he might throw the oinrth right into Brock's face. "He is a most disloyal dire-lord. Not one I care to trust with my life."

"Unlike me, Suprin?" said Davn, grinning.

"Oh, you are most loyal, Arkist. And you will have your

reward for gaining my freedom for me. But first the important matters.'' Tregher stepped to within one pace of Brock, his arrogant eyes flaming. ''We shall link, Direlord. Now! It is your duty.''

''Wait.'' Anza stepped forward, making a hasty civilian salute as Tregher glared at her in astonishment. ''He is ill, not himself. Let him rest a while longer.''

''He doesn't look like he's resting,'' growled Davn. ''He looks like he's trying to sneak away. With your help, Anza.''

''I wasn't aware that he is a prisoner,'' she said stiffly. ''I am a medic, not a guard.''

''But you were perhaps assisting him in his disloyalty?'' asked Tregher softly.

Anza's dark eyes flashed. ''I am only a medic, Nairin. He is the dire-lord.''

''Indeed he is,'' said Tregher, and Brock released his breath slowly in relief. Anza could look after herself, it seemed. ''You mustn't corrupt my people, Brock. That is wicked of you. Come now. Let us link and get it over with, and then you may go and do as you please. I will not hold you to my service.''

Brock stared at Tregher, hating him, wondering how Tregher could have found it in himself to betray his people, his suprin, his throne. There was no use in active resistance; Davn was standing ready to shoot him if he tried to escape. Tregher's gloved hand reached out and took the ceremonial dagger from Brock.

''A dangerous ambition, power,'' Tregher said. ''It can corrupt so quickly. Even Sedkethrans, it would seem, are not immune. I hope, Ellisne, that you are making note of this extraordinary behavior.''

''Indeed,'' said a feminine voice marked by a soft accent which made Brock stiffen.

He stared, barely concealing his dismay, as a tall Sedkethran woman in the brown robes of a healer stepped gracefully forward through the contingent standing alertly at Tregher's back. As she stopped beside the nairin, she lifted a gloved hand to pull a cord. The hood of her cloak fell back, revealing a slender, fine-boned face of haunting beauty. Her skin was so white it seemed to glow against the shadows, and her eyes shone with a brilliant luminescence that burned into Brock with accusation.

She hurled one word at him like a blow: ''*Promadi*!''

Outcast. The word with a hundred shameful meanings. The word that proclaimed his failure as a Sedkethran, his denial of the Writings, his refusal to submit to the elder council.

Brock stared through her, rejecting the shame she sought to arouse in him. "I am still the dire-lord of the Held," he said to Tregher. "I bring you the words of your father."

"Yes!" said Tregher eagerly. "Speak them!"

"You are a traitor to the Held. You betrayed the defense keys to Colonid agents in exchange for your own safety. Utdi's death lies to your blame."

"Arrogant fool!" Tregher lifted his arm to throw the oinrth.

"Wait!" said Davn, stepping in the way. "Must he die before he talks?"

"He has said too much already," said Tregher, seething, but he slowly lowered his arm. The serpent, disturbed, lifted its black head with a hiss.

"You have the dagger your father wore," said Brock. "Let that be enough."

Davn growled, and one of the Chaimu warriors struck Brock behind the ear with the bludgeon end of his staff. Brock staggered beneath the blow, his whole head ringing. The precarious control he was maintaining over his body slipped, and for a moment he was nauseous with pain.

"Stop it!" cried Anza. "He is injured. Davn, please!"

"He isn't too injured to insult the Superior Life." Davn glared at Brock, who was staring desperately at Ellisne.

Stop this, he pleaded. *Is this justice?*

But she ignored him. Her face was a beautiful, cold mask. It was as though his thoughts bounced off a mirror.

"You will obey Suprin Tregher's commands," said Davn implacably.

Brock stood without moving, his left arm held stiffly against his body. The goda band was vividly green against the bandages. Tregher's eyes fell to it.

"You go too far. The corbydium bracelet is not yours to wear!" said Tregher, his face dark with anger. "Take it off. Now."

"The band is locked by the suprin's own mindprint," said Brock.

"Take it off! Or by Meir I swear that you will see your hand severed from the wrist!" The oinrth was erect and swaying on Tregher's wrist. Its tongue flickered out. Its eyes glowed like jewels.

Brock watched the reptile, wondering if his reflexes could move fast enough to dodge it. He had no intention of surrendering to Tregher's demands.

"Arrogant fool!" Tregher pulled back his arm to throw the oinrth.

"Suprin, no!" said Davn. "If he dies, you can never—"

"It does not matter," said Tregher with a hiss of fury. "I will not be defied."

"But will you agree to be served by this one?" asked Ellisne. Her voice, artfully modulated, calmed Tregher visibly.

"In what way?"

"The dire-lord has been seriously injured. In order for him to surrender to your commands, Suprin, he would have to lower internal discipline techniques. I am sure he is not really desirous of defying you. But rather, he doubtless cannot control his thoughts sufficiently to unlock the bracelet. Nor if he were to link minds with you, could he keep his pain from being transmitted."

Brock turned his face away, not from shame at this frank explanation of weakness, but to hide his astonishment at her unexpected assistance. Would Tregher believe her? Had she bought him time?

Tregher bared his teeth in contempt. "He defies me out of ambition, not concern for my welfare."

"But it's true," said Anza. "The dire-lord is hurt. If only, Healer Ellisne, you would—"

"No," said Brock sharply, backing up a step. He did not trust the healer. She was a member of Tregher's party. If she touched him, she could probe freely. And once she discovered that he had indeed been named successor by Suprin Utdi, he would not only be in danger from Tregher, but he would be in worse peril from the magstrusi of Felca. She would tell them. As a stated member of Sedkethran society, she could do nothing less.

"No," he repeated, meeting her compelling gaze only to look away hastily. "I do not permit treatment."

"You have no choice," said Tregher. "I command it, Dire-lord."

"And I do not submit to your commands—"

The Chaimu bludgeon thudded off his skull, sending Brock to his knees. Through waves of dizziness he saw Ellisne coming toward him, stripping off her embroidered gauntlets and reaching out her pale hands.

"No!"

"*Merc sic t'*," said Rho, kneeling beside him to help hold him in place. "Let her help you, Dire-lord. You need help, *sic*?"

And then her icy hands were upon him, flesh merging with flesh and thoughts with thoughts as his pain seemed to flood from him like the blood from a wounded man. Her mind was inside his, sifting through the barriers he sought to erect against her. But she was no novice healer. He could not resist her.

Stop fighting me, she said. *What do you fear*?

I do not permit treatment!

Atrox. Her hand pressed against his chest and the dull ache there subsided. *I sensed this. Why do you resist? This is a serious injury. You should be returned to Felca for treatment.*

Promadi! he retorted, taut with fear. She was close, too close. She was threading through his Disciplines. Soon she would know.

Even an outcast may be treated. It is a basic right of—No! You must not! You could not do this! It is forbidden for a Sedkethran.

Utdi gave me the command, Brock said, trying to reach through her horror. *I am sworn to save the Held.*

Not at the price of galactic destruction. She withdrew her hands abruptly, breaking off the flow of comfort. *You are sworn first to Felca.*

No. You must listen to me. You must understand—

Promadi ga! She jerked back and rose to her feet, sweeping out an arm. "Kill him!" she said aloud. "You must kill him now, for he is a threat to us all!"

"YOU FOOL!"

Ton's slap caught the colonel across the jaw and sent her spinning back.

Taken by surprise, Falmah-Al managed to keep from falling by grabbing a chair. She righted herself, lifting a hand to gingerly touch her jaw. The whole side of her face felt numb until she touched it, and then suddenly pain stung it.

"You're finished, do you hear! I want you out, and I'm calling up to the ship for you to—"

"Wait a minute, Nls," she said sharply. "You're over-reacting—"

"Am I?" His voice was icy. The sunlight glinted on his silver hair as he turned from the window to glare at her. "Am I indeed? I spent twelve hours as a prisoner. They could have killed me. Or they could have filled me with slow-activant drugs and monitoring devices to make me their spy, their puppet!"

"But they didn't. My security team gave you a thorough examination. Perfect check out. The Held wanted you only for an exchange. We'll still get them—"

"Damn it, their capture is not at issue here! Your incompetence is!"

"This city is not secured, not with its underground tunnel network," she retorted, trying not to scream back at him. "My people followed procedure flawlessly. The fact that Held rebels were able to execute a surprise offense from those tunnels is—"

"—a very big mistake on your part."

50

"—is something which has gone into our tactical study files," she finished grimly. "And they will not be able to do that again."

"I am so relieved, Colonel," he said sarcastically, coming back to his desk. "I can now rest easy, knowing that you are in charge of my safety. Knowing that at any moment, I can be picked off by one of their assassination squads while you are in a completely opposite sector with your precious Major Millen."

She flushed, thankful now that she had taken the precaution of fitting herself with a miniature camcorder. Nls Ton would regret his jealous outburst, she vowed.

"The major and I were investigating the area where the suprin's corpse was discovered," she said. "We found the absence of his dire-lord significant. Certain accoutrements of the suprin associated with his rank were also missing."

"Thievery," he said, waving a hand impatiently. "Stop trying to deflect attention from your own criminal incompetence."

"I am doing my job correctly, Governor," she said crisply, hating him and hating herself for having ever loved him. He had used her achievements as a springboard for his own ambitious career. She had meant nothing to him but a tool, and she remained a tool now. But this time she would not let him discard her. She had her own ambitions. "And I think my report is worth more attention than you seem willing to give it."

"The only thing worth consideration at this moment is how fast you can be transferred out."

"The only thing worth consideration is can I get you the goda locations."

Ton stared at her, his face slowly changing color. For the first time since his release he became still. "How? If you're bluffing to save your skin—"

"We've been doing further cultural research," she said, moving briskly away from the personal arena although she really wanted to shove her bootheel through his teeth. "The suprin's body was given ritualistic attentions before it was abandoned. It is our theory that whoever was with the suprin at his death probably was told the goda locations."

"Yes, and that does us a tremendous amount of good," said Ton angrily. "You're stalling, Colonel." He punched a button on his desk. "Communications, get me a link with Captain Sala. Yes, on the ship."

"I am not stalling," said Falmah-Al. "You are so desperate to alleviate your humiliation by blaming me for what was a brilliantly conceived and executed Held operation that you are refusing to look at the possibilities before us. Don't you see, Ton? Your capture gave us an excellent opportunity to put an agent right into the rebels' midst."

"Who?" he said suspiciously, frowning. "Not the nairin. He can't be trusted."

"No, but he can be bought."

"In exchange for what? We spared him his miserable life, and we shall have constant trouble—"

"I have studied his profile. He is anxious for power. He feels a need to dominate. Historically, the quickest way to undermine rebel actions is to make token acceptance of their demands. If we give Nairin Tregher a little power over his own people, he will be all too happy to assist us in return."

"You mean make a dictator of him," said Ton slowly, obviously not liking the idea. "No. That would split my own base of authority."

"Not if we set up the prison camps on the western hemisphere as planned, and leave the nairin in charge of their administration. Prisoners make the best guards." She smiled slightly.

Ton's own lips curled in return as he grudgingly nodded an acknowledgment. "It is a use for him. But we still have the problem of neutralizing the godas."

"Nairin Tregher will find out where they are located," she said. "And he will give them to us."

"But suppose he can't find out. Suppose the suprin died with the knowledge. Or else it is locked away—"

"No, it is supposed to be shared with the successor at the moment of death. If the successor is not present, then a surrogate is found to deliver the message. I am certain the dire-lord is whom we seek. And being loyal to the throne, the dire-lord will be eager to deliver everything to Tregher, who will in turn give it to us."

The intercom buzzed. "Sir, link established with Captain Sala."

Ton sat still a moment, then he pushed the button. "Cancel that."

"Yes, sir."

"All right, Falmah-Al," he said, as she hid a sigh of relief. "Try it. But if you foul up on this one, that's it. Clear?"

She saluted, her face expressionless. "Quite clear, Governor."

As she left the office, she switched off the camcorder with a mental note to file it away with the other material she was collecting on Nls Ton. She had just bought herself sufficient time to prepare several contingencies. Although he was certain to try again to get rid of her, she would be ready for him.

The implant set upon Tregher enabled her scanners to locate him immediately. She marked his position on her maps with a small grim smile and activated the buzzer which would give him a subliminal but overwhelming urge to contact her agents dispatched nearby.

"I do not understand," said Izak with a frown as he watched her. "There is an agent surgically altered to resemble one of the Chaimu guards. Why not work through him? It is more direct."

"Yes, and a stupid waste of infiltration," she snapped, tired of Izak's ineptitude. "Why install him in that position only to betray him at first opportunity?"

Izak stiffened. "I thought only of saving time."

"Short time spans are not always the most efficient." She waved a dismissal. As soon as Izak was gone, she unlocked a small, highly classified scanner and activated it with a feeling of excitement. It was new equipment, its existence known only to the upper echelons of security personnel. Recent leaps in cyborg technology had created several useful spin-offs. This optic scanner was one of them. Her agent did not even know that one of his eyes had been replaced with an advanced cam that linked directly to her scanner. Without her activation it operated according to normal optic functions. But she could zoom to incredible magnifications if she chose, and a corder preserved every detail for further study.

When she activated the scanner, initially she saw nothing but a dark blur. Falmah-Al frowned. Had she been misled? Was it not yet ready for field use?

Then the agent moved, and she realized his line of vision had been blocked. She released a small sigh at her own impatience and increased magnification. The area where the nairin and his men were standing was dark and poorly lit.

She leaned closer to the screen, longing for audio. She had expected them to be congratulating themselves on their small *coup*. Instead they appeared to be arguing. The nairin's ugly face was thunderous as he gestured. She saw the serpent he carried lifting itself, ready to strike at . . .

She gasped, astonishment catching her in the throat. A Sedkethran male half-dressed and heavily bandaged was arguing back. She had never seen one of the species exhibit more than a token emotion. But this one looked as angry as Tregher. Her finger stabbed the magnification control again, and the picture leapt toward the Sedkethran's face. Falmah-Al blinked and rubbed her eyes but the scar she saw on the creature's cheek was not her imagination. It was the intricate mark of a dire-lord.

"On a Sedkethran?" she said aloud, and cursed her agents for never having brought her this information. It explained his elusiveness. He could vanish in thin air any time he chose. What a perfect choice for the bodyguard of a suprin. But she had never seen one of the spineless creatures who would fight before. This one was different, very different.

She zoomed back slightly to study him, noting the slope of his bones and the eerie paleness of his skin. Bloodless creatures, the Sedkethrans. Aloof, unflinchingly honest, dedicated to using their talents as empaths, they were among the few non-human species permitted access to the Imish Collective. This one was tall, as tall as the Chaimu shouting at him. His eyes, slanted and a pale grey green color, blazed with vehemence as he gestured. One of the guards struck him, making the patrician features twist with pain.

"*Gazal*!" swore Falmah-Al. "Tregher, don't you know what you have?" She twisted in her chair to reach for the intercom. "Technician Patterson, have you got your transender hooked up to any power supply?"

"It's still on side generator four, Colonel. But operational."

"Good." She kept an eye on the optic scanner as she spoke, and nearly cursed aloud as her agent swung his gaze away. "I want you to grab someone for me. A Sedkethran at the following coordinates—"

"Excuse me, Colonel. A Sedkethran? They don't scramble on normal transender signals."

She'd forgotten. "All right, Patterson," she said with a grimace. "Then a Chaimu." The screen showed a female Sedkethran abruptly backing away from the dire-lord and gesturing what was obviously a command. One of the guards, a big new-human in charge armor, aimed his weapon at the dire-lord. "No! Patterson! Grab a human, coordinates seven mark five, eastern subsector two. Got it? Now!"

"Sending," said Patterson. If he succeeded in grabbing the guard before he fired he would have had to file coordinates with extreme rapidity. There was a sudden blur, and the new-human disappeared. "Got him, Colonel. Further orders?"

"Have him disarmed and held in a security cell," she said, grinning at the confusion moving across her screen as the nairin gesticulated and shouted and guards milled about. "Raw meat to your table, Patterson."

"Glad to oblige, Colonel."

Falmah-Al cut communications and called a deputy into her office. "Dispatch, priority," she said, stamping her signet onto a flimsy and tossing it at the young woman. "I want Millen to personally lead a squad down to eastern subsector two. This message is to be given to Nairin Tregher. Millen is to see to the details. Go."

The deputy saluted and hurried out. Falmah-Al got up to pace about her office. She was close, very close to having the dire-lord in her possession. With the location of the godas to her credit, even Ton wouldn't be able to stop her rapid ascent on the political ladder. She stopped in midstride, cutting off her own ambitious dreams, and punched the intercom.

"Library access," she said. "Reference: Held culture. Specifics: Dire-lord. Function. Duties. And any bio material available upon individuals who have held that office."

"Acknowledged. Ten minutes until relay."

She returned to her pacing, keeping an eye upon her optic scanner as the screen cleared again to show a pair of Chaimu guards dragging the dire-lord through a doorway. Her agent's attention remained focused upon the nairin arguing with the female Sedkethran. In disgust Falmah-Al switched off the screen. The dire-lord was a series of contradictions that intrigued her very much. Sedkethrans abhorred war. They committed no acts of violence. They committed no crimes. Able to walk through walls or appear anywhere they chose, they restricted themselves inside rigid codes of behavior. Deviations were not permitted.

"But you are a very large deviation," Falmah-Al muttered to herself. "You are a warrior, pledged to protect the life of the Held Suprin. Yet Sedkethrans do not fight. Interesting. Very interesting indeed. I must know more."

Ten minutes later the library began to chatter information across her viewscreen:

DIRE-LORD. HIGHEST HELD WARRIOR RANK BELOW ROYALS. CROSSREFERENCED TO HELD COURT ETIQUETTE. DIRE-LORD NOT SUBJECT TO COMMANDS OF HONORABLES. DIRE-LORD ANSWERABLE ONLY TO HELD SUPRIN. POSITION GAINED THROUGH RIGOROUS TESTS, INCLUDING TRIAL BY COMBAT. POSITION GRANTED FOR LIFE.

FUNCTION. DIRE-LORD RESPONSIBLE FOR PHYSICAL SAFETY OF HELD SUPRIN AT ALL TIMES.

DUTIES. DIRE-LORD ATTENDS SUPRIN AT ALL FUNCTIONS, BOTH OFFICIAL AND PRIVATE. DIRE-LORD TESTS FOOD. DETECTS ASSASSINATION DEVICES. SURVEYS ANY OFFICIAL SEEKING AUDIENCE WITH SUPRIN.

CURRENT DIRE-LORD. FIFTH IN SERVICE OF SUPRIN UTDI XII. AWARDED CHAIMU NAME BROCK AT INVESTITURE CEREMONY. SEDKETHRAN. ORIGIN FELCA OF STAR SYSTEM PRAXOS.

NO FURTHER INFORMATION.

Falmah-Al stared in frustration at her screen. No further information. But she needed to understand this creature. She needed a means of prying him open to her questions.

"Library access," she said. "Cross-reference Dire-lord Brock to planet Felca. Data spill."

"Acknowledged. No further information."

"So you've been blotted from the official records," she said thoughtfully. "Why? Even that seems too much for the secretive Sedkethrans." She recalled watching the female healer who had seemed to actually be urging the guards to shoot the dire-lord. That was odd too. Oddities and contradictions marked a puzzle, and a puzzle marked a secret. A secret was something a chief of security should always know. Falmah-Al smiled slightly to herself. She would have the female brought in for questioning, too.

* * *

Across Impryn, trailer sleds rumbled slowly over the multiple layers of streets criss-crossing each other, devoid of anything but the most cautious traffic. Each trailer blared the same announcement in stilted Held dialect:

"ATTENTION! ATTENTION! ALL CITIZENS MUST REPORT TO CENTRAL FOOD DISPENSARIES IN THEIR SECTOR TO RECEIVE IDENTIFICATION TAGGING. FAILURE TO REPORT WILL RESULT IN TERMINATION."

"It's started," said Brock to one of the Chaimu guards busy positioning him at the broken end of the bridge which had once spanned the Marupish. Brock could feel the sway of the structure against the current of the wind. Below him the river churned black and sluggish on its course. It was swollen with debris, and corpses bobbed and tumbled in the foam. Oily threads of orange or purple followed in the wake of crushed and leaking barrels of noxious chemical waste dumped in during the fighting. Beneath the bridge structure, folzone factories and glastel works stood silent, robbed of their usual noisy productivity along the water's edge. The whole city was silent, except for the trailers blaring out their ominous message.

"Don't you realize what that means?" insisted Brock as his hands were shackled to the jutting rib of a girder. "Identification tags. Marked and labeled. Then off to labor camps."

"Shut up."

"The Colonids are old-humans. You know what they think about anyone who doesn't belong to their species. You know what they'll use you for."

With a snarl, the Chaimu shoved Brock painfully into the bridge railing and stalked away with a gesture to his companion who followed him. Ellisne remained, a tall slender figure, graceful in pale silhouette against the gloominess of the cloudy sky. The wind whipped at her robes, plastering them to her body to reveal every feminine outline. Her features were set in a careful mask. Even the fire in her eyes was banked, muted down to a glitter.

Brock straightened with a wince and tugged at his bonds in one futile gesture. The shackles were fission locked, lightweight, but inescapable. If only he could *flick*, he thought, resisting the frustrated urge to jerk at them again. The limitations of his disability chaffed him more and more. He shoved away the fear that his atrox might never heal, that he would be doomed

57

for the rest of his life to have to travel conventionally along distance instead of around it, that he would find walls and locked doors, that he would be hemmed in, trapped, frustrated.

"How can you participate in this of your own free will?" he demanded. "Everything the Colonids say and everything they offer is a lie. And if you help them, then you betray—"

"I am not the traitor, *promadi*!" she said, her stony facade cracking. "Tregher works for peace. He has made the agreement to submit in order to save his people's lives. The killing must end. But you would do more than revive the killing. You would destroy Felca!"

He stared at her, cold with astonishment. Had she read more than he thought? Did she already know everything?

"Ellisne—"

"I have had mystic training," she snapped. "In the Writings it is said that Felca is Goda Prime. We are devoted to peace. You know that. You studied the Writings too. But you fled your training. You rejected the teachings of the magstrusi, you who were destined to be a magstrus yourself. You threw everything away just to live among these Chaimu with their sybartic pleasures and their celebration of inward decay. You threw away the opportunity to restore life in order to learn how to kill. You glory in death, *promadi*. Your hands reek with blood. And now you are not content with bringing shame upon shame to your own people. You must also destroy us. Why?"

"Do not call me *promadi*," he said stiffly. "My name is Brock."

"Lie," she retorted. "It is a Chaimu name which you have adopted because your own was stripped from you by the magstrusi to shame you."

His head came up. Memories of the shaming flooded his unwilling mind. He remembered the sticky, unpleasant warmth of a winter day and how the magstrusi had ringed him in the shadowy glare of Felca's dim sun. He was supposed to cower beneath their contempt. He was supposed to quiver under the lash, to permit himself to be beaten back into submission. He was supposed to fear the awful loneliness of exile hanging over his head as a threat. But he had shunned fear as he had shunned repression. He had simply walked away from the circle, refusing to participate in their cruel ceremony. It was his last day on Felca.

"We Sedkethrans stand outside politics," Ellisne was continuing. "What does it matter which empire rules the galaxy? Does such a trivial justification underlie your desire to destroy Felca? Don't you realize what will happen to your people, your home, your world if Goda Prime is activated? The atmosphere will be sheared off. Everything will be laid waste. Forty million people will be murdered. And for what purpose? Your revenge, *promadi*? Your glory? Do you truly hate Felca so much?"

"Hate," he said. "How swiftly you refer to the emotions which you refuse to experience."

Her eyes became vivid beams of color, boring into him with astonishment. "You use the accusation of a non-Sedkethran. For what purpose? You know we control emotions only during our work, to protect our patients. You—"

"Olbin sent you here, didn't he?" said Brock with sudden insight. "Why? To spy on me? To persuade me to come back? To make sure I die?"

Confusion and guilt spilled across her face before she turned away to face the emptiness of sky and river. Skiks dived and played in the air, chattering their cry.

"You were their best pupil," she said quietly, keeping her back to him. "You gave them hope for the first time since the second Chaimu dynasty. You hurt them very deeply."

She turned suddenly, her eyes meeting his in a plea. "Brock, please: Put away the anger and hatred which lie within your heart. Do not destroy Felca for a cause that is not ours."

He heard the sound of an airsled coming, and said, with a pleading of his own: "Ellisne, open your eyes to what the Colonids are. At least the Held left us alone. The Colonids never will."

"I will have to probe you for them," she said as though resigning herself. She, too, glanced toward the approaching sled. "I will have to tell them where all the godas are. It is the only way of stopping you from your madness."

"And when you tell them," he said grimly, "they will destroy the godas, Felca included. Felca most probably first of all. Enjoy that guilt, *promadise*."

She flinched. "No. There will be no need to dest—"

"The Colonids had no need to destroy Mabruk either," he said sharply, his words almost drowned out as the sled chuffed directly over them and began to descend. "A defenseless planet devoted entirely to producing children and to conducting medical research. Destroyed. Blown to ashes. Think about Mabruk when you betray me."

ELLISNE'S ESCORT OF armed guards fell back at the doorway, leaving her to enter the room alone. She had been brought through darkness and pouring rain from her spartan cell at the detention center to this small, elegant villa on the broad embassy avenue, which had somehow escaped the bombings. There had been no explanations, and since she was aware before she even entered the room that it was empty, it did not look as though she would be told anything soon.

The room was large, designed for receiving the plentiful number of guests normally gathered for embassy functions. Its furnishings were opulent, reflecting an expensive taste for tholan-woven fabrics, fist-sized jewels cut into intricate boxes by the court jeweller Muzl Obtar, long carpets, and living glow-tapes which gave off a soft light flattering to the complexion of court ladies and *dalmas*. Ellisne was surprised. She had not expected Colonids to know or care about maintaining glowtapes.

Glancing only once at the black monitor globe floating in an unobtrusive corner, Ellisne crossed the room to gaze out one of the tall, narrow windows. The soft warm light of the room reflected back at her from the black mirror of the night. Rain beaded down the heavily shielded glastel, blurring her reflection into a puzzle of rich colors and melting shapes. The room was not heated, but she found it too warm because of its stuffiness. It had the smell of having been closed off for a while.

Ellisne took off her wet cloak, laid it neatly over a footstool, and folded her hands within the wide sleeves of her simple robe. She had not seen Brock since the Colonids had picked them up at the bridge and taken them to the detention center. His parting words to her about Mabruk had been well designed to strike deep. Doubts had unsettled her for the rest of the day. She was still uneasy. And he was as wise as the Magstrus Olbin had warned her. Those slanted eyes, grey-green like the heart of ice, were impossible to read. But they saw everything. And she had the uncomfortable notion that he had read her far more deeply than she intended anyone to. More deeply perhaps than even Magstrus Olbin had?

No! She moved away from the window in denial. She had come to Darjahl Imperial because it was her duty. The magstrusi had chosen her to control a potentially explosive situation. At the time she had been sent, she had not seen their wisdom. Now, after having read the mind of the *promadi* Brock and seen the dreadful intentions within him, she realized that the instincts of the magstruši were correct. Felca was in serious danger. She must not let the *promadi* deflect her from her purpose. She must close her mind to chaotic emotions. She must shut out the truths he had spoken.

But to deny a truth was to twist it. And that was a greater wrong.

Confused, she moved to a chair, but did not sit down. She longed to be with the *promadi*, asking him all the questions clamoring within her. Yet she feared him as she feared no other, not even the powerful magstrusi. For he was an attractive danger, fascinating in the mass of contradictions he offered, making blatant displays of forbidden emotions one minute before retreating behind a mask of formality the next, speaking with earnest persuasiveness yet foretelling the destruction of all she upheld. He revelled in that which was not permitted, yet his mind worked along the lines of a magstrus. She thought of that contact, trembling as she remembered the power of his mind which had so nearly swamped hers. Yet he was injured and lacking the amplification of his atrox. She drew in a breath. If he were well, what would be the range of his abilities?

"There is anger within him," Magstrus Olbin had said at the council meeting where she was chosen to come here as a control, "but no evil. He refuses to focus his abilities into their full potential."

"He wastes a great gift," Magstrus Pare said. "One which we need!"

"Better to lose the use of that gift than to see it turned against us."

"Syllogisms!" snorted Magstrus Pare against the murmurs which rose around the council chamber. "He is a random factor which should be restrained. Or we shall all come to regret our leniency!"

"We already do," she murmured aloud, picking up an Obtar ruby box to see if she could find the trick of opening it. Puzzles were always mental exercises on Felca, designed to teach rather than to amuse. The confusion within her made it a relief to seek occupation for her hands.

"Exquisite, isn't it?" said a man's voice in accented but fluent Held Formal.

She turned in time to see the speaker step through a doorway where previously there had been only a wall of carved paneling. A panel closed silently behind him, and it was as though there had never been an opening at all. The opulent intricacies of Held culture did not distress her, but she was perhaps dismayed that so much energy should be devoted to the trivial. She put down the jewel.

The man approaching her with an enormous, sleekly furred quadruped at his side was old-human. There were no physical or genetic differences between old-humans and newans. When the Held had encompassed this species centuries earlier, some had been able to adjust to the concept of there being other sentient life forms; others had elected to be placed in isolation. Thus, the Colonids had been shipped out to fringe worlds and cut off from Held culture. And now they had returned. The illogic of political idealisms did not interest her. But she eyed this man warily now, recognizing him at once from the holographs she had studied before coming. He was tall for his kind, with long flat bones. He had once been muscular, but now his body was soft beneath the tailored lines of his clothing. Jowls blurred his jawline, and his thick silver hair shone with almost metallic luster in the light from the glowtapes. He was Nls Ton, a man who had survived the tough climb from military service into the political arena. In his youth he had been known as Ton the Butcher.

Something of that old cruelty still emanated along his mental projections. Although he wore, as did all Colonids, a device which protected his full mental patterns from being read, she could still pick up enough to warn her not to trust him. Power overlaid earlier patterns, but she could not keep herself from drifting slightly back in revulsion as he walked toward her.

Again confusion distracted her. Could the magstrusi truly desire her to assist this man against one of their own kind? Brock is *promadi*, she reminded herself sternly and shook the distractions away.

She was not an osmatic, but a sudden fear smell alerted her. Ton had stopped. The animal beside him blinked round tawny eyes. The tip of its striped tail twitched nervously. The false smile on Ton's face faded. He stared at her.

She realized with annoyance that she was drifting, subconsciously allowing herself to fade, and quickly corrected her appearance. He was afraid of her because she was not human.

Deliberately she took a non-threatening position by sitting down. "You see?" she said in a soft voice designed on all tonal frequencies to be reassuring. "I am not really a spiritual apparition. I can sit on solid matter and not fall through."

The tense set of his shoulders relaxed slightly. He resumed the false smile, but behind it his eyes remained as wary as her own.

"I am Governor Ton," he said, coming no closer to her. His pet stretched itself out full-length on the floor with a yawn that revealed sizable fangs. "I understand you are here to assist us, Healer Ellisne. Forgive my suspicions, but why should you wish to do that? Felca is a full-fledged member of the Held. We are, therefore," he said, baring his teeth in a delicate little smile, "enemies."

A stronger wave of distrust engulfed her. She closed it off, refusing to let emotions distract her at this moment when she needed all her senses alert.

"Felca's neutrality is well-known," she said without inflection, speaking in perfect Imish. "And our healers visit the Imish Collective as frequently as they are permitted."

"To spy perhaps?"

The monitor had moved imperceptibly closer. Ellisne avoided looking at it. She suspected the harsh, abrupt mannered Colonel Falmah-Al was watching this meeting through it. She wished she were dealing with the colonel directly. Falmah-Al dealt straight on. She did not layer every statement with subtle traps and altered meanings as the governor was attempting to do. Ellisne suddenly remembered that last moment with the *promadi* on the bridge, when he had been staring into her eyes, trying to convince her to believe his reasons. He intended to destroy her world. Why then was it so much harder to ally herself with Governor Ton, whose objectives were her own?

"Sedkethrans are not spies, Governor Ton," she said, her voice still containing reassurance. It did not seem to be having any effect upon him.

"Your species is ideally suited for the job. My troops call you ghosts. How can we design surveillance protectors against ghosts?"

"That does not change the facts." She stared up at him. "You distrust my offer. Let me speak plainly. Felca is opposed to war in all its forms. Our dedication to the preservation of life leaves us no other position. Yet, because of the terrible escalation of hatred between your forces and those remaining within the Held, we fear goda weapons will be unleashed."

"Goda . . . excuse me. What sort of weapons?"

His attempt at feigning ignorance was clumsy; Ellisne found herself becoming increasingly impatient with him.

"I assure the governor that these terrible weapons are known to Imish military personnel. Perhaps the governor should seek information later from Colonel Falmah-Al."

The smile dropped from Ton's face. His eyes flickered to the monitor hanging overhead. "Continue."

"The destruction would be terrible. Countless lives would be lost. Godas were built at the apex of Chaimu technology, and even at that time they were too frightening to contemplate using."

"Yet you have held them over us constantly as a threat! Do you know what it is like, Healer, to grow up under fear, never knowing if you live close to one of those weapons, never knowing when some Chaimu whim might detonate them?"

She stared at him, longing to say yes and not daring to utter the word. "But you have ceased to fear them. You came—"

"Yes, we came. Once we found out our worlds were not booby-trapped we came out! And we have won! We have beaten you!"

She sat there with her hands folded in her sleeves, but her hands had become fists. He was toying with her, throwing war rhetoric at her to goad her into unwise words. Why?

Couldn't he understand what she was offering? She strove to uncurl her fists, and when calm was restored to her, she spoke into the silence:

"We do not want the dire-lord to succeed in what he proposes."

"The dire-lord is a Sedkethran. So are you. Why betray him to us?"

She suppressed a sigh. How many more times would he test her? "Brock is an outcast from Felca. Should he ever return to his home planet he would face severe punishment and retribution." She paused a moment, then added, "Of course if I cannot be certain that we do indeed have the same objectives in this matter, and if I cannot have your assurance that the godas will be destroyed or rendered permanently inactive, then I will not help you."

Again a long silence stretched through the room. The animal began licking its paw with slow, self-absorbed swipes of its tongue. Ton clasped his hands at his back and began to walk slowly back and forth in front of her. He frowned as though seeking the right words.

"I believe that our objectives are the same, if you are being truthful. However—" He paused, staring at her as she stiffened. "Healer? What is wrong?"

She rose to her feet, rigid against that sharp burst of pain transmitted directly to her mind. The Disciplines came to her aid, numbing it, but she could hear the cry in her mind.

"Healer Ellisne—"

"What are you doing?" she cried, turning fiercely on Ton. Flinching back, he drew a weapon, but she paid no heed.

"You are torturing him, trying to make him talk! Are you mad? He will never tell you what you want to know. I can get you the information easily, painlessly. I have only to read his thoughts. I made you that offer openly, without tricks, and you still prefer to hurt—"

"Stay where you are!" he said sharply. "We aren't fools. Why should we trust you?"

Fury scorched through her, rising up so strong even her inner reflexes could not hold it down. She glared at him. "Barbarian!" she shouted, and *flicked* to the detention center.

As she materialized in the quarters she had been assigned, another burst of pain rocked her. She lifted both hands to her temples, locating Brock within the building, and *flicked* directly to his cell.

65

The sight before her was appalling. For a moment she could only stare at the interrogation machine he was strapped to.

"Where are the godas located?" blared a speaker overhead, startling her. A light blinked on the control bank of the machine, and Brock's body jerked violently against the restraints. She reeled from his pain and braced herself, fighting her own immediate urge to grasp his arm and draw out his torment. But that wasn't the way. She must first find out how to free him.

"Where are the vaults containing the Held treasury?" blared the speaker. "How many Heldfleet ships escaped the battle? Where are the rebel bases located? Where are the godas?"

The track cycled relentlessly. Brock lay there panting and limp, his wrists swollen and bloody from the jolts of power that threw him against his bonds. She was studying the control panel with desperate intensity when a relay clicked over and a different light flashed.

"Method 7 ineffective," announced the speaker. "Switching to Method 8. Mehedrine barbathol will be applied." With a soft whir a panel opened in the central core of the machine and a hypo was extended.

"No!" she cried and grabbed it from the robot arm.

An alarm sounded with an ear-splitting whoop. "Intruder in Cell Nine. Warning. Warning. Intruder in Cell Nine."

She looked over her shoulder at the door, hearing the sound of running footsteps in the corridor. There wasn't time to figure out the controls. But if she pushed the wrong one, something even more terrible might be done to him.

"Brock!" She grasped his shoulder and shook it, steeling herself against the sensations which flooded across her empathy threshold. Grogginess, pain, disorientation . . . she pushed through them to reach him. "Brock! Tell me how to free you from this thing. Hurry! Brock!"

His eyes swam open. He gasped, responding to her touch. "Left panel. The dial."

She pounced on it, and the straps released with loud clicks. There was a shout outside the cell door. It crashed open. She had never *flicked* another adult before, only children. She wasn't sure if she could do it. But there was no more time. Ellisne grabbed Brock with both hands and *flicked* just as disruptor fire burned across her back.

Her scream echoed after her through layers and layers of

greyness. She spiralled dizzily, lost, not knowing where she was going, unable to grasp her senses enough to direct their impetus through interstitial time. Then through foggy mists of agony she felt Brock's mind steady hers. He reached through her, became her, to guide them. And in that moment of oneness, there were no secrets on either side. She thought dimly, *The magstrusi were wrong to punish him. He is not what they fear him to be.*

Then they were tumbling to the ground, safely back in the physical dimension once again. She landed on her knees and crouched there, gasping. It took a second before she became conscious enough of her surroundings to realize they were outside in the darkness of the night, buffeted by wind and slashing rain.

"Ellisne?"

His voice reached her faintly, muffled by the water drumming around them as though it meant to drown the world.

"Ellisne?"

She started as his lips brushed her ear, but she nodded this time in response.

"Can you stand?"

She nodded again, feeling oddly ashamed as his hands took her arm and steadied her. She was supposed to be helping him. "I am a poor rescuer."

"What?"

"Nothing." It was impossible to speak in such wild weather. Besides, she needed to conserve her energy.

"This way."

He guided her along the street, weaving back and forth as they stumbled in unison, leaning on each other for support. His pain was fading; hers was stinging more and more fiercely. Gripping each other's hands with flesh made slippery by the rain, they shared the discomfort, halving it, dissipating it by gradual degrees.

"Here."

He pulled her suddenly to the left, and abruptly the rain was cut off. She could breathe again. She gasped, sinking down beneath the small shelter of a half-fallen structure, and wiped the water from her face. He crowded her, his body big and awkward in the small space. There was water beneath them, and she was beginning to shake as her body temperature dipped below even what was comfortable for a Sedkethran, but at the moment she was too grateful for the shelter they had found to find fault with it.

"How bad is it?" asked Brock.

She stiffened with a gasp as his fingers gently touched her back. "A graze, I think."

"I think so too. Otherwise you'd be down by now."

How matter-of-factly he spoke of being shot and cut down by weapons! Where had he learned such behavior? Why had he sought to learn it?

"You changed sides a little late," he was saying as she frowned at the water gushing over the edge of their shelter. "But just in time. Thank you."

"The Imish are fools," she snapped, her anger returning. "I offered to obtain the information for them, and instead they tricked me. They are illogical brutes. It would have been painless, civilized—"

"Suprin Utdi would have utilized your offer," said Brock. "But you cannot expect Colonids to behave according to Held standards."

She bowed her head, ashamed to think she had made such a mistake. "The magstrusi expected it," she said after a moment.

"Magstrusi! *Cuh*!" He grunted an explosive Chaimu oath. "I hope you now see their blindness."

"I shall not speak against their wisdom as you do, with bitterness and hatred," she said in rebuke. "I remain obedient to the Writings."

He hunched his shoulders. "And does that mean you intend to take me back to the Colonids as soon as the rain stops?"

"No," she said quietly, miserably torn by shame once again. Would he sense her lie?

"You are thinking of Falmah-Al," he said, his voice gritty. "You are thinking you can trust her even if Ton is treacherous. Who do you think ordered me placed on the interrogation machine?"

"I am caught by a dichotomy," she said, stung. "What they do is wrong, yet that is only because they are afraid. Their civilization is young, still half-savage. They exhibit many faults, but at least they understand that the goda destruction should not be unleashed. Brock, you must surrender this goal."

He was silent for so long she began to hope that finally the teachings of his youth were going to influence him. Surely he must see the truth of her argument. Surely he could put the sword out of his heart.

"I held Suprin Utdi while he died, Ellisne," he said at last.

She gasped, appalled not only by the recklessness of such an action for one half-trained, but also by a greater fear. What had he *seen* in sharing death? What had he dared reach for?

"That's very dangerous—"

"I know." He shifted and she felt his eyes staring at her through the darkness. A thousand nuances seemed to play through those two words. "But I loved him as a father. I could not deny him, not even to obey my fear, not even to save the few things Sedkethran which I still honor."

She sat stunned by what he was revealing. Magstrus Pare's fears were true! Brock was daring to reach for the unattainable. *We are not permitted to evolve*, she wanted to say. Instead, she stumbled over the accusation and said, "Parents are put aside at Change. Why do you constantly seek to regress, *promadi*?"

He laughed softly. It was a peculiar sound that startled and affronted her. Sedkethrans did not laugh; he was deliberately seeking to provoke her.

"Regress?" he echoed. "Must you twist everything to fit the narrow restrictions set upon your mind?"

"I have completed the training of a healer," she said stiffly. "I have entered the round chamber of the magstrusi, and when I have learned the full measure of all the Writings then I shall—"

"—aspire to be a mystic," he finished. "Perfect. Your mind runs along each groove set for it in exact order. They must be very pleased with your progress."

She drew herself up. "Yes, I—" She stopped, suddenly aware that he was mocking her. Anger struck her sharply below the atrox.

"Yes, indeed. That is why you were sent here as a control, isn't it?"

She felt robbed of breath. He wasn't on that level. He wasn't supposed to be able to discern such things!

"But I can, Healer," he said with anger. "Do the magstrusi truly believe that just because I fled the round chamber all those years ago I have remained frozen at that point? Do they truly delude themselves, hoping that I have learned nothing further on my own?"

"Self-training is not permitted. It is error."

Again he laughed. "Of course it is." He seized her wrist with such roughness she cried out. "Why won't you listen? Why won't you see? You've had enough training to know that we are nothing more than Chaimu creations—"

"Blasphemy," she whispered, her lips trembling at the magnitude of his error. She longed to tell him the truth, but managed to seal off the impulse. It was better if he did not know. She sought a way to move him farther along the wrong path.

"Felca is Goda Prime," he said. "It is not a planet. It is a weapon. Sedkethrans are designed to operate that weapon."

"No! We do not wage war. We are healers—"

"Chosen by the ancient Chaimu to populate Felca, to take care of the survivors of a goda attack."

"No!" She tried without success to break free of his grip. "We are our own selves. We have our own origin. We are not—"

"Why aren't emotions permitted?"

"Emotions interfere with healing—"

"How can they? Is not the emotion of caring important to one who is ill? Love? Tenderness? Do they not help? Of course they do."

"You are not permitted to heal. You do not know."

"Nevertheless I have helped others. As I tried to help the suprin."

She arched against the limited space of their shelter, trying to get free. "Forbidden!"

"Why? Because I don't have the healer's shields to prevent me from merging too well with my patient? From learning too much about what it means to live? To think? To feel?"

"*Promadi*! Evil! You should be destroyed!"

"Then why didn't you let the Colonids destroy me?" he asked, pulling her back as she attempted to throw herself out into the rain. "I have broken every code held sacred on Felca. Why save me? Is it because deep inside you know I am right, Ellisne? Is it because somewhere beneath the iron bars of your training there remains something honest within you that wants to face the truth as it is and not as it has been told?"

"No!"

"I think there is." He drew a deep breath and winced, but she felt nothing cross their touch. He was now shielding himself completely from her. "I must experience all emotions. I must find out what it means to be whole. I shared the ending with Utdi, and it was not just the passing of the Superior Life into a new vessel—"

She gasped, shaking with horror. "Surely—"

"It was also the sharing of race memories, back to the days of the ancients who created the Held. I now know what manner of creatures they were just as I know what their descendents have become. I have taken a step."

She closed her eyes, shaking her head. He was too strong. He could not be controlled. "On Felca we are taught that there is a point we may not cross. We are not free to sacrifice ourselves for others. That is wasteful."

"Of course." He released her wrist and leaned back, rubbing his chest. "I sacrificed my atrox to save Utdi."

The sadness in his voice made her think that at last she had found the weak point in his logic.

"Yes," she said at once. "You have condemned yourself to this dimension for the rest of your existence, and to what purpose? To save the suprin's life? But that life was not saved. Therefore, your sacrifice was wasted. You achieved nothing. You lost a great deal. The Writings are correct, as always."

"They are false!" He sat up. "I lost much, yes. But I gained more. I gained all that Utdi knows and was. I came that much closer to becoming what is real. And I was named suprin, not Tregher."

"No!" Again shock numbed her. "It is not permitted! You follow falsehood down a dangerous path, *promadi*. You will find at its end terrible things—"

"I already see them," he replied softly. "Many variations spreading out before me."

An odd note in his voice caught her attention. He sat rigidly, staring past her at the rain with his hand suspended in midair.

Puzzled, she caught his hand, her mind reaching for his, and saw with horror that he was in multiple timestreams. There was the Chaimu army chanting out their war songs, hundreds of thousands of them standing on a broad plain beneath a fringe-world sun. Their hoarse voices rose in unison, creating a terrifying sound that swelled and rumbled across the earth. There was a sense of falling through a void of dense blackness, surrounded only by unfamiliar frets of

71

chromium and glastel, then sudden flashes of color against the blackness of space as a cluster ship separated into a hundred swift wedges, all hurtling toward a Colonid battlecruiser as insects swarm toward the face of an immense bulox. There was the opulent glitter of the Held throne room, with the sun striking down through the ocular window in the ceiling, splashing the people assembled with blood-colored light. The *promadi*, seated upon the throne in Chaimu robes, the shameful scar on his face crossed through, beckoned to her and Magstrus Olbin, bent and translucent with age. Together they walked forward, and within the wide folds of her sleeve she held the dagger that would kill the *promadi*. . . .

"No!"

She jerked back from his mind, panting for breath. "No! It isn't true! I could never kill! I will not become what you are, not even to stop you! I won't—"

"Ellisne. Gently. Hush." His hands caught her clenched ones and he held her tightly in his arms until she calmed enough to be ashamed of her blind panic.

"You're tricking me. You can't really see multiple timestreams. You can't really see the future. I will never use a dagger to kill someone."

"I hope not, Ellisne," he said, giving her no comfort at all. "But none of us can ever say what we will or won't do. Circumstances change. Or have you forgotten that yesterday you demanded that Arkist Davn kill me?"

She felt lost, sucked this way and that by tides of confusion. She longed for Felca and its calm order. She longed for the dull complexity of her studies. She wished she had never been sent here. Dealing with the *promadi* was a test, and she feared she was failing it. Brock's hands gripping her arms seemed to tell her of the blood upon them, reminding her of the countless lives he had taken in his determination to live in a way he was not created for. For the first time in her life, she knew fear for herself. Would he kill her?

"I think it has to do with the *skial* in the suprin's bloodstream, combined with the strain on my atrox," he was saying. "It is happening less often."

She frowned. "What else do you tamper with? You see alternate futures. Do you see the past as well? Do you dare alter—"

"I'm not a fool!" he retorted. "Time is too complicated a grid for anyone to dabble with alternatives."

"But the temptation is there."

"One more reason for my destruction, I suppose." He released her. "Will you tell Olbin immediately? He will probably replace you with an avenging magstrus."

Relief shot through her. He did not intend to kill her. And in its place immediately came anger. He did not think her a sufficient threat. He considered her a mere student, not strong enough to be a danger to him.

"Why should he?" she retorted. "Olbin sent me because he knew I could do what was necessary to deal with this situation."

"By now Olbin should know that simple arguments will not deter me."

She wanted to cry out in despair and did not know how. "But why? Why, if you want to make the Sedkethrans evolve into what you think you are becoming, do you want to destroy Felca? You will kill millions of people—"

"I must stop the Colonids," he said grimly. "I think the rain is easing up."

She gripped his sleeve to keep him from ducking out. "Why must you? One master is as good as another—"

"There! You admit it!" he cried, turning on her fiercely. "We are the Held's creatures, put on Felca to unleash Goda Prime at the suprin's command."

"The suprin is dead. The Held is defeated," she said wearily, tired of this circular discussion and its impasses. "There will never be such a command given now if you will have done."

"Of course," he said as though surprised. "I should have realized that long ago. The magstrusi want the Colonids to win. They want the Held to be destroyed."

"Stop separating yourself from us," she said in exasperation. "You are Sedkethran too. Surely you understand that this is a logical solution to an ancient problem."

"No, I do not understand." He ducked out from under the shelter as the rain slowed to a light drizzle and then stopped altogether. He stood in the street, staring at her as she followed more slowly. Her limbs were stiff and tired. Her sodden clothes clung uncomfortably to her body.

"The Held gave us freedom," Brock said. "Freedom to twist reality into lies of Forbiddens and Disciplines. Freedom to change and grow if we chose. As I have chosen. The Colonids will take away that freedom."

"Why should they harm us? We are permitted to travel through the Imish Collective, giving assistance as it is needed. We are among the few alien species they trust."

"They *trust* no one," he said harshly. "And it is time you saw that. You are a means to an end, Ellisne. They will use you to stop me and then they will dispose of you."

"Individual outcome does not matter—"

"Then think about Felca! When they find out the Sedkethrans won't join in their ways, when they find out the Sedkethrans will not swear allegiance to their bloodstained banners, when they find out the Sedkethrans expect to be left alone to meditate and contemplate and travel as freely as they did under the Held, they will close an iron fist around Felca and crush it."

"You are speaking from fear. You do not know these things." She stared up at him. "Or are you seeing another time-stream?"

"No, Ellisne," he said quietly. "I am speaking from years of fighting them. I am speaking from years of watching the casualities pile up, of seeing their treacheries undermining treaty attempts, of seeing the vids of Mabruk exploding just because they wanted to be sure there would be no future generations of Chaimu to rise up against them. There will be no more Chaimu children because of them, Ellisne. Specifically because of Colonel Falmah-Al, whom you admire. It was her idea to destroy Mabruk and its irreplacable genetic banks."

"I have told you they are an immature civilization. They tend to fear things they do not understand. But in time—"

"In time, they will go on destroying things they do not understand. The Chaimu were tolerant of differences. Do not expect the same from the Colonids."

"They call themselves Imish."

"Yes. And do you know who Im was?"

"An ancient leader."

"The man who would not accept Chaimu authority over human. The man who led the humans in so many futile, bloodbath wars the Chaimu isolated them out of mercy to save the human race from extinction. Far, far back in the dimmest times of human history before they knew anything about the rest of the galaxy, they conducted such wars against each other. They called those wars *jihad*. Holy wars. An impossible contradiction in logic, don't you agree?"

She frowned uneasily. How could Brock raise so many confusing questions within her?

"But they have evolved, *promadi*. That was thousands of years ago. They have changed."

"Have they?" He started to walk away.

She darted in front of him. "Where are you going?"

"Where would you have me go?" he asked. "Back to the Colonid headquarters and turn myself in? Why, then, did you jeopardize your own standing with them by making that spectacular rescue?"

It was true. They would not trust her again. She had failed.

"I must find Rho," he said when she remained silent. "If he is still alive, I will need his help. We have to contact Esmir Eondal if possible and find out how much of Heldfleet has survived."

He stepped around her and started up the street, then stopped and glanced back. "I don't advise you to go back to Falmah-Al. She'll kill you."

Ellisne made an effort to compose herself. "I must return to Felca. I have failed."

"Then your best chance of getting there is to come with me," he said drily.

It was true. If he was determined to destroy her home, then she might as well be there to die with the others. A Sedkethran could not live alone. She wondered when he would realize that.

He walked on, and after a moment she followed him slowly, her head bowed in humiliation. Her hand clenched inside her sleeve, and she imagined what the hilt of a dagger must feel like. Perhaps it was best to let him go to Felca. Perhaps it was best to let the magstrusi deal with him. They would stop him. She was not sure anyone else could.

RHO WAS WAITING for them near the base of an immense statue of Suprin Prime, twelve meters tall, hewn from stone and metal with an artistic skill no longer to be found in the Held. In sunlight the intricate armor would be gleaming with bronze luster; the weapons on the wide belt flashing; the uplifted hand in the heavy gauntlet spearing the sky. But tonight in the darkness the statue was only a tall, shapeless mass seen dimly in the light of the double moons breaking now and then through cloud cover. The statue was located in a public park in the central section of Impryn. The Marupish bordered the park on its east side. Emptied office buildings stood like sentinels on the west. There was a constant whisper of foliage swayed by the breeze coming off the river and the faint gurgle of rainwater sluicing along park walks into drains. Normally the city would be alive, luxuriating in the intrigue of the darkness. Lights would be shining from apartments, reflecting back and forth at each other across the river. Exquisite barges would be sailing upon the water, tiny floating islands of pleasure where the wail of music for the dancing *dalmas* and the gruff chatter interspersed with booming Chaimu laughter would echo across the rippling waves. There would probably be a parade—since Impryn was the city of a thousand cultures, there was always a holiday to celebrate—with whistling Slathese acrobats leading the way along the broad avenues into the park. There would be flame throwers and dancing youths in costumes that glittered in the torch light. Officials in masks would scatter baubles of money or food to the gawking populace. And the Gwilwans, resplendent with purple throats and green-scaled backs, their long claws gilded for the occasion, would roar and shake their crests at each other, laughing madly while they strained against the leashes of their keepers. Or the park itself would be ablaze with light, the leaves of the clipped shrubberies shimmering with waterdrops like cascades of diamonds. There might be a Meir festival going on, with a stately ritual performed here at the base of Suprin Prime while crowds swayed, hypnotized from the mantras and colorful clouds of hallucinogenic smoke. Young honorables, momentarily freed from the shackles of watchful tutors and bodyguards, would be cavorting along the winding paths with their friends, merrily drunk or grappling with the creatures of pleasure purchased for the evening. Along the wide Tis Avenue bordering the park, exclusive shops would be open at the foot of the office buildings, displaying priceless wares from every corner of the galaxy to tempt sophisticated appetites. Visitors from other worlds would stroll by, sighing among the crowds of warriors on leave and junior embassy officials released from duty. Patrolmen and monitors would be scanning the wealthy crowds with unobtrusive efficiency, ever on the watch for pickpockets and con artists dressed in glitter and false smiles.

But tonight there was none of that, only silence as an empire bowed in defeat and shame. Darkness shrouded the glitter. No lights shone. There was no incense on the air, no costly perfumes, but only the stench of decay from the river and the lingering smoke of fire and bombings. Now and then a patrol sled rumbled overhead, following the rubble-strewn streets, spotlights spearing down sporadically in search of trouble.

Brock did not like meeting here. It was too open, too near Colonid headquarters. There were too many patrols about. Yet by now he was sure those searching for him were busy scanning the outlying districts where slums jumbled against each other and the streets were layered thickly like warrens. He was probably safer here. But he still did not like it.

The scuff of a footstep caught his attention. He focused in that direction.

"Rho?"

"*Merc sic!*" came the answer. A thin wiry figure oddly

77

thick at the back emerged from the shadows. "*Ch'n tic st, nmen 'at k.* Dire-lord, I feared you gone forever. I feared the voice in my thoughts was a dream. But I came, and it is you!"

Rho grinned, baring his poisonous fangs with a delighted hiss, and slapped Brock on the arms in his enthusiasm.

"Yes, it is I," said Brock, thankful to have one man's simple loyalty to depend on. "I was afraid you'd be dead by now."

"No, I am hard to kill. I am house-boy now. I clean rooms. Work hard. Assignment." Rho's long forefinger tapped the tag fastened to the front of his coveralls. His leathery wings, no longer discreetly concealed under a loose tunic, extended in a broad stretch before he furled them again. "We were given a choice. We could all go with Suprin Tregher to the western exile camps or we could be assigned positions here among the Colonids."

Brock nodded. "How many elected to go with Tregher?"

"Most all. *Sic*, it is hard to know with accuracy. Some are still hiding in the slums, but they will be found easily now." Again Rho tapped the tag he wore. "Centralization of all inhabitants. No tag means death." Rho shrugged and stared past Brock at Ellisne, who stood a few paces away in silence. "Healer? Change sides again, or trick?"

Brock did not bother to look at her, but he sensed her restlessness at Rho's pointed question. He wished he could be sure of her. "She got me away from their interrogation machine. Beyond that . . ." He made the Chaimu hand signal of uncertainty.

Rho whistled the Slathese equivalent of a nod, but his eyes narrowed on Ellisne once again.

Brock stared north in the direction of Heldfleet Central, which was located just beyond the edge of the city. It had been one of the first targets to be bombed, but he wondered if the underground backup equipment had been damaged.

"Rho, I need access to a transmitter. I have to contact Eondal. Whatever vestige of the fleet remains, I need to coordinate with them. I also need a ship."

"Ah," said Rho, whistling. "This I have thought about too. To join Heldfleet—"

"No, I have another purpose."

"Galactic destruction," said Ellisne sharply, startling Brock into turning to face her.

"Not quite," he said, tired of dealing with her. She was as blind as her teachers. He had thought he sensed an opening within her, a willingness to listen objectively that he could reach, but he had been wrong. "The Colonids think they have defeated us, Rho, but they're still afraid."

"*Sic*," said Rho, his voice growing hoarse with awe. "The godas. The arkist and all his men were questioned a long time about them. I took off my weapons and pretended to be a medical orderly. The others think I am coward, but I waited for you. I did not go to death camps. Do you still intend to activate?"

The question was loud against the silence of the park. Brock hesitated, feeling once again the conflict of inner loyalties. Felca was my home once, he thought wearily. All the things Ellisne has said have their own bits of truth. The universe can go on with new masters. He sensed her stiffen behind him as though she sensed his trouble, and with a flash of anger he realized she had been using Influence upon his thoughts.

Fool! he shot furiously at her. His mind, clearing again, burned away the doubts. *I would rather destroy Felca myself than let the Colonids do so.*

She did not answer. Her shields were drawn up tightly. He felt his thoughts bounce off, and he turned away with a frown.

"Yes," he said firmly to Rho. "We activate. But first the transmitter."

"Not to be reached," said Rho after a moment, cocking his narrow head to one side. "*Ch'tk ta 'a sis*. Most guarded of all. As you have said, they fear such an attempt."

"What about underground access?"

"No!" said Rho sharply, clicking a negative. "No, no! Dangerous. They have filled the tunnels with nust gas. All levels."

"Don't expect me to *flick* you there," said Ellisne.

This time Brock did not even bother to glance at her. "You couldn't do it," he said and did not trouble to explain that Heldfleet Central was armored even against Sedkethran infiltration. There were a few substances which his species could not pass through, and ungstan carbonix was one of them. He wondered if she even knew of the organic metal's existence. Probably not.

"I could steal a stri-jet and fly in," offered Rho, but without much enthusiasm.

"No, you'd be shot down. A ship then. We can use its transmitter once we're off Darjahl Imperial." Brock twisted the goda band on his wrist, thinking of the star charts he would have to match the codes against. He knew the identity of one goda. He needed to know the other two as well. "Have you any weapons?"

Rho sorrowfully tapped the tag on his chest. "No chance yet. No armor for you either. They confiscated all and destroyed it."

"Damn." Brock sank down on one knee as a patrol sled rumbled over the river, and the others joined him in the shadows. The breeze coming off the water was cold on his bare shoulders. His bandages, imperfectly bonded with his flesh, were soaked from the rain, and absently he began to strip them off. Ellisne reached out as though to stop him, then remained silent.

"I go on duty soon," said Rho. "I will be missed. Our time is shortened."

"What is your routine? Do you live where you work? Or are you kept in barracks?"

"Barracks. Security loose. We are all supposed to be non-military, therefore low-threat." Rho grinned broadly. "Each shift goes on ground shuttle to work assignment."

"Are you counted?"

"In barracks, yes. On shuttle, no."

Brock lifted both brows. "Very loose security. How many guards on each shuttle?"

"Two. One guards the workers. The other drives." Rho cocked his head to one side, his eyes bright upon Brock's face. "I understand. *Merc*! The driver calls in shuttle ID and destination. You could probe for a new destination code—"

"No," said Brock. "They all wear protective implants to prevent that."

Rho hissed, then brightened. "But a less complicated plan comes to me. Why not gain port entry through one of the supply lines?"

"Too dangerous. Those transender points are constantly offloading—"

"No, no! All lines down. Colonids fear them. Ground transports haul everything to a central shuttle pad."

"What about power?" asked Brock, considering the suggestion with increasing satisfaction.

"Most power returned to city. I can channel power access to transender lines if needed," said Rho. "*T'k cha*, it requires only a computer link. And we will be in before they notice any power drain."

"You realize, of course," said Ellisne, "that they will be expecting you to make such an attempt at the spaceport. You—"

"We're going," said Brock curtly. "Are you?"

"Why do you insult me with such childish games?" she asked, rising to her feet. "You will not dare use the transender. You intend to hijack one of their ground transports and then steal a shuttle. They will shoot you out of the sky, and you will have a glorious end according to the Chaimu view. But you will still be dead."

"Ellisne—"

"No." And with a repudiating gesture of her hand, she *flicked* from sight and was gone.

Brock let out his breath in a heavy sigh of relief as Rho glanced from where she had been to Brock's face.

"She will warn the Colonids?"

"Yes, I think so."

"*Merc*! And I thought she was fooled."

Brock rubbed a thumb thoughtfully over his scar. "But I am serious about trying the transenders."

"Dire-lord, you know it is impossible. Not for me, but for you—"

"Why?" asked Brock, pushing away his own doubts. "I can no longer *flick*. My molecular structure should be cohesive enough for transender scrambling."

"I don't think you should try—"

"But I'm going to anyway," said Brock grimly. "It's our only chance to get out of here. We'd better hurry. They might just try covering both plans."

Despite their best efforts, it was nearly an hour later before Rho picked the fission-lock on a transender station and they darted inside. Breathless, Brock crouched down and gratefully accepted the ration cube Rho pulled from a pocket. His chest had finally stopped aching yesterday, but being on the interrogation machine had sapped a lot of the strength he'd managed to regain. He flexed his burned arm and winced. The new skin already growing was tender and not very elastic.

"See?" whispered Rho, tapping his shoulder for attention. He pointed overhead at cusp-shaped disks fixed in a sporadic pattern to the ceiling. "Everything has been reprogrammed through City Maintenance. Without this tag, you will set off the sensors."

Brock looked past Rho's shoulder down the narrow, almost tube-shaped room stretching past the counter near the door where shipments were customarily dropped off. It was a small station. There were only about six or so transender points. Containers were stacked haphazardly upon the floor where they had been abandoned when the city was attacked. There were even flimsies still scattered across the counter, and a com-link blipped a forlorn green light through the shadows to tell the departed operators that they had forgotten to disconnect the last call.

Brock frowned. It was not easy to reshape his thinking to these new problems of mobility. He had always simply desired to be in a certain place and *flicked* there. Sensors did not pick up his passage; his molecular patterns were unlike those of any other life form in the Held. Now, however, he dared not count on that. He had only to take a chance with one sensor, and if he set it off, all their chances would be over.

"Put me in a crate," he said. "The whole way. Otherwise, I won't even be able to get out of the cargo room up in the spaceport."

Rho whistled softly in agreement with the idea and bounded off toward the rear of the station. Several minutes later, Brock heard a faint thud and a muffled exclamation. Then a bulky hexagonal carton loomed out of the shadows, suspended on an anti-grav dolly. Rho's narrow ugly face appeared, grinning, to one side as he pushed it toward Brock.

"What took you so long?"

"I had to pick the pressure locks," said Rho, still grinning as he snapped up three locks along the side and lifted the lid. "Campesians and their binary numbers. The first carton I opened was unsuitable. This one I think will pass Colonid scanners, *sic*?"

"Campesians . . ." Already suspecting what it might contain, Brock peered unwillingly inside. The stench hit him like a blow. He drew back. "Rho—"

"Fluid pacs," said Rho triumphantly. "Organic enough to mix with your own readings on the scanner."

"What was in the other carton?"

"Pod fittings. Unsuitable."

"But more comfortable," said Brock, swallowing hard. "All right," he said as Rho looked at him in puzzlement. "Help me in."

As he climbed into the carton and curled up among the squishy, gurgling contents that released a pungent odor each time they were touched, he tried not to think about the possible effects of the transender upon him. Helping to guide the lid back into place, he settled back, closing off his olfactory nerves, and shut his eyes against the complete darkness. Each snap of the three locks marked the finality of his decision. *If I still wanted to, could I go back?* he wondered, thinking of the brutally cold spring day on Felca when he had left the barracks without permission. At that time, there had been no conscious decision of disobedience. He had simply looked at the wall and *flicked* out. It had taken the monitors hours to discover he was not in his assigned place and to come looking for him. He remembered being surprised at how long it had taken them to find him when he was not even actively trying to elude capture. But that day had marked him as a troublemaker, and from then on his every action was regarded with suspicion. *What*, he asked himself now as Rho grunted with the effort of maneuvering the bulky carton around, *would I go back to?*

The training of the round magstrusi chamber? What would he learn now? What questions would he ask? The first merging would reveal the multiple time-streams, a potential always there, now released. Would they share Ellisne's horror and kill him, disposing of him with a silent crushing blow of mental power united against his? It was a technique called merciful extinction, used primarily against patients beyond help. Or would they have compassion upon him and fuse him back to a single time continuum? Were the diverging splits inside him marking the end of his quest to become something real? Had he followed a false path all these years? Had he made himself an exile for nothing? How long was it going to take Rho to link up systems?

As though in answer the crate suddenly bumped and shifted. Rho thumped on the lid in reassurance or perhaps goodbye.

Brock burrowed deeper among the repulsive fluid pacs as he heard a hum of machinery building rapidly to a low-pitched whine.

It is wrong. It is wrong. The godas are wrong.

Brock listened to his instincts. He listened to the deep-seated morals at the root of his psyche, ignored for so long.

I have killed, he told himself, resurrecting an argument he thought he had succeeded in banishing long ago. *There is blood on my hands. Why stop now? It must be done. I must be the one to do it.*

Why? Why him, of all the individuals making up the broad spectrum of the Held?

But he knew the answer. Of all the possible futures fanning out from each step of each road he took, there were long stretches of inevitability where, having once started along that path, there were a certain number of consequences to go through before he came to the next point of intersection. There, and only there, could he choose another road, another future, another range of possibilities. But in the meantime, he had to follow what he had started. Right now, he was still in the middle of the road he had taken when he first became a dire-lord. It had been the second intersection of his life. He could have chosen a solitary existence as a hermit mystic on a barren world far away from other life. He could have concentrated upon evolving into pure thought. He could have sat for years within himself, tracing out each tendril of consciousness to its source. Instead he had turned sharply aside into a way of life foreign to everything he knew. He had taken punishing physical training. He had thrown himself into the patterns of a life where sensation was valued above mental purity. He had learned to kill. He had forced himself to experience emotions as fully as possible without guilt. He, more than any other creature alive, wanted to rule the Held.

When he could no longer hear the whine, that would mean the transender had activated. It was still building. The sound was becoming a part of him as he tensed, waiting for it to happen. One was supposed to relax, he knew, but all the same, his hands clenched hard on two fluid pacs, releasing such strong odors he choked with nausea.

I have learned to feel fear, he thought in surprise. *I have finally learned what it means to be a coward.*

Because he knew he couldn't live in the transender beam.

That to even try it inside a container would only increase his chances of coming out on the other end scrambled hopelessly with inert matter. That relying on his damaged atrox was illogical because an injured organ did not cause one's molecular properties to change. The container was his coffin. If he didn't get out now he was dead.

Brock lifted his fist to pound on the lid. "Rho—"

The whine of the transender lifted to a subliminal pitch, and just as he realized he couldn't hear it any more he knew it was too late to get out.

"YOU REALIZE," SNAPPED Falmah-Al with a restless glance over her shoulder, "that if you are wrong this time we are going to be finished with you."

"Threats serve little purpose," said Ellisne, maintaining an outward composure she could not feel inside.

She and the colonel stood on a glastel observation deck overlooking the shuttle landing pods of the spaceport slowly orbiting Darjahl Imperial at its standard operational path of 35,000 kilomyls. Beyond the wide, slightly cupped field hung the black backdrop of space. If she turned about and looked in the opposite direction, Darjahl Imperial filled her vision with variegated patterns of brown land mass and green ocean. Colonid troops stood alertly at their posts, waiting for the stolen shuttle to come in. So far, nothing had happened. Ellisne closed her eyes, unaccustomed to feeling such nervousness. She hoped the *promadi* and his friend Rho had had enough time to reach the spaceport via transender. Falmah-Al was already pacing the observation deck in visible impatience with an ambush that was not taking place. She would not wait much longer.

Hurry, thought Ellisne, opening her eyes out of fear that Falmah-Al would guess the truth from her slightest action. *I have given you all the time I dare by this trick. Hurry and steal your ship.*

She did not permit herself to consider the terrible risk the *promadi* was taking with a transender. Brock was so reckless with his life. She knew, from the few times she had merged with him, that he had damaged his atrox seriously from his wild attempt to save the suprin's life. It was astonishing that he had survived *flicking* such a tremendous distance, much less carrying someone with him. Even the magstrusi could not *flick* that far. But Brock threw himself at every challenge with a force and determination that was foreign to her. It was not the Sedkethran way to conquer. Achievements came through calm, rational planning. Why was he so determined to be different?

She shied away from the question, unwilling to return to thoughts of their discussions. He blasphemed against the Writings, violated the Forbidden Codes, twisted the Disciplines to suit his own purposes. He was *promadi*, outcast. Why, then, was she helping him? Why did she stand here gripped with concern for his survival?

The Elder Council would want an answer to those questions. She was not sure she could provide any, not even to herself. Brock horrified and offended her, yet his arguments appealed to sentiments deep within her. She could not help but wonder if she had a latent rebelliousness which had been sealed off from her conscious mind. Was Brock breaking open that seal for her? Was that why her thoughts kept returning to his words and her curiosity struggled against prudence? She had long ago mastered the techniques of serenity, yet Brock had managed to quickly overthrow her self-mastery. She had experienced fury, fear, and distrust as never before. She had even shouted at him, wanting to strike him. And the thinness of her civilized veneer shocked her. Was he using Influence upon her? She had saved him from the Imish once, and now she was jeopardizing her own safety a second time in order to divert them from his method of arrival at the spaceport. Why? If the Imish eliminated him, then the magstrusi would not be forced to act directly to stop him. They had trained her, and they were depending upon her now to control the *promadi*. Why, then, was she so confused and acting contrary to her decisions?

"Aha!" said Falmah-Al, throwing herself at the glastel wall as a warning alarm signalled the opening of the hangar forcefield. One of the landing pods glowed, indicating that its magnetic coils had been activated to pull the shuttle down.

Ellisne moved slowly to the colonel's side, her eyes fastened upon the incoming craft. Disappointment mingled with sharp relief welled up within her. So he had not dared try the transender after all. And she had not betrayed her own duty, but him instead as she was supposed to.

"Good," said Falmah-Al. "This could be it." She unhooked a communicator from her belt, and shot orders at her men waiting out of sight below. Her eyes, dark and gleaming with a hunter's excitement, stabbed at Ellisne. "Now we'll see. Millen is ready to move—"

Her communicator beeped. "Colonel, looks like a false alarm. Their ID codes check out in proper sequence."

The shuttle whine was muffled but not quite silenced by the insulation of the glastel. It was descending slowly, carefully, positioning itself directly over the glowing coil of the landing pod. Ellisne realized she was holding her breath. She forced herself to release it. She even dared a quick mental scan. The patterns were not his.

"Damn!" Falmah-Al glared at Ellisne and gestured at her men. "Millen, check it out! Move!"

The squad ran out to surround the shuttle with heavy disruptors aimed and ready. Ellisne watched the major enter the hatch first, half-crouched and competent. The violence in Falmah-Al rolled like a wave over Ellisne, who winced and stepped back from the windows. She did not want to watch. How had Brock adjusted to the lust to strike and kill?

"Colonel?" said Millen's disembodied voice over the communicator clutched in Falmah-Al's white-knuckled hand. "Strike activity. Deputy personnel. All cleared."

Falmah-Al muttered something in her language which Ellisne did not understand. "Stand by, Millen." The colonel's dark, definitely hostile eyes lifted to meet Ellisne's. "Nothing. They've had ample time to steal a craft if they were going to. Are you sure you heard them correctly?"

Ellisne met her gaze directly, betraying nothing. "It was the plan they discussed, Colonel. I am not responsible if they fail to carry it out."

The colonel's brows flashed together. "Be careful, Sedkethran. I am growing tired of your games."

"But I—"

"You have delivered none of your promises! You said you would take the goda locations from him, but instead you helped him to escape. And now you are trying to be clever again." Falmah-Al drew her weapon and aimed it at Ellisne. "Do you expect me to trust you, ghost?"

"You did not hold your end of our bargain. You were

torturing him," said Ellisne, trying not to stare at the disruptor. Her heartbeat quickened. "I could not permit that."

"If you had returned to us with the goda locations I might believe you," said Falmah-Al. "As it is, move! We're going to check on the dock surveillance."

Ellisne obeyed, going down the steep metal steps from the observation deck ahead of Falmah-Al. Colonid troopers were everywhere, helmet screens snapped up to reveal watchful eyes and suspicious faces. She knew they were covering the shuttlecraft in Impryn as well as the landing pods here and the loading docks for the larger ships. Brock had no chance to get through, providing he had even tried.

Had the transender killed him by now? she wondered. But surely she would have felt something. She had attuned a portion of her thoughts to his pattern, ready to recognize it should he succeed in reaching the spaceport.

There was plenty of activity in the branching corridors, although over half of the spaceport had been closed down. But supply freighters, fully automated and sent out on regular schedules before the final battles, were still coming in. They had to be docked and unloaded, and the cargoes had to be sorted and sent planetside to waiting distributors. Passengers, stranded when their liners were confiscated, waited at terminal gates in dejected little groups, their finery bedraggled now, duffles heaped at their feet, fingering their identification disks as they slowly moved through processing. Ellisne, pausing beside the colonel as their guard escort impatiently cleared a path through a jam of people at an intersection where a processing counter had been set up, noticed that newans had been separated from those of other species. Their processing was going much quicker. She frowned, disturbed by fresh evidence of the Imish inability to deal easily with alien life forms.

"Where are you sending them?" she asked.

Falmah-Al glared at her. "Come along. It doesn't concern you."

Ellisne had no choice but to follow, centered in the phalanx of guards. The looks directed at her were hostile.

"Sedkethran traitor!" shouted a voice. "How much did you pay to buy your freedom?"

Falmah-Al didn't even pause. She flicked a finger, and one of the guards moved swiftly into the crowd to isolate the speaker and strike him down with a savage blow.

"No!" said Ellisne in dismay. "You mustn't—"

But one of the guards prodded her around the bend in the corridor away from the angry voices and cries of pain.

"That was not necessary!" said Ellisne. "I refuse to be the cause of violence—"

"It wasn't done on your account," said Falmah-Al. "The Held has been placed under Imish martial law. Displaced civilians have been ordered to stand quietly in silence. That rule is strictly enforced."

Ellisne might have protested further, but at that moment they had to step aside to the right wall of the corridor to make room for a line of bulky containers hitched together on anti-grav dollies. A slender, long-armed Slathese in silver work coveralls was in charge. He carried a simple propulsion control unit and was slowly steering the cargo along.

Seeing him, Ellisne involuntarily gasped. He was keeping his eyes strictly on his work, trying to arouse no suspicion. Ellisne glanced away from his face and stared at the containers, her mind reaching out to each one. Where was the *promadi*? One of the containers held organic mass on a low order, but she picked up no mental patterns.

"What is it?" asked Falmah-Al, startling her. "What has caught your attention? Major By-Rami, scan these containers!"

Rho's eyes flashed a single accusing look at Ellisne as the guard checked the identification tag fastened to the front of his coveralls.

"This worker has been processed, Colonel, although I'm not sure about his code prefix in this area."

"What species?" asked the colonel.

Ellisne could sense the anger boiling out from Rho at her. Plainly he thought she had betrayed him. But she had not mentioned to Falmah-Al that Brock had assistance.

"Slathese," she answered quietly, knowing that if Brock was not here he must surely died in the transender beam. She had not felt the loss, but that was no certain indicator. The *promadi* had lived cut off from his own kind for many years. In death why should he have reached out to her? Shame and an unexpected wave of regret touched her. She felt responsible, as though she had failed him. "From the planet Slath. They—"

"Never heard of it," said Falmah-Al contemptuously. Her eyes raked Rho up and down. "You," she said in a passable Held dialect. "Where are you taking those?"

"Dock 7-A," he answered sullenly, keeping his eyes down.

Ellisne saw his fingerpads twitch, extending clawtips slightly. *Don't be foolish,* she told him, but his mental shields were up against her.

"That's an outward-bound dock," said By-Rami with a frown. He lifted a thumb to wipe away a trickle of perspiration from his forehead. The helmets looked hot, and the air in the spaceport was inadequately circulated. "We aren't shipping anything out."

"Merc sic," said Rho in exasperation, twitching one tall pointed ear. "Campesians always sending wrong shipments and crossing invoice destinations. These fittings belong to the new construction sites in the Darnaug system. We can't have them taking up space in off-loading. My boss say take them to Dock 7 so they are out of the way."

"What's in them?" asked By-Rami.

"Pod fittings and fluid pacs. Ordinary construction materials," said Rho sharply as another guard stepped forward with a scanner. "No illicit substances!"

They scanned each container, but the guard shook his head. "Nothing clear on these readings. What's in this one?"

"Fluid pacs. *Sic!*" Rho fanned a hand in front of his face. "You wish to be opened? Not pleasant."

"Organic contents, Colonel."

Falmah-Al gestured impatiently. "We don't have all day."

Rho hissed to himself and snapped open the locks. He barely opened the lid when a noxious odor flooded out. By-Rami backed up hastily.

"Gazal-ma!" he said, then shot Falmah-Al a nervous glance and held back the rest of what he'd been about to say. "All clear, Colonel."

Rho slammed shut the lid as they waved him on. His eyes flickered once to Ellisne, then he switched on the propulsion unit and headed on up the corridor ahead of them.

Go safely, she thought sadly. She hoped he did succeed in escaping. The Slathese were gentle people who kept to themselves and caused no one any trouble. Rho's cause was over. She would hate to see him end up in an Imish labor camp. Now that the *promadi* was dead, there was her own survival to be considered. Escaping from the colonel would not be too difficult although her craft and pilot had been impounded. Could she steal another ship? She did not know how to operate one, so to engage in a criminal activity would not help her. Perhaps she could seek Rho's assistance.

Falmah-Al's communicator beeped for attention. She frowned and plugged a small module in her ear for private transmission, then glanced at By-Rami.

"I have to return to Impryn. Tell Millen to maintain alert status. As for you, Sedkethran—"

"Permit me to wait at the transender terminals," said Ellisne quickly. "He would be most foolish to try such a thing, but just in case—"

"*Gazal!* I'll deal with you later," said Falmah-Al impatiently. "You have been useless to us. The rest of you, with me."

She strode away, gesturing vehemently to By-Rami at her side. Ellisne stood there a moment, watching them leave her. They thought she was still their prisoner. After all, with all coming and going so carefully monitored, how could anyone leave the spaceport without authorization? Ellisne could not *flick* to the planet surface, but even if she managed it she would still be in Imish-controlled territory.

Rho was her only chance to get away. She now wanted only to return to Felca, to seek the peace of her work, to forget the disturbing challenges Brock had presented. She was not accustomed to failure, yet was it failure? Her home was no longer threatened by the *promadi's* madness. The magstrusi would be pleased. Yet, as a healer she considered death a failure. And now that he was dead, she dared admit to herself that she had had other feelings for him, feelings of attraction that were Forbidden for one of her training. She would have to overcome such disturbing emotions during the journey home.

But first, she must convince Rho to trust her.

She waited until the colonel and her men were out of sight, then she gathered herself and *flicked*, arriving in the vast cavern of the docking area just as Rho unlocked one of the containers and helped the *promadi* climb out.

"No!" Astonishment caught her in the throat like a blow, and she spoke more loudly than she intended, making Rho's head whip around. "No! It cannot be possible! I scanned those containers myself, and there was nothing—"

With a furious hiss, Rho sprang away from Brock and came at her with lightning speed, his wings outstretched and his claws extended.

"*Th't ak!* You will not betray us again!"

Crying out, she dodged his grasp. But a leathery wingtip clipped her arm and sent her spinning. This time she had to *flick* to one side to elude him.

"I didn't betray you!" she said desperately, looking at Brock who had sagged limply beside the container. "I kept them occupied with the shuttles to give you a chance to take the transender."

"Yes," said Rho, baring his poisonous fangs. "And now you appear to help us again, by leading them here."

"No!" She stumbled and fell, *flicking* barely in time to Brock's side. She reached for his arm and shook him, pouring her entreaty through that touch.

For a moment there was no response. She felt as though she were pouring herself into a void. Dead? But his eyes were open. His lungs and heart were working. Rho seized her, his claws slashing her arm as he jerked her away from Brock.

"Do you want Brock to die?" she asked, gasping from the pain. "Or do you want me to help him?"

Rho's orange eyes returned to sanity, then he hissed and shook her violently. "You will help him die! You came here only for that purpose."

"Untrue. I came here to stop him from activating the godas."

"We are Held," he spat. "Godas are only way to defeat Colonids."

"Felca is Goda Prime!" she cried in despair of ever making him understand. "Don't you see? How can I stand by while he destroys my home?"

"Felca?" Rho stared at her, visibly stunned. "Your planet? Your birthing place? The reservoir for your spawn? This is a goda?"

"Yes." Her eyes implored his, willing him to understand. "How can we pay such a price, even to rid ourselves of these new masters? How can we?" She looked down at Brock, who had closed his eyes. He was pale, almost transparent, but his breathing was stronger. Was he listening? Could he possibly, finally understand? "It is Brock's home too. He has forgotten—"

"*Shstk,*" commanded Rho, his head whipping around. He listened for a moment, then said, "There is no time for this. If he needs you to live, then you will come. But if you do one more wrong, I shall be quick to the throat. Help me get him into this ship."

Together they maneuvered Brock to his feet. His features were slack, and although he opened his eyes when Ellisne supported his weight alone, freeing Rho to unlock the ship's hatch, Brock stared through her without recognition. She lifted a hand to the nerve points on either side of his throat, concentrating on penetrating the shock clouding him. No wonder her scan earlier had not picked up any mental pattern; she could not detect any now. She frowned and dropped her hand in alarm. Had the transender permanently erased his mind? It had managed to reassemble his molecular structure correctly, but. . . .

"Now," said Rho, pulling down the hatch.

It was a small ship, adapted for dry internal dock unlike its larger sisters which could only be accessed by airlock in the vast space hangars. This little craft had probably been pulled inside for storage.

They carried Brock up the steep ramp into the belly hold of the ship and left him slumped in a corner while Rho slapped the hatch closure controls and climbed up a ladder well into the main part of the ship. Ellisne followed him, watching as he lifted himself into a seat fashioned to fit far different contours and belted himself in. He sat, fierce with concentration, and stared at the complicated array of controls before him. She looked at them too, aware of her severe limitations in this area. She knew only of life and the patterns that sustained it. Mechanical devices and the mathematics required to operate them were beyond her knowledge.

"Can one person navigate this?" she asked.

He whistled without glancing at her. "It was chosen as best for that purpose." As he spoke he pressed a fingerpad to a switch. She heard a responding whine below her feet.

"Won't there be someone monitoring—"

"Yes, yes! Systems control will catch us the moment we request open doors." Other lights were blinking on around her as power levels warmed and instrumentation panels came on-line. "We must be clever." He flashed her a threatening look. "And you must try no more tricks."

"I told you—"

"Go below and stay with the dire-lord. I will think of a way to ease us out of here when traffic is heavy. Perhaps we can tandem a freighter. I think we are small enough to fit along the superstructure."

She did not understand what he was talking about, but she

did not intend to argue. Climbing back down the ladder into the hold, she paused a moment as the lights went out. But almost at once they came back on. The whine of the engines was stronger here. As soon as she knelt beside Brock, his eyes opened and his hand flashed out to grab her wrist.

The touch was like an electrical shock. His mind leapt at hers, insistent, hungry, desperate. He drew energy and strength from her, taking more and more until she gasped dizzily and managed to break free.

"Come here." His voice, deep and raw, rang with Influence. His eyes were huge in his pale face. They compelled her so that she found herself swaying in his direction.

She barely held herself away from him. "Stop it!" She lifted shaking hands. "Stop!"

"Help me."

Again she had to fight herself to keep from obeying. Frightened, she did not dare meet his gaze again. "I will help," she said unsteadily. "But it must be what I give, not what you take."

"Of—of course."

To her relief the Influence faded from his voice. He slumped back against the bulkhead and let his head roll to one side. She had to fight her own fear to reach out to him, but he gestured to stop her before she was able to grasp his hand.

"I am better," he said. "Not just yet. Not until you are ready."

She drew in a deep breath and nodded, composing herself by slow degrees. Now that her emotions were compressed once again beneath the Disciplines, she realized that there was a change in him. His guard seemed to be down. His inner shields were weak. At this moment he was not holding her at the distance he had before. She felt herself on the verge of an Understanding. But it eluded her grasp.

"You are stronger than a magstrus," she found herself saying. "It would take the whole council to crush me, but you could do it alone. You made me afraid."

To her surprise, he gave her the formal gesture of apology. It was the first time she had seen him conform to any of the rituals of their culture.

"Shock perhaps," she said when she could find her voice again. "You did really dare try the transender. You are reckless beyond comprehension. The expectation that a damaged atrox would change your essential molecular structure was worse than illogical. It was stupid. I am at a loss to understand your survival."

"It was a surprise to me as well," he said, then abruptly leaned forward with an eager flash of his eyes. "Ellisne, just think of it! I have discovered more abilities. Just as I was able to *flick* from the ship down to the planet with the suprin when the need arose, so was I able to hold myself sufficiently stable for the transender to reassemble me. Mental power, Ellisne," he said, his whole face lighting with a degree of enthusiasm that was not proper. "Incredible mental power that seems to grow each time it is drawn upon. What is it? What source? Why can it be tapped only during the severe stress of survival attempts?"

She drew back, stunned by the implications of what he was saying. Her eyes, wide and disbelieving, moved from his face to his long, well-shaped hand which was unconsciously twisting the goda band around and around his wrist. Then anger at his presumption spread through her, and for the first time she longed for the ability to command a whip of the magstrusi.

"Silence!" she said sharply. "How can you dare to utter such questions?"

The eager smile faded from his face. "How can you dare to close off knowledge?"

"You are seduced by the corruption within your mind. You deliberately throw yourself into danger in order to increase these abilities—"

"Yes!" He stretched out his hands as though to grab her by the arms, but she flinched back. "That is what I have been trying to show you, Ellisne! How can a person grow if he does not take risks? The Sedkethran have shut themselves off into a stagnant culture for centuries. It is a crime against all that they are and could be."

"We have evolved to precisely the point where we wish to be," she said, shutting off the doubt he raised within her. "Why should we go farther?"

"Why shouldn't we?"

She frowned, averting her head. "Our civilization is advanced to the point that our citizens suffer no discomfort. We fill a useful place within the society of the Held, and—" she stopped his protest with a sharp look—"I am sure we shall also find our niche within the Imish Collective. We are peaceful. We have no crime. What will you replace these things with? Would you have us all evolve into magstrusi?"

There, it was said. She was breathless at her own daring, but the arrested look in his eyes made her glad she had used boldness. She had been sent to control him, and this might be her only opportunity to succeed. She pressed further:

"They are noncorporeal. And your avid desire to increase your mental powers suggests you also wish to join this state. Will you be happier thus? You say you want all Sedkethrans to change. Will they be happier as pure mental energy? Will they be more useful to society?"

He was looking confused and uncertain. He hesitated before answering, and she was filled with a sense of triumph.

"I am not a magstrusi," he said slowly. "Therefore I do not have an absolute with which to answer your questions. I am not so limited."

She frowned. "You—"

"Why must there always be answers?" His eyes held hers, boring in with a fierceness she could not evade. "All I know is that we could be much more than we are. When I discover another ability, I must use it. Otherwise, it is as though I spurn the gift and the responsibility of having it. Am I so arrogant? Are you?"

She opened her mouth, but his words seemed to impale her. She hunted a response in vain. "I do not understand," she said at last, hating the weakness of her own selfevasion. "I am not certain I want to understand. There are grave dangers in what you do. Multiple time-streams are a trap from which it becomes impossible to escape. The ability to *flick* incredible distances is another trap. One desires to travel farther and farther, until one never emerges from interstitial time at all. The indulgence of emotions creates mental instability under which the Disciplines are fragmented and rendered ineffective. You are dangerous. You delude yourself with these quests."

He stared at her oddly. "Do you know what I have learned to do from using the transender? I have learned to blank myself. Scan me. Go ahead. Try."

She frowned, annoyed by his foolishness. "But I do not have to search. You are right in front of me. I can sense you easily—" She broke off, bewildered. Between telepaths there always existed a faint stasis field of mental energy, usually ignored as one ignored one's own heartbeat and respiratory functions. Mental pattern emissions, even from shielded minds, were always existent. It was how one recognized telepaths, even of unknown species. No one could shield their mind so completely that they vanished. Only death could achieve that.

But . . . he was gone! She stared at his handsome, scarred face, her eyes wide with concentration as she scanned and probed, seeking to break his concentration. But it was not even the same as reflecting off a shield. He was simply not there! He was sitting less than a meter from her. She had only to reach out her hand and touch his flesh, but if she closed her eyes she could not have detected even the faintest glimmer of his existence.

The ship rumbled around them, and she was jolted by a sudden acceleration. Brock threw out a hand to grab onto something, and his patterns returned. She loosed her breath, unconsciously relaxing from the tension which had knotted her. The ship jolted again, almost flattening her to the deck. She gasped, robbed of breath by the g-forces, then apparently Rho found whatever boosted the internal compensation field, and the heavy pressure eased.

Brock was counting audibly in rapid double digits. Then he broke off with a lifted fist which she recognized as the Chaimu gesture of victory. "Past initial detector range! Luck must ride on Rho's shoulder. We should have been blown to bits by now, or at least recaptured."

"How do you—"

"Wait," he said, concentrating.

She felt a shudder in the ship.

"Ah," said Brock knowledgably. "Warming up to jump point now. We'll shift into implosion drive at any second."

By the hatch ladder, Ellisne saw a panel suddenly flash red with warning. She was not used to deep space travel, and her few trips had always been accomplished by comfortable passenger liner where such things as warp jump and implosion points were unnoticed. She was grateful for Brock's warning, for the lurch into faster than light speed left her momentarily dizzy as though she had suddenly been dropped down a dark chute too fast.

Brock laughed as though enjoying the unpleasant sensation. The sound of his amusement was totally foreign to her ears. No Sedkethran laughed. She wondered from what species he had imitated the sound. Human perhaps? She could not exactly remember the Chaimu manner of showing mirth. Ah, but what did it matter? He distracted her too easily.

"At last we're on our way," said Brock, getting to his

feet. "I'm starving. Would you like some food? That is, providing this ship has any. If it was stored in internal dock, it may have been thoroughly cleaned out."

She dropped her eyes to hide her shock and disapproval as he began opening the lockers at one end of the tiny hold. Sedkethrans regarded all bodily functions as strictly private and never to be shared. To eat in someone's presence constituted the greatest rudeness. Even to mention it bordered on direct insult.

"I . . . no," she managed to say as he began pulling packets out of one of the lockers. "I require nothing at this time."

He looked sharply at her over his shoulder, then his eyes softened.

"I understand," he said quietly. "It was the hardest taboo to overcome when I first left Felca. I'll take some rations up to Rho and leave you alone for a while."

The kindness and sympathy were unexpected after his deliberate attempts to shock and annoy her. She rose to her feet, uncertain of what to say. Just when she thought she understood her position against him, he did something unexpected.

He smiled slightly at her, looking tired as he passed her to go to the ladder. He paused with one foot on the bottom rung.

"When I blanked out a moment ago, what did you feel?"

She frowned, not wanting to be reminded of it. "Alone. I felt alone, as though I were the only Sedkethran alive. That's how I couldn't detect you when you were in the container. I thought you were dead." She paused, then something in his expression prompted her to add, "There are no other Sedkethrans near Darjahl Imperial, are there?"

"None."

"I had never been cut off before. It's terrible, frightening." She rubbed her arms, wondering how he had stood it. "So alone. To be so very alone."

He held out a palm to signify his understanding. "It is what exile feels like all the time, Ellisne. I have been alone a long time."

She lifted her head quickly. "By your choice, *promadi*."

"Yes." His eyes were dark with memories. "I had a choice, Ellisne. To be whipped almost constantly by the magstrusi for thoughts that violated the Forbiddens, or to live in exile away from Felca."

"You did not have to think such thoughts," she retorted.

His mouth tightened, and suddenly his eyes were hard as though she had been unforgivably stupid. "You are a healer. If a sick child were lying at your feet and you were told you must not touch it, what would you do?"

"Impossible," she said, impatient with such a ridiculous question. "The situation would not arise. It would be illogical to deny me—"

"But if there were such a situation. Ellisne, whether you blind yourself or not, it could arise under the Imish. What would you do?"

"There could be no hesitation," she answered, trying to imagine his postulation. "I must assist those who are injured. I am a healer."

"Yes, precisely. And when a thought comes into your mind, how do you chase it away?"

"The Disciplines are designed to—"

"Ellisne," he said reproachfully. "Don't evade. You forget that we have shared a little. Your desire to heal has not always kept you from taking risks with your own health, has it?"

Sharp grief caught in her throat. She remembered the child she had been assigned to monitor during Change. She had been only partially through her training as a healer at that time, but already her abilities had earned her commendation and the notice of the magstrusi. The child Pretka was a frail little thing, never very strong, and unsuitable for training in the usual occupations. But she had had such an avid desire to learn that Ellisne could not resist teaching her whatever she asked for. Death was an understood future, but Ellisne had not expected it to come so soon. She had permitted her emotions to override her experienced judgment, and she had nearly died herself by trying to save the child even after it was too late. To hold someone into death was dangerous, but she had risked it foolishly. How had Brock read that memory? It was hidden.

"There is hope for you, Ellisne," Brock said softly. "In you there are also questions. If you will stop denying them and if you will learn not to be afraid, perhaps you will be able to reach out to another person as you once did to the child. Until all Sedkethrans learn to trust each other, we are a doomed people without a soul, without a future."

"Displaying emotion, is that what you mean by trust?" she asked, unable to hide how deeply his words had struck.

"It is a step in that direction," he replied, holding out his hand to her.

She stared at those long fingers and the flat palm marked by more than one scar. Old hurts and doubts emerged within her. She remembered the early days when she had wanted to encompass the universe in her eagerness for knowledge. What had she gradually become? A healer, who could not always save her patients? An acolyte of the magstrusi, who would never be granted the position of knowledge which they enjoyed? She knew a moment's blind surge of resentment toward the mystics for holding themselves so tantalizingly out of reach. Even Brock, with his great talents, had been denied a share of what they had. Was that why he had turned elsewhere? Could she blame him?

Then shame dampened the anger and she hastened to conform herself back under the proper thoughts. Brock was dangerous. But she would not let him succeed. She would not forget what he intended to do.

Ignoring his outstretched hand, she lifted her eyes to his waiting ones.

"Is learning to kill the next step, Dire-lord?" she asked coldly and watched him flinch.

He withdrew his hand, fingers curling slightly like leaves of the brill herb when they are dried too rapidly. Without a word, he turned and climbed up the ladder out of sight.

BROCK STUMBLED AS he climbed out of the ladder well into the cockpit of the ship. He dropped several of the ration packets, and the brightly colored squares skidded across the deck behind Rho's chair. Startled, the Slathese turned to glance at Brock over his shoulder, then that narrow ugly face of bone and sinew brightened with a wide grin. He lifted a fist.

"Victory to the Held! We are free, Dire-lord, and without pursuit."

"Excellent." Brock grinned back, and they saluted each other. "How did you do it?"

Rho whistled, ducking his head to one side. "Fitted ship to superstructure of out-going freighter. *Merc, ch't k!* Also put our sensors on reverse jamming frequency and tied in functions to freighter's autopilot. We split from it before going into warp drive. Their sensors picked up nothing."

"You make it sound simple," said Brock, not concealing his admiration. He glanced at the viewscreen, but Rho had it switched off according to proper procedure for solitary piloting. Without the distraction of other crewmembers, a pilot could become mesmerized by the panorama of space and fly himself right into a solid body. "Too simple," he added, unable to help thinking it had been suspiciously easy. "But that was a very sharp piece of piloting, Rho."

"All Slathese are good pilots." Rho glanced at him as though reading his troubled thoughts. "The Colonids are careless perhaps, or I am clever, or perhaps they let us go. Do you think we are leading them to the godas?"

Brock frowned. "It's a possibility we had better watch for."

"*Sic*. I have sensors on long-range, but they. are not very powerful. This is a non-military craft."

"We'll have to stay alert." Brock switched on the viewscreen and stared at the pattern of stars against the infinite black reaches. He thought of the lovely Ellisne, who was so close to breaking free if only she could see it. And he thought of Felca with the aching beauty of its glaciers and polar walls, remembering the shine of moonlight over the ice with the aurorae playing across the night sky. He used to stand upon Moba Glacier, a solitary figure caught up in the splendors of the night, the wind cutting sharply through his body as he dreamed of what it must be like to visit each star twinkling above him and to see all the infinite varieties of the thousand cultures of the Held. The earth and the sky had seemed his friends when he had no other. They had provided refuge from the mind-numbing exercises of training. The cold wind had been an exhilarating bracer that took away the lingering sting of the whippings. How he hated those crackling bolts of energy, like miniature tongues of lightning, which the magstrusi used to punish and teach. But each night when he crawled stealthily out of the sleeping barracks and fled to the refuge of the glacier, the bare crags of the mountain passes and the low growls of the moving ice all spoke to his eyes and his ears, his mind and his soul. It was the Sedkethrans he hated, not Felca. *How can I destroy it?* he wondered in anguish.

The suprin would not have had patience with his inner conflict. Chaimu were accustomed to giving orders and carrying them out, secure in their trust of hierarchial tradition and rank. That simplicity had made it so easy to serve the suprin. Brock had no responsibility except to do his job well. Now, he felt as though he carried the fate of the entire galaxy in his hand. The responsibilities crushed him from all sides. How he longed for someone to share them with. But no one followed him except simple, faithful, loyal Rho. He wished Ellisne would not remain so closed. He had tried reaching past the crust of training to the soul he was certain she had, to the compassion and kindness he had seen at unguarded moments in her eyes. Why couldn't she see that he needed someone to help him bear the horror of what he must do? But why should she help him? She thought he was a monster. Perhaps he was.

He sighed and glanced at Rho. "I'm lucky to have you."

Rho looked surprised, but not displeased. "I lost all my family, all cross-siblings and side-siblings, to fighting Colonids on the out-worlds," he said. His slanted eyes grew fierce. "I am descended from Kesmail the Mighty, who of my family was the first to serve the Held. I am the last. It is upon me to share in the Colonids' defeat. I heard some of what she said to you, Dire-lord. I know she is against what we do. But she is wrong, *merc*? She does not understand that they wish only to destroy all that is Held, not to govern it. They do not understand the concept of mercy. They are afraid of all that is not of Im because they are afraid that toleration is weakness. Is that food which you have brought?"

"Yes." Called back to his original purpose in coming up, Brock bent and scooped up the scattered packets he had dropped. His fingers still tingled numbly from aftereffects of the transender. Handing Rho a couple of packets, he tried to tear one open for himself and failed.

"Permit," said Rho, reaching over to do it for him. Rho's eyes studied him closely, but the Slathese made no comment other than, "What course do I set? Then I can turn ship over to autopilot and sleep. You should sleep, too."

Fitting himself into the seat at navigations, Brock nibbled hungrily on the compressed food bar. It contained few of the nutrients he required, but for the moment it would serve to fill his stomach. He studied the controls for a moment, wishing he had more than a rudimentary grasp of their operation. But a dire-lord's function was to protect the life of the suprin, nothing more. He was not supposed to be distracted by any other interests.

Finally he asked Rho, "Will this control call up the star charts?"

"*Sic.*"

Brock nodded and after another slight hesitation began slowly keying in the goda codes to the astrogation computer for cross-matching. The process, once he had entered everything, took only seconds.

He stared at the chart blinking steadily in three places. *Felca*, he thought numbly. *I loved you once. Was it to learn to destroy you that I entered the coliseums of the Chaimu and felt the hot splash of blood upon my hands?*

An odd sound from Rho pulled him from his thoughts. He glanced at the Slathese, who was sitting rigidly, eyes locked on the chart, and fangs bared.

Rho panted. He seemed to find it difficult to speak. "Those are the godas?"

"Yes." Brock's gaze went back to the chart. He blinked, forcing himself to look at the other two besides Felca. The Dena Minor system. . . . Slath was located there.

"Rho—"

The Slathese hissed. His hand, claws extended, clamped down hard upon Brock's wrist. "There are five planets in my system, Dire-lord. *Which?*"

Brock swallowed with difficulty. He wanted to reassure the Slathese. He wanted to find words that would take away shock and disbelief. But what words existed?

"The fifth," he said at last. His voice was hoarse. "The outermost."

There was an imperceptible easing of the grip on Brock's arm. Rho ducked his head. "Slath is the third. Could it survive the shocks if Amul left orbit? Could it retain its surface and its atmosphere?"

Brock shook his head helplessly. He was not an astroscientist. "I don't know. The fourth planet will certainly be laid waste. Slath may suffer damage. The extent—"

Letting his voice trail off, he looked at the third goda. It was the farthest away from galaxy center. It was located in a system he did not recognize on the opposite side of the galaxy from the Colonid borders. An information request from the computers revealed no life forms inhabiting that system. He frowned at it.

"Goda Tertiary is barren. To activate it would harm no one," he said slowly. For once he wished he had never learned to encourage his emotions. They were clouding his thinking. "But it is in the wrong position. Goda Prime, however, is closest to Colonid territory—"

"That is Felca!" said Rho angrily. His eyes, pupils flaring, swung to Brock. "The source of your species. Your spawning place."

Brock withdrew behind the protection of the Disciplines. He was not sure whether he saw dismay or accusation in Rho's expression. "It is the only inhabited goda," he said neutrally.

"You knew this." Rho drew breath with a sharp hiss. "Always you knew this. And she knows it, too. That is why she tried to betray us."

"She didn't betray us. She kept the Colonids occupied away from the transcender terminals while we—"

Rho whistled, gesturing this aside. "I do not say she is on

105

the side of the Colonids. But she is on the side of Felca. She will not let you destroy it. At least Slath has a chance, but your world—"

"We will none of us have worlds soon," said Brock grimly. "If the Colonids have their way, we'll all be nothing more than fodder for their labor camps. Right now we are scattered, demoralized. But once we begin to form cohesive resistance, they will shatter worlds as they shattered Mabruk. The godas are the only things they fear." His eyes shifted back to Felca on the screen.

"But there are how many people living on Felca?"

"The population is small. It is not a hospitable world, even for us." Brock looked sharply at Rho. "I know what you are trying to say. And surely you can guess my response. What are the lives of a few million if the billions populating the Held can be spared?"

Rho clicked disconsolately in his throat. "I have not your strength, Dire-lord. But neither was I exiled—"

"That is not why I am willing to activate Goda Prime!" snapped Brock angrily. "I am not concerned with petty revenge. If the suprin had not commanded me, I would not—" He broke off, breathing harshly as he fought to regain control. A dire-lord was accountable to no one save the suprin himself. He did not have to explain.

"Perhaps," said Rho hesitantly, cocking his head to one side, "it would be better to wait until we contact Esmir Eondal."

Brock shook his head. "There is not time."

"But we are free. We have escaped the Colonids—"

"Have we? I am not so sure." Brock grimaced, trying to put his uneasiness into words. "Falmah-Al would have thought of all contingencies. Stop looking at me in that way! Do you think I am eager to destroy my own—" He broke off, averting his eyes as a wave of emotion overtook him. *I cannot do it,* he thought in defeat. *I am so tired. I cannot keep fighting myself as well as them.*

"If I offend with what I say, I am sorry," said Rho quietly, lifting a clawtip to scratch one tall, pointed ear. "You are renowned throughout the Held, the first of your kind since the ancient days of legend to carry the rank of dire-lord. You have had to try harder than anyone else to become what you are. But surely there comes a time when it is wrong to try too hard, when there is a time to listen and to step aside from the stronger tide."

"Are you saying I should surrender?"

Rho met Brock's bleak eyes without evasion. "You know what I am saying. On Slath we have a proverb. *Ach'tk s. Tass mut 'k onsis sul.* One can fight the universe, but not the heart. You worry much about your soul, Dire-lord. What does it tell you to do?"

Brock stared at the chart without seeing it. Rho's words had struck home. Shame, disappointment, and relief mixed within him. He had battled Felca for such a long time he had fallen into the error of severe logic. Felca was the closest goda, and therefore the primary choice. But if he entered personal value into his decision, that changed his set of alternatives. And if he entered compassion into the decision, he could not act against Rho's system either. That left Goda Tertiary, and the offsetting factors of its inaccessibility. He realized suddenly that he had been guilty of all the narrow, restrictive thinking he hated most in his race. Was it necessary to unleash destruction? The Colonids feared the concept of the godas so greatly they could surely be bluffed. It would be sufficient just to activate Goda Tertiary. He would not have to destroy millions of innocent lives. He would not have to bear that responsibility.

An immense weight dropped from him. He blinked, feeling buoyant, stronger, relieved.

"Plot a course for the third goda," he said. "I think we can use it to bluff the Colonids into scurrying home. We may not even have to rip it out of orbit."

"This is your decision?" Eyes gleaming, Rho let his hands hover over the controls.

"Do we have enough fuel to reach it? What would be our estimated completion time?"

"Three weeks at this speed," said Rho after a moment's rapid computation. "Insufficient fuel. But there are fueling stops gridded along these sectors—" he pointed along the screen—"within an eight-day reach of that system. If we are not intercepted we could get there. *If* we are not intercepted."

"And if we are not detained at any of the fueling stops."

"The risk factor of failure increases with distance," said Rho, then hissed. "*Merc*! I am inconsistent. I urge you first to listen to your heart, then your head. You are the dire-lord. The suprin entrusted you with this task; therefore, you are the best qualified to make the decisions."

Yes, the suprin. Brock got up from his seat restlessly and

stared at the ladder well for a moment without seeing it. His warrior instincts, learned and grafted on with such difficulty, all screamed at him to jump rapidly to the offensive by activating Goda Prime as soon as he could get there. But all that was Sedkethran within him cried out against it. Would Utdi have condemned him for what he wanted to do now?

As though sensing the chaos of his thoughts, Ellisne chose that moment to climb up the ladder to join them. Brock looked at the smooth coils of black hair, the wide pale brow, and those large luminous eyes as they lifted to meet his. Inside, that which was left of the suprin in his thoughts snarled a Chaimu curse. *Forgive me, Utdi*, he thought. *As I tore myself away from the magstrusi, so must I tear myself away from you. I loved you as a father. I admired you enough to try to become Chaimu. But I must be my own self, whatever that is. I must make my decisions as I would make them, not as Magstrus Olbin would or you would.*

As his thoughts faded, he realized he was still staring at her. She was frowning, her lips parted as though she wanted to speak but did not dare. Brock tore his gaze from hers to glance at Rho.

"If you've plotted the course," he said, "lay it in. Goda Tertiary."

Rho grinned broadly as he moved to comply, but Ellisne was still frowning as she finished her climb into the cockpit. There was barely enough room for the two of them to stand behind Rho's chair.

"I don't understand," she said. "Where is this goda?"

Brock pointed at the chart. "There," he said, telling himself that he had made his decisions independently of her influence, yet he could not keep his gaze from moving back to her face to see her reaction. "It is uninhabited and located in a barren system."

Relief flashed across her face before she smoothed her expression back under control. "But I thought . . . we are closest to Felca, which is in a direct line to the Colonid borders."

"Yes," said Brock in a low, rigidly controlled voice. "The Chaimu training in me says attack with Felca. The Sedkethran says surrender. Neither are acceptable. *I* intend to bluff with the third goda. Am I wrong?"

For the first time she smiled at him. She even reached out and took his hand, and the warmth of her approval and relief flowed into him like a rich drink.

"No, you are not wrong," she said firmly. "Trust the deeper voice. Heed what it tells you, and do not be troubled."

"You don't understand," he said. "They may call the bluff. I may still have to pull the goda from orbit. I may have to do more than activate it. I am not taking a Sedkethran solution."

"You are still—" Her eyes narrowed upon him with sudden concern. "This can be discussed later. You should rest."

"*Sic*," agreed Rho emphatically as Brock pulled free of her grasp. "Rest is needed. You will need your energy later, Dire-lord. Trust my piloting. We are steady on course, and the sensors will give us warning if necessary."

Brock could no longer deny his exhaustion, not to himself or to them. "Very well."

He followed Ellisne down the ladder and through a narrow door into the ship's living quarters. These were as cramped as the cockpit. Most of the ship's space allotment had been designed for the engines and the hold.

Ellisne folded out four bunks from wall compartments, and Brock crawled onto one of the lower ones. There was not room enough to stand when all the bunks were down. He stretched himself out with a sigh and a wince for his sore body.

"How will you rest?" he asked her, frowning as he watched her climb onto one of the upper bunks. "There are no suspensor plates."

She smiled remotely as she folded her limbs into a graceful attitude of the Disciplines. "I shall meditate on two levels only. That way I need not fear drifting, but it should permit enough of my metabolism to rest."

He nodded. He had used that method himself more than once, especially before achieving the rank of dire-lord and enough status to command the luxury of his own suspensor plates instead of a conventional Chaimu bed. Meditation served the purpose, but after a while the body still felt unrested and reaction time slowed. Before their three weeks of travel time were up, he would show her how he had learned to compensate for those deficiencies; that is, providing she would trust him enough to let him teach her.

Trust, he thought, shifting his position restlessly on the hard bunk. His body ached; it was tempting to inventory all the damage not yet repaired but he sidestepped the activity as wasteful. His head still throbbed a little from the effort of coming through the transender, and he was very, very tired.

He fought back the weariness, however, aware of her eyes watching him steadily. An old despair he thought he had conquered years ago surfaced. *Will I ever find anyone to share with and trust again? She is momentarily satisfied with a tactically weak decision, but she does not admire me for it. Or does she?*

"Yes, I do," she answered as with a slight sense of shock he realized he had let his shields down. She stretched out a hand as he forced his drooping eyes open wide. "Don't. I will not invade you while you sleep. I just could not help . . ." Her voice trailed off and her gaze fell from his. Her hands dropped from the position of meditation in a small gesture of agitation.

"Ellisne," he said quietly. "At first you hated me. Then you feared me. I will not harm you—"

"I know." Her eyes flashed to his, then fell away again. "I have learned this. And you have learned compassion."

It was his turn to be uncomfortable. "Perhaps."

"I was coming up to apologize," she said after a moment's pause. "I have spoken cruelly to you out of my own insecurities. It is unforgivable conduct. I am ashamed."

"Don't be." He lifted himself up on one elbow. "I have goaded you from the moment we met."

"Yes." Her eyes met his directly then in simple accusation. "You have. And you know—surely you must know—that their orders are not easy to disobey, even if I wanted to do so. You are considered an alarming danger—" She broke off, staring into the distance for a moment. "I bend to the greater wisdom of the magstrusi. I know they sent me to control you for reasons which I need not understand, but . . ."

"Ellisne."

"I am not worthy of the task! I lack the abilities and the strength. As do they! They could not control you when you still were on Felca, and you have grown stronger. Your mental capacities are immense, far greater than theirs. Surely they must have foreseen this. Then why did they send me?" Her eyes were enormous, pleading. "Why? They knew I would fail, yet they sent me. Did they want me to fail? I have been their best pupil, their strongest acolyte since you—" She gasped, and grew transparently pale as realization crossed her face. "That's it, isn't it?" she said in a hollow voice that made him ache for her.

He held himself silent, knowing that she must work through it herself.

She shut her eyes. "They wanted me to fail. They hoped you would destroy me, confuse me, negate my Disciplines so that I could never go back."

Brock waited.

She opened her eyes, and they were dull. Her features were blurring, growing indistinct as she drifted half in and half out of dimensional sequence. "They fear me. That's why they chose me to come to you."

"Yes. I suspected it as soon as I saw you." He hesitated, fearing to go too far when her wound was so new, but then he remembered all the brief moments they had been linked and knew she was strong enough to withstand what she must be told. "You are not the first they have sent into exile, Ellisne."

"But it makes no sense!" she cried, her voice full of anguish. "I am no threat to them. I have done nothing wrong. I have submitted willingly to the training they chose for me. Why should they punish me like this? I can't bear to be alone. I haven't your strength. I can't—"

He thrust himself off the bunk and reached out to gather her into his arms. She was rigid with grief and fear, and her emotions, so long repressed, flooded through him in an overwhelming tide.

"You are not alone, Ellisne," he said softly over and over. "You are not alone. I will help you."

She clung to him tightly, drawing upon the reassurance he offered. His weariness was forgotten as he sat on the bunk and rocked her gently with his chin resting upon the top of her head. Her silken black hair smelled of tyra and hrrym, the gentle herbs so beloved by the women of Felca. Brock closed his eyes and let his memories surge back to better times, when he had been very young, before Change when he had lain in his blankets upon the bank of his mother's bathing pool, when he had not yet discovered that he was forged of rebellion and talent.

"You said there were others," Ellisne said after a long while. "What happened to them?"

"One could not accept it. He went back to Felca and asked to be retrained."

She drew in her breath sharply. "But that cannot—"

"No. It cannot work." He sighed. "The other one simply faded away."

111

"You mean *flicked* and never came back."

Lost in the grimness of his hatred of the magstrusi, Brock did not answer.

She pulled away from him. "Brock, I must ask something which invades your privacy."

He smiled, amused by her sudden return to formality. "Ask."

"When they discovered that you were stronger, that you could not be controlled, how did they send you away?"

"I was not sent," he said sharply, too sharply. "I escaped. I made my discoveries about them before they made theirs about me. But it was a long time before I dared face the truth. We are so ingrained to respect them, to obey them in everything. We never question. We never seek alternative routes. We never disobey. How hard it is to realize they are a dangerous sham, jealous of their power and determined to hold others from what they themselves achieved so long ago." He looked into Ellisne's widened eyes and permitted his anger to soften. "There are Writings that you would have never seen, even if they had not sent you away."

The wounded expression in her eyes made him swear to himself in Chaimu. It was not easy to overcome such a shock. The others had not succeeded, but she must. She must!

Brock stared down at his fists, clenched so hard they were shaking, and knew that he must persuade her to let him help her survive. He needed her. For so long he had been alone, a stranger, an oddity, set apart by his rank and his race. He had filled that void with service to the suprin. He had poured all of his loyalty and abilities into that service, determined to survive, determined to withstand the magstrusi, determined to have some purpose to his existence other than hatred. Now he had lost the suprin. The new place he had carved out for himself had been destroyed by the Colonids. And when he had succeeded in carrying out the suprin's last wish, what would he have? Ellisne's arrival had given him a hope he had never dared indulge before. After all, a *promadi* was shunned by all Sedkethrans as something to be abhorred. A *promadi* could not take a lifemate, could not share, could not enjoy the experience of siring children. A *promadi* was *alone*. With Ellisne, so beautiful and agile of mind, he need never be alone again.

He sensed her withdrawal and quickly gripped her cold hands. "Ellisne! Please don't be afraid. I will help you. If you will only trust me, I can help you."

She shook her head. "You are different, Brock. You are what they have tried to keep from developing for centuries."

He caught his breath. "You know? Great Meir, you are more talented than I thought, to see it."

"Nonsense," she said, frowning. "Anyone can. It shines from you, even when you are hurt and tired as you are now. Why do you think all your excited talk about evolving and trying out new abilities frightened me so? It's not easy to meet someone whose existence has been foretold by the Writings. You are like the ancient ones, the ones who came before. . . ." Her voice trailed off on a queer note, and she clutched his fingers.

"Yes," he said gently, smoothing her hair away from her face. "The ones who came before the Chaimu installed Sedkethrans on Felca, the ones who used to stand shoulder to shoulder with the mightiest legends of the Chaimu Empire, the ones who helped the Chaimu design the godas. We have been bred into tiny, docile entities, restricted and suppressed, hidden from the truth of our true origins. There are so few of us left now who even have the capability to see through the Disciplines and the Writings for what they really are. You are one, Ellisne. Don't be afraid of that! Be proud of it. It is your true heritage."

She shook herself from side to side, pulling away in spite of his hold on her wrists. "I wanted only to be a healer, nothing more. But they made me take additional training. They showed me the Writings. They forced me to acquire a hunger for higher knowledge. And now they punish me for it. Why, Brock? Why?"

He held her still and forced her to look at him. "Ellisne!" he said sharply. "What do you feel? At this moment?"

She tried to pull free, but he would not let her.

"Ellisne! Answer me!"

"Fear. Betrayal." Frowning, she would not meet his eyes.

"Beneath that," he said insistently. "Look! Be honest."

"I can't—"

"You must!" He shook her roughly. "Tell me how you feel!"

She gave a low cry and with sudden strength jerked her hands free to press them to her chest over her atrox. She shut her eyes as though to shut him away. Her face was drawn and colorless.

"I hate them!" It was a cry of sheer pain. "It is all a game to them. It's all a lie. I hate them! I want to make them—"

Her eyes flew open, and she stopped the words with an audible gasp. "No," she whispered. "I mustn't. It's wrong to say such things."

"Say them, Ellisne. You must say them. The magstrusi have hurt you. They have played with your mind and then discarded you with contempt. Haven't you the right to disobey one Forbidden? Just one? Tell me now. What do you want to make them do?"

"I want to make them *die*!"

And then she was in his arms, trembling uncontrollably from the lash of her emotions. He held her close, leaving himself unshielded so that he could share and absorb her grief and bitter hurt. There had been no one to hold him all those years ago. But he had survived because of his own strengths. And now, as his arms tightened about this lovely, stricken woman, he felt the relief of being able to finally trust her. The time-stream where she stood as a future assassin was sealed off. With a sigh, he closed his eyes.

He waited until the trembling had stopped and she was leaning quietly against him, spent from her own emotions and his. Then he gently touched her temple, her ear, and her chin with his fingertip in the formal gesture of request.

"Share with me," he whispered. "Even part way. I know we cannot *flick* together or even drift because of my atrox, but—"

"Hush." She laid a finger gently across his lips to silence him, then touched his chin, ear, and temple in the formal answer. Her eyes glowed into his with gratitude and trust, mirroring that which was awakening in his own heart. "I am strong enough for both of us. Let us share. Teach me, Brock."

THE SECURITY MONITOR focused on Nls Ton as he sprawled on a vast Chaimu bed. His sand tiger slept at his feet. The soft light from glowtapes played across irridescent hangings. Her face expressionless, Falmah-Al pressed a switch and the monitor zoomed in on his face. The soft jowls and slack open mouth repulsed her. He was gaining weight upon the rich delicacies of Impryn. He had stopped his obligatory exercise routine and dispensed the duty of daily troop reviews to his deputies. In private he wore the exquisite robes of a Chaimu honorable, his soft hands caressing the delicate cloth colored in hues none of them had ever seen before. He threw parties for select members of his administration who ate and drank themselves into stupors until dawn. His chambers were decorated with priceless objects spirited away from the plundered treasuries designated for shipment back to Kentra. Falmah-Al had carefully documented every priceless gwirleye secreted away under the lock of his seal. He was amassing an enormous private fortune for himself. She made no effort to remind him of regulations and his violations of them. Ton had always been ambitious, but at long last his greed had overwhelmed his caution. He was governor on the treasure house of the entire Held. Kentra was far away, and the whole Collective was euphoric with victory. Many standards had been relaxed, but that would not last for long. Falmah-Al hummed quietly to herself as she switched the monitor back to auto. She had enough documented on Ton to make sure his head would roll in the next purge. She might even use him to

115

start one. Or she might yet decide to utilize the Fet device her people had located this morning near Ton's chambers. Fet assassins were supposed to be among the best in a culture that accepted poisons and vendettas as a daily fact of life.

She slid her hand carefully over the sleek black surface of the small conical device, feeling the play of temptations. It would be so easy to arm the device and slip it into the security monitor now patrolling Ton's chambers. He need never awaken from his nap.

No! Her hand jerked back as though burnt. She would not use Held ways, not even to exact her own revenge.

Abruptly she left the monitor booth, stepping out past two guards who snapped to attention. Her deputy was a slim young woman in a plain black uniform who was waiting for her with a salute.

"Is my shuttle ready?"

"Standing by, Colonel." Tirza held out a flimsy with the correct amount of deference in her eyes. She was newly assigned and Falmah-Al found it a refreshing change to be able to trust the person at her back. "This message just arrived from Major Millen."

Falmah-Al's stomach tightened. She snatched the flimsy and read it in a glance. "*Gazal atallah Im*," she swore, calling down enough blasphemies to make the deputy gasp, and headed outside for her shuttle at a run.

She sprang up the steps through the hatch and slapped her hand in a loud thump against the bulkhead behind the cockpit. "Molaud! Take it up! *Zist!*" She glared at Tirza scrambling aboard with a clumsy leap just as Molaud activated hatch closure. The engines whined shrilly as the shuttle swung around in a slow arc, already lifting in a maneuver that used an enormous amount of fuel but shaved minutes from take-off time.

Falmah-Al threw herself into a seat and fastened the safety restraints. "Tirza, as soon as we are in the clear, get me By-Rami. Yes, I know he's off the duty roster for this week, but that's changed now. I need him."

The deputy bent over the communications board and as soon as they shot up over the city into a dark bank of clouds that buffeted them with sharp turbulence, Tirza flipped on the speaker and nodded to Falmah-Al.

"I have him on, Colonel."

Falmah-Al leaned forward "Major, you're back on duty.

I'm putting you in charge of the governor's personal security in my place."

There was the briefest of pauses as By-Rami absorbed this sudden change of status. Then he said, "How long will you be gone?"

"Unknown. Deep space," she replied curtly.

"There's been a positive on the scanners?"

She frowned. They were on open communications. She did not answer the question. "I know I can trust you to guard the governor's safety. I'm preparing my official log now on the shuttle. Deliver it to Ton first priority."

"Yes, Colonel. Any *other* instructions concerning the governor's well-being?"

"No." She was not ready to strike against Ton, and she didn't want By-Rami getting too eager. "I've advised the governor against making that inspection to the camps and he's agreed to postpone it. Tregher has become a useless bore. There should be no need for enhanced security, but use your own judgment if trouble arises."

"Acknowledged."

Falmah-Al leaned back, and Tirza cut communications. Damn, damn, damn. Falmah-Al's fingers drummed against the arm of her seat. She'd given the dire-lord all the rope she dared and then some. Ton was sitting back and watching her stick her neck out farther and farther on this gamble, and he made no secret of how quickly he would chop her career in half if she failed to deliver the godas she'd promised. Now it looked like that ghost was going to elude her after all. Deep space! He was aiming at nothing, leading them nowhere, laughing at them. Damn him and his lying ghost-woman! She'd see them both fried. She'd peel them down to their skeletons layer by layer. She'd take them to their home planet and let them watch while she destroyed it just as she had Mabruk. Then there would be no more damned ghosts. Falmah-Al threw back her head and laughed, but there was no amusement in the sound.

Millen was waiting for her at the airlock leading to the trim little courier sloop already prepped for departure. "The cruiser *Im Naga* is waiting just beyond the Mystbellian Cloud for a rendezvous, Colonel," he said without preamble and without a salute.

She glared at him but came aboard the sloop with suitable piping from the crew. It did no good to reprimand Millen for details he considered unimportant. He was the best man she had. She left him alone.

"Welcome aboard, Colonel," said the lean first officer of the sloop. "We're ready to go at your word."

"Then go," she snapped. "We have no time to waste."

"Aye, aye." He stepped to the intercom. "Colonel and party are aboard, Captain."

Minutes later the sloop was easing out of space dock. Falmah-Al, followed by Millen and Tirza, made her way immediately to the small but efficient bridge where a crewman showed her the tiny blip on the long-range scanners.

"It doesn't make sense," said Millen, expressing the frustration she was hiding now. His flat yellow eyes squinted at the screen. "They've been holding this course for days. They've even refueled once. The plotted completion for their current trajectory is nothing. Our charts aren't mapped in that area."

"Heldfleet?"

"Our long scanners could pick them up. There's nothing out there."

"And all the spies can tell us is that the godas are closer in. *Gazal!*" Falmah-Al shook her head. "What is the fool doing? Tregher assured us under authority probe that the dire-lord is determined to activate them. Why, then, is he going in this direction?"

"Perhaps he's on to us."

Her exasperation flared out. "How could he be? Held technology is behind ours. They haven't scanners even approaching the range that we have."

"Still, he could be deliberately leading us wrong."

Her head snapped up. "Millen, what are you saying? Do you suspect that our mental protectors aren't working?" Behind Falmah-Al, Tirza surreptitiously rubbed the spot behind her ear.

"No, no," said Millen with an irritable shrug. "It's just a hunch. It's just a postulated explanation for the dire-lord's actions."

"I don't want guesses, I want facts!" snapped Falmah-Al, slamming her hand down upon the top of the screen. "Say you're right, Millen. Say he suspects we're watching him. Say he's taking his time in an effort to throw us off the trail. He knows, damn him, that we can't afford not to find them soon. The Collective is divided now by those mewling idiots who fear our military successes will cause the godas to be set off. We could all be recalled if there's a turnover in government.'' She clenched her fists. ''I want those godas. And I want them now.''

She nodded at the captain, who was on the other side of the bridge beside his first officer. Both were making a pretence of not listening to her and Millen.

''Gentlemen, how long until we rendezvous with that cruiser?''

''Approximately two days at current speed, Colonel.''

''Increase speed, and open communications to them. I want an intercept course already plotted by the time I come on board. The dire-lord is to be overtaken and stopped.''

''Aye, aye, Colonel.'' The captain's gaze swung away and he began issuing rapid-fire orders in a low, calm voice.

Millen snorted. ''How are you going to force the information from the dire-lord? We tried that once, and it failed.''

''It might have succeeded if the ghost-woman hadn't intervened.''

''I doubt it.''

Falmah-Al drew in her breath with an angry hiss, but Millen's flat yellow eyes never wavered.

''I went over that interrogation machine myself, Colonel. He wasn't responding. He wasn't even close to responding when she rescued him. Half the readouts didn't register, and the rest were unreliable because of calibration errors. He's Sedkethran, not human. Our methods aren't—''

''Stop telling me what we can't do,'' she broke in. ''I want a positive course of action.''

''All right.'' Millen lifted a hand in a casual shrug. ''The dire-lord is running a bluff. He's the only one in the galaxy who knows the location of the godas.''

''Yes! So?''

''So we already know from talking to Tregher and that deputy of his . . . um, Davn, that no one in the Held wants the godas to be activated. The suprin must have ordered Brock to start galactic annihilation. Otherwise, I don't think he'd be doing it.''

''Perhaps,'' said Falmah-Al impatiently. ''His motivations are of little concern.''

''Aren't they? If he's running under orders he'll never surrender his information, no matter what method we try. What we must do is call his bluff.''

"How?"

"By threatening to blow him out of space." Millen's lips curled to reveal white, evenly spaced teeth. "If he dies the godas can't be activated. Because no one else knows where they are. The Collective will be safe."

Falmah-Al frowned, considering it. "Good, but it isn't sufficient just to destroy him. I want those—"

"Of course. I am merely stating the worst scenerio first."

"But he still has no inducement to tell us their locations. I have read about dire-lords, Millen. They go to the death for their suprins. He may even be eager to die at our hands." She turned away. "No, I don't like it. I want those locations. It isn't enough to merely plug the hole. I want—"

"Power." Millen's eyes met hers as she glared at him. "I haven't seen you this ambitious in a long time, Colonel."

"It's necessary."

"Then convince the dire-lord that you want to deactivate the godas. Sedkethrans abhor war. Build on that argument."

Falmah-Al shook her head skeptically. "He may be a Sedkethran, but he's also a deviant."

Millen cocked his head to one side and sent her an odd look. "And I thought you always claimed you could outnegotiate Ton if you ever had the chance."

The barb hurt more than she expected, but she hid it by turning her back on the major. "I'll consider your suggestions," she said stiffly.

"Kezi," he said as though in apology.

"Yes." She flashed him a brief look to stop him from saying more there on the bridge. Inside emotions battled her. Why was she such a fool? She had wasted her youth loving Nls Ton, who had discarded her after she bore two dead children. And now she wanted a half-breed mercenary when her whole career and standing in society would be destroyed at the first hint of anything more than professional comradeship with someone who was not purely human. Why did she throw herself into these no-win situations? Keeping her feet professionally was difficult enough; she did not need to battle her heart as well. Only Millen's own coolness toward her had thus far kept her safe. If he changed now . . . if he softened . . . she would be lost.

She moved away from him, aware of his gaze upon her, aware of those odd alien eyes that both repulsed and compelled her. Oh, to be far away and free, where she could wear the traditional drapings of an Imish woman for the privacy of her man without spies or recriminations! But that was not what she really wanted. She thrived on the challenges of the military. She lived for the chance to rise high upon the ladder of power. The soft ways of a woman were only her fantasy, discarded as she had been discarded.

"I'll consider your suggestions more carefully, Major," she said in a neutral tone of voice and left the bridge for the refuge of her quarters.

Brock was seated in the cramped corner of what constituted the galley, engaged in trying to resynthesize the contents of a food packet into something more palatable when the sharp whoop of alert sounded. He swept everything into a bin with one motion and ran for the cockpit where Rho and Ellisne were seated side by side. Rho was hissing, and Ellisne's face was an expressionless mask. Only the darkness of her eyes and her hands clenched rigidly on the edge of the control console revealed her fear.

"Rho! Status!" snapped Brock, looking at the viewscreen and seeing nothing but innocuous stars scattered across a field of black.

"Sensors just picked up a heavy battle cruiser closing on our starboard side, bearing 0 mark 5." Rho stabbed around on his board, and the alert abruptly cut off. "Interception in approximately forty-five minutes."

Brock covered his dismay by switching the screen to their starboard and increasing magnification to maximum. All he got was a blurred shape too dim to distinguish any characteristics.

"Held or Imish configuration?"

There was a pause while Rho checked the readings. "*Merc*! Imish power emission."

"Meir above," said Brock softly, feeling as though he'd been kicked in the stomach. Either they'd inadvertently crossed someone's scanning range and were being checked out, or else Falmah-Al had decided he'd gone far enough. "I hoped we'd finally found Heldfleet."

Rho whistled disconsolately. So had they all.

"Increase speed," said Brock, snapping back to the matter at hand. "Evasion maneuvers."

"If we burn more fuel we won't make it to the next fueling stop," said Rho.

"If they catch us we won't need to refuel," said Brock grimly.

Silently Rho switched helm controls to manual.

"Ellisne," said Brock. "Call up astrogation. We've got to find a place to hide. Look for dust clouds, nebulas, asteroid belts, anything in close range."

But she was already shaking her head. "There's nothing. Nothing close by."

The shape on the viewscreen had become clear. Brock stared at it, his mind clicking rapidly through alternatives, and did not need Rho to announce that their pursuers had increased speed.

"Twenty-five minutes to interception. Dire-lord, if we try to go any faster we'll shake apart."

Brock could already feel the shudders beneath his feet. The engines were groaning. Ellisne tapped her finger on the fuel level indicators. A green light blipped steadily at communications.

Trying to escape was a futile gesture. They were no match for the big cruiser, and there was nowhere to hide. Space had never looked so empty.

"*Cuh*," said Brock in a Chaimu grunt of exasperation, and opened a communications channel.

"This is Captain Gahiani of the *Im Naga*. Surrender your ship. Repeat. Surrender your ship."

Ellisne had downed magnification considerably, but still the cruiser with its blunt utilitarian lines filled the screen, dwarfing them.

Brock drew a deep breath. "*Im Naga*, this is a nonmilitary vessel. Veer off."

There was a crackle of static, and then a familiar voice came on: "This is Falmah-Al, Dire-lord. Surrender or be destroyed."

"Go ahead and shoot, Colonel," said Brock. "We have no intention of surrendering." He cut communications and made a chopping gesture with his hand. "Now, Rho! Hard about!"

The ship rolled over with a scream of her engines. Bracing himself with the holds provided, Brock grinned. "Again!"

Rho complied. "It won't work, Dire-lord," he said grimly, the safety web cutting into his shoulders as they tumbled in the opposite direction. "They're too close. We can't elude a tractor beam for long—*S'hk t ahc*!"

The scoutship suddenly lurched with such violence Brock

was thrown to the deck. Normally he would have been able to *flick* in time to save himself from harm, but he was helplessly slammed into metal. Dazed, he lay there, unable to breathe, unable to hear or see. He was barely aware of Rho cutting power. A sudden intense silence fell over them as the ship bucked lightly under the pull of the tractor beam. *I could have been to Felca by now*, thought Brock and sagged with defeat.

Then hands were gripping him, shaking him, pulling him up. And Ellisne's mind touched his:

Are you hurt? Brock!

He opened his eyes and gasped as air swelled back into his lungs. He felt battered, bruised, old.

"I'm all right," he said aloud, not wanting her to sense his despair, and climbed slowly to his feet.

"*Dgits*," said Rho with a contemptuous hiss. His eyes were bright with battle fire. "They've got us."

And there was nothing to do but stand there and watch the viewscreen as they were pulled helplessly into the bowels of the big ship.

FALMAH-AL, TRIM AND pacing in her black uniform, was waiting for them when they were dragged into what was a spacious chamber for a starship. It was fitted with a round conference table of black stone, sliced thin and highly polished, with nine backless chairs ringing it. She had reached the far side of the room where crossed swords displayed over a purple and amber banner hung upon the wall when Brock was shoved in roughly by his guards. One of them struck him hard in the back with the butt of his heavy disruptor, and Brock fell to his knees with a grunt.

"Enough!" Falmah-Al shouted.

But before the guard could move aside Brock snaked out one leg in the vicious third strike of *harchi* and sent the man sprawling with a cry. Brock was immediately on his feet, holding down the momentary pain of the blow he'd taken, his eyes sweeping the other guards standing ready for the order to shoot him.

"I said enough!" Falmah-Al came forward with a gesture that brought the guards to stiff attention. Brock relaxed a fraction, and took advantage of this first opportunity to study the woman who was his enemy. He had seen her likeness before in intelligence reports. But prints made from holographs, although easier to smuggle across enemy lines, also failed to exhibit the fiery vital force of this slight, dark-haired woman. Like most old-humans, she was small of stature, possessing a wiry body in superb physical shape and an acquiline face marked by chiseled bones. Her dark eyes, almond shaped and slanted just a bit beneath heavy black brows, were stern and cynical.

Brock's attacker lifted himself up awkwardly, only to gasp and fall again.

Brock's eyes met Falmah-Al's. "His leg is broken."

Her face was flushed with anger. She barked commands and the injured man was dragged out. "I am growing very tired of you, Dire-lord."

Brock stared through her in the Held manner of supreme indifference. "Then kill me and put an end to your troubles, Colonel," he said as Ellisne and Rho were brought in.

Ellisne gasped, but his mind shot out to reassure her, and she remained quiet.

"Dire-lord, please," said Falmah-Al with an abrupt change to a more pleasant tone. The sight of Rho's long ugly face and tall, pointed ears brought her brows sharply together. She started to speak, then returned her gaze to Brock and held out her hands. "You seem to think we are barbarians. I promise you we are not. Do you think we hold life so cheaply? It is sacred to us."

"Nothing is sacred to you except the total destruction of the Held," snapped Brock.

"We are finished with war," said Falmah-Al. "We seek now to build. Why won't you believe this? Why are you so afraid?"

He did not reply.

Her eyes swept over him, studying him, measuring him. Brock moved his own gaze to the man in grey fatigues standing watchfully in the farthest corner. He was a mixture: half-human, half-Varlax. Brock frowned slightly in surprise. He thought the Colonids avoided close contact with other species. Perhaps the man was a spy, but that did not explain the uniform with rank bands of a major.

"Three of you," said Falmah-Al with a brief smile. "Such a small band of resistance. Has it not yet occurred to you, Dire-lord, why the Held does not follow you? Your people are tired. They have lost the will to fight year after year. They can't face more bloodshed and loss of loved ones. And why should they have to? We are not monsters. One government is being exchanged for another. Oh, I realize that we seem harsh now. But transition is an uneasy time. We really are as tired as you of fighting. We want peace. It is time for peace. It is time for an end to fear and despair."

"An appealing argument," said Brock. "But one without purpose. I am not inciting what remains of the Held to resistance. I am merely traveling to a quiet corner of the galaxy to be out of your way."

Falmah-Al snorted. "Really?"

He could feel Ellisne's distress sawing through him. She was not used to lying. Despite the tenderness of their sharing, he knew he would continue to shock her. *Give nothing away, my beloved.*

"My suprin is dead. I do not serve Tregher. There is nothing else for a dire-lord to do but remove—"

"Liar!" Falmah-Al barked.

Brock's gaze shot to the half-breed and saw the watchfulness there. Danger seemed to ring itself more tightly about the room. Brock eased out a breath and decided to cut this game short.

"I will tell you nothing about the godas. You waste your time." As he spoke he felt Rho's touch briefly upon his arm. A warning? All of his senses were alert, expecting attack at any time from any direction. *They will have to kill us, my friends. We have nowhere to run.*

Brock, is there no way to deal rationally with them? asked Ellisne, her thoughts mingling warmly through his.

"You persist in misunderstanding us," said Falmah-Al, pacing back and forth on the other side of the table. "We don't want to use the godas for war. The war is over. We want to deactivate them, so that they will never again be a threat to us."

"They are no threat now."

"Aren't they? For centuries we have lived under their horrible threat. Can you imagine what it means to grow up in such an atmosphere, what it means to plan your future when at any time a Chaimu whim could mean annihilation, what it means to bear children without any certainty that they will live to be old? You think we are fierce, savage barbarians. *You* have made us so, Heldman! We had no choice but to come out and put an end to this threat hanging over us day after eternal day!"

"You will use them," said Brock.

She snapped something scornful he did not understand. "How could we? Fearing the godas as we do? They are horrible, something to be destroyed. And we shall destroy them, render their terrible threat void forever, never to be activated again. Tell me the locations, Dire-lord. If you have any compassion for life, if you have any mercy in your alien heart, tell me!" She leaned forward, placing her hands upon the gleaming black surface of the table, and stared at him

126

earnestly. "There is no chance for our peoples to live peaceably together until you do."

Brock hesitated, caught by her persuasion in spite of his suspicions. If only he could reach past that mental protector she wore! Then he would know the truth. But his mind, while powerful enough to crush her, still could not penetrate the distorted patterns made by the protector. He could only study her external manifestations: the dilation of her pupils, the expression on her face, the movements of her hands, the rapidity of her heartbeat, the smell of her. Her voice rang with the passion of sincerity.

Behind him, Ellisne stirred. "Brock," she said softly, her voice filled with hope. "If it could be true!"

"Yes," said Brock, frowning at Falmah-Al. She was tense, eager. Too eager. He still did not trust her. "If it only could be true. And if the godas were deactivated, what would stop you from eliminating every member of the Held who is not human or acceptably humanoid? While you remain afraid, we have a little safety."

A slight measure of respect entered the colonel's dark eyes. She spread out her hands. "Very well. If you cannot bring yourself to trust us, then we must try other, less pleasant methods. Either way, Dire-lord, we shall have the godas. They must be deactivated. Now . . ." Her eyes moved thoughtfully from him to Ellisne and then to Rho. "Who will be first? Not you, Dire-lord. You have proven yourself to be too stubborn. But perhaps you are less stoic when it is your friends who are in pain."

"No!"

Falmah-Al lifted her brows and waited, but Brock bit back his protest, clenching his fists helplessly.

"Let me deactivate them," he said. "It will be done. I give you the word of a dire-lord."

To his rage, she laughed loudly and scornfully.

"The word of a dire-lord? You wish me to let the three of you go and hope that you will keep your word? Oh, no, ghost. I would be canned out of the service quicker than you can *flick*. No, we shall deactivate the godas together. Where are they?"

"Tell her, Brock. Please," said Ellisne. She clutched his tensed arm, pouring reassurance and pleading into him. "Let us put an end to this."

Perhaps she was right. Brock struggled with himself, but

all he could see was the suprin, burned and dying, reaching out for his hand, giving his trust and his final command. He bowed his head. He could not tell Falmah-Al.

Fury flashed in her face. "Millen!" she snapped, pointing at Ellisne. "Take the female!"

At once Brock seized Ellisne's arm and pulled her protectively behind him as he faced the major. Beside him Rho hissed fiercely, baring poisonous fangs. They were ringed by pointed disruptors from the guards lining the room. There was nowhere to run, and nowhere to *flick* except into the cold death of space. Brock held down despair. He could not let anything happen to Ellisne! After so many years of loneliness, he had found in her something infinitely precious. He could not bear to lose her to these animals.

"Forget it," said Millen in a harsh voice. "You can't resist us, unless you're particularly eager to die."

Death, whispered Ellisne to Brock. *Let us die together if we must, but let this be ended*!

No! he shot back. *We're not going to die. Felca is not worth suicide.*

But Brock—

It is not worth your life!

Brock lifted his chin and shot Falmah-Al a bitter, defeated look. "All right," he said. "I'll tell you the location of Goda Prime—"

"*Merc ch' t*!" broke in Rho, unfurling his wings in such agitation one buffeted Brock and Ellisne. "It's in Dena Minor system, fifth planet. You deactivate it, perhaps then we trust you. Torture of Ellisne unnecessary, you who would not be called barbarian." And he hissed insolently, his eyes glowing orange.

"Rho!" said Brock in dismay, but the Slathese angrily averted his face.

"Good!" said Falmah-Al in satisfaction, seeming to take Brock's shocked protest as all the confirmation she needed. "Major, escort our prisoners to the brig. I have a new course to relay to the captain."

For Brock the trip to the force-shielded cells was a blur. He took no notice of details. His mind spun over and over with the same question that he blurted out as soon as their guards shoved them into their cell.

"Rho! Great Meir above, *why* did you tell them that? It wasn't necessary. I was going to—"

"You are dire-lord," retorted Rho with equal fierceness as Ellisne backed away from both of them, her eyes dark with fear. The Slathese slashed a finger across his throat. "Up to here you are filled with Chaimu pride. It is fact, *merc*? It is your training. How would you bend to their threats? How would you choose between she who has become your heart and the home which you mourn having left?"

"I don't—" began Brock fiercely and then broke off the denial. He frowned at the Slathese who had shown him so much loyalty and devotion, trying to see past the fierce defiance and bravado for the anguish that must be tearing at Rho. Brock had long ago faced the responsibility of being the eventual destroyer of Felca. He had been prepared to sacrifice it for Ellisne. But Rho had acted on the moment, and now his eyes were dull and his cheeks sunken.

"And what about you, my friend?" Brock asked softly. "How were you able to choose?"

Rho shut his eyes and turned away. "*Aya!*" It was a thin, keening sound that sent an eerie chill through Brock. "Don't ask me, Dire-lord. Don't ask me that."

Brock drew back, seeking some way to thank Rho. What could he say that would offer comfort? "When the suprin was dying, I asked him who would follow me in carrying out his last command. He said those who were Held would follow. Son of Kesmail the Mighty, you are truly Held."

It was the highest praise a dire-lord could bestow. Rho lifted his hand as though in acknowledgment, but his face remained averted.

"Brock." Ellisne stepped forward. "We must believe that they are going to keep their word." Her gaze met Brock's, warning him to probe Rho no further. "We must believe that they have said the truth. Are they so different from us, growing up in terror and dread? They deserve a chance to prove their compassion."

"Very well." Brock bowed his head in outward submission to her argument more for Rho's sake than anything else. But his eyes remained hard, and beneath his atrox his heart thumped angrily. "One chance," he said. "One."

Dena Minor was a cramped little system of planets spinning around a yellow dwarf. As the shuttle launched itself down from the *Im Naga*, Rho pressed himself hungrily against the tiny port in an effort to see Slath among the stars scattered in constellations unfamiliar to Brock. Ellisne sat slumped in her seat with her eyes closed. Brock gently smoothed a strand of hair from her face, then turned his gaze to the rear of the shuttle where Falmah-Al sat with Major Millen, discussing plans in low but excited voices.

"A celebration . . . the Collective's brightest moment . . ."

"No brighter than your record for achieving this, Colonel."

Brock sighed, not bothering to listen to more. The change in all the Colonids on board the ship had been noticeable since Rho's admission. Troopers patrolled the restricted areas accessible to the prisoners with a definite bounce in their step. Smiles were frequent, and laughter rang out along the ship's corridors. Even the capture of Darjahl Imperial and the stunning defeat of Heldfleet had not aroused such high spirits. Brock frowned, surrounded by self-doubt and guilt. Had he been so wrong? Had Ellisne and the Sedkethrans been so right? All the Colonids seemed to talk about was deactivation. The deputy lieutenants seated on the shuttle between the prisoners and Falmah-Al also had their heads together, arguing in genial whispers over the merits of *sagei*, the fiery Chaimu drink of fermented panta fruit, good mellow Walica brandy, or Bensha bloodmix—whatever that was—and whether they should team up for the dancing over coals.

I was wrong, thought Brock wearily. *I misjudged these people as much as my Chaimu masters, more so, perhaps*. His fingers sought the goda band, smooth and warmed by his flesh, and turned it about his wrist. Had he been so warped by bitterness and rebellion that he had lost all compassion himself? Had he been so eager to escape being a puppet of the magstrusi that he made himself one of Suprin Utdi's instead? No, not even now would he criticize his suprin. Utdi had been a corrupt hedonist with many faults, but he had been a leader of judgment and insight as well.

With a sigh, Brock leaned back against the flat hard cushions of the seat which were covered in drab, scratchy, hardwearing material. The whole interior of the shuttle was strictly utilitarian without a single splash of color or attempt at aesthetics. Use over beauty; conformity over creativity; discipline over freedom. These might as well be the battle cries of the Colonids. They seemed to oppress his very soul. He did not care what Ellisne and Falmah-Al said; it was *not* merely an exchange of one government for another. It was an exchange of philosophies and tolerance. Diversity would be

130

hammered away. And then what future would the galaxy have? The Colonids drew all of their fierce energy from tackling insurmountable challenges. They had spent centuries united in an attempt to defeat the Held. Now they would turn their energies to converting everyone to Im. And when that was accomplished they would collapse, as the mighty Chaimu honorables had following a glorious reign of great achievements. Now those achievements were dust, remembered only as legends by the hedonists who had given the Held away.

Brock rubbed the scar on his cheek, feeling unspeakably depressed.

Closing his eyes, Brock settled himself down into the old patterns of moving from one point of Discipline to another, taking comfort in the earliest lessons of childhood, so worn, so old and familiar now. And as he did so, he felt himself drift slightly out of time sequence, as he had not done since the injury to his atrox. Startled, Brock opened his eyes. Was it possible he was healing?

But even as the thought flashed through him he felt the gentle touch of Ellisne's fingers upon his and the warmth of her conscious merging into his. Disappointment pierced him, but he layered it hastily in the secret recesses of his mind so that she would not be troubled. Why did he keep hoping for what was gone forever? What he had felt was only the soft eddies of Ellisne's thoughts becoming his.

What is wrong, my dearest? she asked him, her concern spilling over him like the soft fall of heated water. *You're troubled still.*

He gave himself a little shake. *It is nothing, I have been a fool.*

You tried to do what you thought right. We all face choices and change. I do not regret mine.

He looked into her eyes, so trusting, so completely his, and forgot his worries in the fresh thrill of passion. And as the shuttle turned in a slow arc down through the scudding clouds of Amul, tarnished lightly by the setting sun, they drifted together, one to another, and shared until an abrupt tap on Brock's shoulder disturbed them.

Falmah-Al was standing by his seat, her dark eyes impatient. "We've landed, ghost. If you've given us the correct coordinates we should be sitting directly over the spot. Come on!"

AMUL WAS A barren, hostile world with a thin atmosphere and no sentient life. The rock-strewn valley in which they had landed along with a second shuttle containing Falmah-Al's excited technicians was hardly more than a slit carved between jutting mountains. The sun was setting with a last feeble blaze of gold crowning the horizon, and a cold wind swept the desolate cliffs hanging above them as they gathered between the shuttles. The Colonids and Rho wore light atmosphere masks; Brock and Ellisne required no environmental assistance. Falmah-Al's shoulders were shivering beneath the slash of wind, but Brock threw back his head in a deep rush of pleasure. The air was so dry, so thin, so cold; how easy it was to breathe after the thick, humidified soup on Darjahl Imperial.

A disruptor poked him in the ribs.

"Get on with it," said Millen. "We don't want to be standing out here in the dark."

"Give me a moment to concentrate," said Brock slowly. He was reluctant to begin. He still felt that he had failed the suprin. But Ellisne's eyes were upon him, shining with encouragement. At her nod, he grasped the goda band tightly and closed his eyes as he opened his mind to the instructions imparted to him by the suprin.

At first he understood nothing. The patterns were so old, so faded. They had been handed down through generations, passed from one dying suprin to his successor countless times until they almost ceased to have any meaning. Brock narrowed his search, fastening upon one symbol at a time so that the rapid progression of patterns was slowed. His body swayed slightly from side to side as the goda band seemed to grow warmer upon his flesh. Opening his eyes, he did not see the intent faces ringed about him. Instead his eyes sought the cliffs, examining each against the symbol held in his mind until he found the right one.

"There." He pointed due north at the crag towering above the end of the valley. "See the cuts in the side? The elements have almost worn them away."

"Where? I see nothing." Falmah-Al was at his shoulder, crowding him as she sought to follow where he was pointing.

"About halfway up."

"*Gazal*, it's too dark. Tirza, lights!"

The female deputy sprang to action with a swift command. Seconds later a powerful spotlight stabbed at the mountain from one of the shuttles.

"I see it," said Millen.

"Aha!" said Falmah-Al triumphantly. "At last! Father Im is with us. Come!"

Millen caught her arm, his Varlax eyes hooded by the gathering shadows. "It's too dark to climb up there now. We should wait until morning."

"No!" Falmah-Al jerked free. Her chiseled face was fired by impatience. "I have waited too long for this. We are going now. Rig out plenty of torches."

"Formation!" bawled Tirza.

Falmah-Al and Millen took the lead in the trek up the long slope, with Brock, Ellisne, and Rho in the center of the technicians, and the guards bringing up the rear. The going was treacherous with loose stones and uncertain footing, but the climb itself was not steep enough to be difficult. Rho moved lightly along ahead of Brock and Ellisne, his eyes fixed on the night sky spread out above them. A bright steady planet hung just to the right of the mountain peak.

"What a lovely evening star," said Ellisne.

"It is Slath," replied Rho. "On a spring night like this the young males are flying across the path of the moon to vie for the favors of the ones they love. And the little *marsans* are giving their low cry in the river reeds by the thousands. Beneath the citadel, the village lights of the cluster are shining out from cliffs such as these."

Brock heard the longing in Rho's words. "When were you last home?" he asked.

"Many years."

"Do you miss it? Do you wish you were there now?" asked Brock.

Rho's orange eyes met his. "Yes," he said simply. "But it would not be the same."

For a while there was only the sound of labored breathing muffled by masks and the ring and clatter of boots over stones. Then one of the technicians up ahead who was talking earnestly to Millen slipped on loose shale with a sudden cry. His torch flew up end over end as it was thrown into the air. Arms windmilling wildly, he almost regained his balance and Millen made a grab at him but missed as the man came tumbling down straight at Ellisne, who stood frozen in his path.

"Ellisne!" shouted Brock, but it was Rho who was the closest to her. He leapt at her, knocking her to one side out of the way.

"Catch him! Someone catch him!" shouted Falmah-Al. "He's going over the edge!"

The technician just behind Brock grunted and scrambled forward in a futile attempt to check his colleague's progress, but he was too slow. He'd never catch the man in time. Brock hesitated only an instant before throwing himself at the edge of the trail. He might not be able to *flick*, but he could still move faster than any Colonid alive, and he felt the old familiar blur as his muscles bunched and snapped out.

"Brock, no!" screamed Ellisne, but his outstretched hands were already reaching out to the technician's jacket and grasping hard on the tough cloth.

He felt the unyielding impact with earth, the sharp grunt as the breath was knocked from his lungs, the tear at his shoulder and back muscles as the technician rolled over the edge and shot out into the air, slowed only by the drag of Brock's weight. There was the metallic taste of dirt in his mouth, and the raw sting of a stone scraping his cheek. But their wild impetus was slowing as Brock dug his boot toes into the ground, and then they were stopped, with Brock hanging off the edge all the way to his waist and the man sobbing below him in his grasp.

"Get them!"

There was a rush, and hands grabbed at Brock's legs, dragging him and the technician back to safety. Brock got to his feet, breathing hard, and pulled the technician upright beside him.

"Are you hurt?" Brock asked.

The man's trouser leg was shredded, he was trembling all over, and he could barely stand on his own from the shock.

"Egel!" blurted out someone else, shining his torch mercilessly into the man's face. "Are you all right? Say something."

"*Gazal*," muttered one of the guards in disgust. "Our best technician. Stand back from him, ghost."

"Have you ever seen anyone move that fast? I haven't," said someone else. "Truly, Egel, Im was watching out for you."

"Yes," said Egel shakily. His eyes, wide and still full of stark terror, stabbed only briefly into Brock's before he yanked himself away.

Millen came down with a reckless slide of dirt and shale. "Is he all right?"

Egel nodded and tugged at his jacket to straighten it. Brock stepped back and slapped the dust from his clothes, angered as much by the lack of thanks as by his own involuntary eagerness to save a Colonid life.

Millen glanced at Brock and seemed about to say something to him, then shrugged and turned away. "Let's move on," he said.

The earlier excitement faded, to be replaced by an ever-tightening constriction of tension. *If I were human*, thought Brock, trudging on up the slope, *I would be weeping*. He lifted his face to the cold slice of wind, letting unfamiliar smells fill his nostrils. That he was following the killer of Mabruk so docilely shamed him. Had the end of the Held truly been on the day of defeat, or was it now at this moment when he walked up to deactivate the Held's last hope? He had never suspected that all the struggles of his life would culminate in such humiliation. Already he could see how it would be played. As soon as Falmah-Al finished celebrating the end of this goda, she would demand the others.

Brock bowed his head as he fitted his foot into a niche and boosted himself up over a boulder after an agile Ellisne. A broken dam began with a tiny crack. Once he gave in to Falmah-Al here, he could not keep her from the others.

But shame on another level also burned him. What was wrong with him that he mourned the end of the godas? Did he crave power so strongly? Had he become that corrupted by the ways of the Held? His memories played over the words of the suprin naming him the successor instead Tregher. Was he fighting for his own ambitions?

He was afraid to look into himself for the answers. After all, why should he? The war was over. He had his life and he had Ellisne. That was enough.

Reaching up to scramble over another series of boulders rolled together like a child's set of balls, Brock was startled when he found his wrist seized in a powerful grip. Millen dragged him up and onto the ledge just under the scored marks now illuminated by at least a dozen torches.

The Colonids parted as Brock walked up to the wall of stone and ran his hands over the cold, gritty surface to find the activation points. One of the codes in his mind surfaced abruptly, and he was speaking it aloud almost before he realized it.

There was an answering rumble from within the mountain that made the Colonids start uneasily and reach for their weapons. But the scored stone slid into a hidden recess with a slowness that marked the extreme age of the door. Blackness yawned at them, absorbing the torchlight shone at it.

"Steps," said Falmah-Al, and her voice rang out like a huntress. She thrust a torch into Brock's hand. "Lead, Dire-lord."

On impulse he started counting the steps as he went, but after a thousand he ceased the exercise. The steps, all evenly cut and unworn, led straight down without any turns or landings. Walls rose up on either side so narrowly Brock's shoulders seemed almost to brush them as he descended with Falmah-Al right on his heels. He held the torch steadily before him, and kept his free hand running along the wall on his right. By the thousandth step he was conscious of atmospheric changes in the air, changes in temperature and pressure. There was a slight buzzing in his ears, and those behind him were panting audibly. His fingers stiffened as they touched a slick, highly polished surface very different from the roughly hewn stone they had been following. He stopped abruptly to catch his breath, and only Falmah-Al's quickness saved her from bumping into him.

"Go on!" she ordered, poking him in the back with her torch. "What's wrong?"

"Ungstan carbonix," he said beneath his breath, a little frightened now. It was an organic metal highly dangerous to

Sedkethrans. They could *flick* into it, but coming out was unlikely. He shuddered, remembering the boy in his barracks who had recklessly accepted a dare to stick his hand into the wall surrounding the Temple of the Writings. The boy's screams were still as sharp and terrifying as on the day the tragedy had occurred. Brock could still remember the whine of the scalpel as a grim-faced healer performed an emergency amputation.

Falmah-Al poked him again. "What did you say? Ungstan what?"

"Nothing." Brock shook off his fear. The metal was simply here to serve as insulation for the control room when the goda was activated. As long as he did not touch it he would not be harmed. Sending a warning to Ellisne, he drew his hand close to his side and continued on more slowly. They must be nearly there.

But the steps continued endlessly downward until even he was short of breath. The muscles in his legs burned and trembled. He paused again to rest.

"Don't stop!" said Falmah-Al raggedly. "It can't be much farther. Unless you have tricked us."

"No tricks," said Brock, gulping for air that was nearly nonexistent down here. They were going too deep. It was not safe to go so deep. He could hear the others muttering among themselves. Hope lifted in his chest. Perhaps they would give up and turn back.

Falmah-Al poked him sharply in the back, nearly making him lose his balance. "Go on."

"Colonel," said Millen but as they started moving again he did not finish his protest.

Ten steps farther down, just when Brock's lungs seemed to be collapsing and his head was becoming light and dizzy, the steps ended. It was a tiny space; barely enough room had been hewn out of the mountain for the door blocking Brock's path to swing open. Someone whooped, and they came clattering down the steps after him, crowding him as they all tried to see.

"Stand back!" barked one of the officers, and the Colonids quietened.

Brock waited until they were silent, then he spoke the second code. Nothing happened.

"*Gazal-ma*!" swore Falmah-Al. The muzzle of her disruptor jammed under Brock's right shoulder blade. "Open it!"

"Quiet!" he snapped back, his nerves nearly as frazzled as hers. Even the careful shielding of the Disciplines could not forever withstand the turbulent emotions of the Colonids. They weren't telepathic. They had never learned the necessity of keeping themselves under control.

Carefully he ran through the sequences again. He had the correct code, but the age of this machinery was immense almost beyond comprehension. None of it might function now.

He spoke the code again, giving it perfect Chaimu inflection. There was a pause, during which the disruptor in his back seemed to grow enormous, and then slowly, ever so slowly the door grated open.

There was a puff of old air in his face, warmed to the correct temperature for Chaimu comfort, and recycled at the correct rate to avoid staleness. Brock inhaled it gratefully and stepped through into a chamber approximately the size of a standard cruiser's bridge. Sensors did not register him, but Falmah-Al's entrance made lights blink on in dazzling illumination. The colonel froze at the low sound of a hum.

"We have activated it," she said in an appalled whisper.

Brock smiled. "No, that is merely life support systems kicking on automatically to full operational levels. Despite what you may have heard about the Chaimu love of luxury, they are not wasteful, Colonel. Whenever they are absent from a place they close energy levels down to standby."

Falmah-Al's eyes snapped to his, but instead of looking angered by his insolence she almost smiled back. "I see," she said quite mildly. "Explain everything to me."

Brock glanced about at the complex control banks. Everything had been covered with dust shields. Everything was shut down. He expected there to be a response along with the kick on of support systems, but nothing else had come on. An ironical urge to laugh surged through him.

"It's dead," he said aloud, grinning at the colonel. "After all of your years of terror, there's nothing to fear after all. And after all of my guilty soul-searching, there's nothing here at all."

"What?" Falmah-Al frowned at him as though he had gone mad. "What are you saying?"

"I'm saying that we have been pursuing a cloud, a phantom, an illusion. There's no goda here any more."

"Impossible!"

"Look." He pulled off a dust shield and recklessly slapped at a panel of controls with the flat of his hand. Someone gasped. "Nothing! See? It must have died long ago. Age finally conquered the best of Chaimu technology."

Rho closed his eyes and mumbled something, but Millen brushed roughly past him as he came up to join Falmah-Al.

"Did you hear, Major?" she said.

"Yes, I heard." He looked grim. "Egel!" he shouted. "Get your crew working to check out the power sources."

"It can't be," whispered Falmah-Al, her face white and drained. She stared slowly about the control room as though unable to believe what her eyes told her. "After so long. To finally be here and find *nothing*. . . ."

Brock shook his head, his eyes meeting Ellisne's relieved ones briefly. All of that self-torment for nothing. He did not realize until now just how much he had dreaded making a decision in this room. And now he was spared all of it.

"Perhaps we are going to be able to make peace as you have hoped," he said formally to Falmah-Al.

She slowly turned her head around to face him, and only the fury burning in her eyes gave him a split-second's worth of warning before her disruptor struck him across the mouth and sent him sprawling to the floor.

"Peace!" she spat as though the word were filth. "What do I want with peace, Held scum? I want an operational goda. And I want it now! I know you can activate this one. You are lying to us, trying to trick us. But I know you must key in a special code. Get up!"

Slowly, under the menace of her aimed disruptor, Brock hauled himself to his feet and straightened, ignoring the desire to press his hand to his cut and swelling lip. He tasted the sour sting of blood, colorless and bitter, and spat some of it out of his mouth.

"Brock—" said Ellisne, starting toward him, but Millen swiftly blocked her path with a drawn weapon. "Stay back," he said harshly. "You aren't going to vanish with the dire-lord this time."

"I was right," said Brock with growing fury. "All the time when no one else believed it, I was right. You do intend to destroy us, all of us—"

"It is what you intend for us!" she retorted.

"No. I meant only to drive your people away, back to your own territory where you belong. That is—"

"Liar!" She motioned with the disruptor. "Get over to those controls and activate them!"

"They are dead. I've told you—"

"And I don't believe your lies!" Her head whipped around. "Egel!"

The technician glanced nervously up from the scanner he had unpacked. "Power sources are still intact, Colonel. But I don't know yet how to reach them."

"The dire-lord knows." She almost whispered the words. Her dark slanted eyes glittered at Brock. "And the dire-lord will tell. Is that bracelet you wear perhaps the key we seek?"

With a shock he realized he was twisting the goda band around and around his wrist. Brock dropped his hand immediately. "I'll tell you nothing." He thought of the whips of the magstrusi that had never tamed him, of the fire branding the swirled scar into his flesh and how he had not flinched even the slightest bit, of the terrible rounds of killing in the Chaimu arena in order to learn, in order to survive. The Colonids could never torture a dire-lord enough to make him talk. His chin came up, and he met Falmah-Al's eyes with a gaze like steel. "You fear us telepaths because you do not understand us. Well, understand this. With my mind I could crush you where you stand."

"And I can kill your friends while you threaten me," she retorted. As she spoke, she aimed her disruptor and fired at Rho, enveloping him in a nimbus of raw energy before he crumpled limply to the ground.

"*No!*" cried Brock in a roar and rushed at her. A wall seemed to come out of nowhere, knocking him back. Dizzily he staggered, every molecule suddenly on fire, and through a blind haze glimpsed Millen's grim face above a blazing disruptor before the world went black and crashed upon him.

HEAT SHIMMERED THROUGH him, baking his flesh, searing his entrails, frying the layers of his mind. His nervous system twitched in spasms like shorted-out circuitry. He seemed to be fighting, but he wasn't sure what. He could not see or hear or feel. He was only aware of the heat, that awful fire which tormented him until he writhed helplessly, crying out without sound. Why was it so hot?

The scar . . . they were branding him with the scar! He should be proud. He had worked so hard for it, trained for it, killed for it, and now the white-hot iron was sinking into his flesh. He could smell the nauseating stench of burning meat while the pain exploded through his head. No! He did not want to serve! *No!*

"Brock! Brock, my beloved, please. Let me help you. Let me reach you. Brock, please stop fighting me."

Gradually he became aware of the words, first as a low hum buried beneath layers and layers of pain and discomfort, then as a louder continuum of sound, then finally as distinct words, recognizable and making sense.

Ellisne!

He tried to speak her name and failed, but the effort bumped him through to the upper layers of consciousness. He stirred, blinked open his eyes, and sank down again. Cool hands pressed against his burning face, incredibly soothing. He grasped them, pressing them harder to his flesh.

"Brock, oh, please . . ."

"Ellisne." This time he said it. Pleased with himself, he

tried again to open his eyes, but they were gummy and would not focus. His lids were incredibly heavy.

"Let me help you," she kept saying. "Don't keep me out. I can't help you if you won't let me." Then abruptly she paused. "Have I permission to assist the dire-lord?"

"Ah . . ." Something within him relaxed, and her healing strength surged through him like a tide of renewal.

"Sleep," she murmured, her relief and joy trembling through him. And with those emotions came her love, a gift as pure and delicate as the finest lattice of ice crystals worked in harmony. Her heart sang to his as he responded, and after a moment she forgot the calm ministrations of her profession and held him cradled tightly in her arms with her soft hair brushing his face as she cried softly over and over: "You're alive. Oh, my beloved, you're alive!"

"Ellisne." His fingers slid up the loosely woven sleeve of her cloak. Her voice was louder. He could hear other things now: the scrape of her shoe upon the floor, the little choke in her throat, his own breathing. He realized he was lying on the floor. It was a stone floor, very hard and cold. He concentrated on the comfort of that coldness, letting it seep through him to gradually dissipate the lingering fire of the disruptor. Brock frowned as memories came rushing back to him. Disruptor . . . Millen firing at him . . .

"Rho!" he said in anguish, jerking upright despite her attempt to hold him down. His eyes met hers, searched them.

"He is dead," she said softly, her beautiful eyes darkened with sorrow. "I offer thee my grief, beloved. There was nothing I could do for him."

Squeezing her hand, Brock averted his face to hide the savagery of his anger from her. He remembered it all now: Falmah-Al's duplicity, her threats, her cold-blooded aim at Rho. He never had a chance. True, faithful Rho, a Heldman to the last, shot down on a madwoman's burst of spite.

"Barbarians," he whispered, his voice raw with hatred. Crimson stained his mind, filtering down through his vision, and making Ellisne gasp. Deep inside came the thrumming of Chaimu war chants, ancient, alien, yet disturbingly compelling to that portion of life force which was ancient within himself. He remembered the nights in the grottos beneath the training arena when those who had been selected to duel the following morning squatted around blazing fires, Chaimu scales glistening as slaves poured warm oil upon muscled bodies. The rooms glowed red from the baleful heap of coals and the hallucinogenic smoke until only the gleam of the brightly polished weapons remained clear in the haze.

Brock shook his head as though fighting that dizzy influence once again. He had not been able to kill until his trainers finally managed to fill him with the drugged smoke.

"Brock!" said Ellisne sharply, giving his hand a shake. "Come back. You have slipped so far away. I cannot feel you."

His eyes lifted to hers, but he did not see her. He saw instead Falmah-Al's face, grimly smiling as she shot Rho down. He saw old battle scenes on the fringe worlds, where Colonid forces butchered Held shock troops and were mowed down in return. The killing did not ever stop. The Colonids did not know how to stop it, or themselves. They did not even know that they should try.

"All the stories are true," he said hoarsely. "All the old tales of the atrocities, the cruelty, the unspeakable disregard for life . . . they're all true. She'd won, Ellisne. She'd forced us, tricked us into bringing her here. We gave her a goda, the ultimate weapon of the galaxy, and it was not enough for her. She enjoyed killing him."

"Brock, don't."

"I saw her face. She wanted to kill. She wanted to hurt me in here." He pressed a fist to his chest. "What if she had shot you instead?"

"Hush!" Ellisne's arms held him tightly. "Brock, do not torment yourself in this way. I am safe. You are safe. It is enough."

"No, it is not enough!"

Thrusting her away, he levered himself unsteadily to his feet and took two swift strides across the tiny cell of stone which held them. It had been a storage area of some kind. A short stack of dust-covered cubes still stood in one corner. Others had been dragged outside, judging from the trail left in the dust on the floor. He struck the closed door with his fist, and Ellisne jumped to her feet.

"Brock, do not let this fury eat at you. You must rest. There is nothing we can do now. She has tricked us. It is over—"

"Never!" he snarled. "Not while there remains breath in my body."

She looked at him doubtfully. Her face was a peculiar color

in the light shining from the halon lamp designed more for preservation of perishable chemicals than for illumination.

"What are you going to do? What can you do?"

"We're getting out of here. And then I'm going to stop her."

"Brock!" Ellisne grasped his arm. "How can you? She has too many guards. They'll kill you."

"No, I'm not going to jump her here. We've got to get away. Find another goda." As he spoke Brock was examining the door. He touched the latch. Unlocked. His brows shot up. "Well, now. They must have thought they'd killed me too."

"They nearly did. Brock, please try to think rationally. We can't get away. The only way out is through the control room and back up those steps. They'd see us."

"I don't think so." Brock grinned at her and gripped her by the arms. "Remember my ability to blank myself out? I think I can blank you as well."

"Yes, but that won't help. Their scanners might not register us, but their eyes would."

"They have to sleep sometime, and I can take care of the guard on watch."

"Brock, you mustn't kill!" she said in alarm. "Their atrocities do not free you to imitate them."

"Ellisne," he said sternly. "When we first shared, you learned what manner of creature I am and have been. You know what I have done."

"But you need not continue. You are not dire-lord now. Your suprin is dead. That released you from your duty."

"I am not free until I carry out his last command," said Brock grimly. "Don't you see? I've handed a goda to Falmah-Al! Do you think we've come through every horror of war imaginable in the past few years? Just wait until she activates this thing. She'll command the galaxy. She can even hold her own Collective in her power if she so chooses."

"But why are you so certain she will activate it? You said yourself that it's dead. It's too old. The machinery no longer functions. Her technicians may never discover—"

"And what if they do?" he shot back. "Egel has already said that the power banks are still intact. All they have to do is decipher the controls. Not such a difficult task for a people whose technology currently outstrips the Held's own. Egel."

Brock scowled. "I wish I had let him fall to his death. Why didn't I listen to my instincts? I *knew* I should not trust her!"

Brock lifted his head, and his eyes bored into Ellisne. "We must go to Felca. I thought—I hoped—that the responsibility had been lifted from me. But it hasn't. I can no longer avoid it."

"But if you activate another goda, what is left but complete annihilation?"

Is this my destiny? he wondered with a stab of pain. *To destroy all existence? Is this why the magstrusi tried so hard to cripple me? Was their wisdom greater after all?*

"But what if I don't?" he asked quietly, feeling a great weariness invade his soul. "Is Rho's death to mean nothing? Is it to have no vengeance? Falmah-Al will put the Held under a reign of terror greater than any history has ever known."

"Just as the Held did to the Imish Collective."

"It isn't the same. The Held never carried out its threat."

"But the chance was always there."

"Was it?" His eyes met hers. "Then why didn't the suprin order activation when the Colonids destroyed Mabruk? What greater provocation could there be? The death of billions of innocent people, most of them children. The destruction of irreplacable genetic banks. It is a crime beyond comprehension, and surely one undeserving of mercy. Yet no action was taken. Do you think, had the positions been reversed, that the Colonids would have forbore the ultimate retaliation?"

She caught her breath sharply. "Brock, please. I understand what you are trying to say. But there is a flaw in your logic. You have forgotten that the suprin did order retaliation. You have been trying to carry it out ever since he died."

Brock lifted his hands, then let them fall helplessly to his sides. She was right. Her thinking was flawless, pointing out all the errors in his own. And yet, his heart told him he was right.

"There is a time, Ellisne," he said slowly, "when logic becomes so absolute it creates an aberration in what is just. Whatever reasons and motivations have been mixed together, I know only that until this time I was never entirely certain within myself whether I would commit destruction."

"On the scoutship you had decided only to bluff," she said. "You had made your decision, Brock. Are you going to undo it now?"

"Falmah-Al has changed the circumstances. You heard what she said. You know what she intends. If you doubted my ability to remain uncorrupted by the power of commanding a goda, what do you think of hers?"

Ellisne's face clouded. "Brock, I—"

"Goda Prime is the closest to where we are now. It is our only chance of stopping her. Ellisne, I can't fight you. If you go against me, then I—"

His voice faltered and he put out a hand to the wall to steady himself.

"You ask me to decide?" Her voice was shrill. "You wish to include me in this responsibility? But you know my opinion."

"Yes, but opinion and decision are not the same."

She sighed. "You sound like Magstrus Olbin. Oh, Brock, why do you torture me so? You know I cannot fight you. I will not fight you. That is finished. We are one."

He held out his hand. "Then help me."

Slowly, almost hesitantly she took his hand. "Blanking exhausts you with the tremendous energy it requires. Why can't I simply *flick* us—"

"No! This place is lined with ungstan carbonix. It's too unstable here." He expelled his breath harshly. "We'll have to do it the hard way." He listened a moment, letting his mind quest lightly beyond the door of the storage cell. "Come. I think it's time to try."

He opened the door just far enough for them to slip through and bowed his head as he focused hard on blanking himself and Ellisne. He wasn't sure he could project sufficiently to conceal her as well as himself, but as soon as he made the effort of slipping his mind out of time sync with reality he found it much easier than it had been the first time. It was almost like *flicking* mentally instead of physically. The problem was, of course, that previously there had been no physical effort required of him, and this time he had to navigate a stealthy path through the control room and back up the steps. That required conscious, active thought. Would it register on the scanners? He still had to try.

Already his energy was draining rapidly as he projected the shields around himself and Ellisne and slipped through the door with her hand grasped tightly in his. The storage room had been carved from a natural fissure in the stone, and it was set slightly back from the curve of the control room walls. Porta-lamps dimmed down to a mere glimmer of light provided the only illumination. Monitors rotated the room on auto-alert. Designed to be heat sensitive, one skimmed the air right over Brock's head as he and Ellisne froze but its scanning field was not triggered. Brock smiled briefly to himself as he noted the deficiency in their security systems. Until the Colonids completely adapted to dealing with non-human life forms, the Held still had a few advantages.

His breathing pattern changed, and with a jolt he realized his concentration had slipped. Angry at himself, he focused down again. As soon as he had himself back under control he eased forward again with Ellisne drifting like a shadow behind him. She was helping by sliding herself slowly back and forth between dimensions. It did not take so much effort to blank her out that way.

Another monitor circled overhead, pausing near Brock and Ellisne to extend an antenna. *Why were they so cautious*, he wondered, then shut off the thought hurriedly. Speculation could come later. He stepped carefully over the legs of a guard snoring on a thin pallet spread out on the cold stone floor. Most of them were asleep in the center of the control room, huddled together beneath the orange glow of a small heating unit. *Who had gone back for all the equipment*? Some of the guards, obviously. There were not as many in evidence now as there had been before.

Three of the panels were open beneath the control boards, and circuit boards hung outside by their multicolored wires like entrails spilled from a dead body. Tools littered the floor. Brock was surprised that Falmah-Al wasn't working her technicians on continuous shifts.

Slowly, taking his time, Brock edged around the sleeping bodies, ignoring the urge to eliminate Falmah-Al and her henchmen now while they were helpless. This goda was no longer a secret. Other Colonids would come to replace Falmah-Al and her ambitions with ones equally dangerous. He moved past the outermost sleepers on silent feet, not even daring to breathe. No one appeared to be on sentinel duty; the monitors were serving that function. Ten steps to the exit. Eight steps . . . four . . .

The soft chink of metal upon stone and the scrape of a foot froze Brock. Ellisne's dismay was a sob in his mind. Slowly, ever so slowly, his whole body tensed, Brock turned his head to look back over his shoulder. Egel was rising from where he had been crouched out of sight by one of the control panels.

His face could barely be seen in the inadequate illumination. He held a pair of needle pliers suitable for work on delicate glass and microsine fibers in one hand. His eyes blinked once, twice, three times in the pale blur of his face. Brock stared back, Ellisne drifting slowly into solid form at his side. Seconds blurred by, stretching the suspense to an intolerable level before Brock realized that Egel wasn't going to sound the alarm. Suppressing a sigh of accute relief, Brock continued on to the exit and took the steps quickly, two at a time, until his breath was short and fast, humming in his ears, and his heart thudded beneath his atrox.

Then, and only then, did he pause to rest and let his mind slip out of its careful discipline.

"Brock!" Ellisne's whisper was no louder than a breath of air. "He let us go! Isn't he the one you saved from falling?"

"Yes." It was one very good way of saying thanks. Brock closed his eyes a moment in the complete darkness, then started on up the steps.

The rest of the guards were huddled between the parked shuttles at the foot of the mountain, trying to shelter around the baleful embers of a dying fire. Brock crouched down on the ledge far above them, his nostrils drawing in the crisp cold air. On the horizon a band of palest gold merged into the smoky expanse of sky. Dawn. There was not much time. He glanced at Ellisne and nodded. She drew a deep breath, took his arm in a firm grip and *flicked* them down to the shuttles.

"Which?" whispered Ellisne as soon as they materialized at the rear of the shuttles.

Brock listened to one of the guards coughing. It must have been a long cold night for them. Fruitlessly so, since they could have been more comfortable and equally alert sheltering inside the crafts. He lifted a brow at the iron discipline of Colonid military forces and pointed at Falmah-Al's shuttle. Her transport would be deemed more important; it should be carrying more fuel.

Ellisne *flicked* them inside and obediently moved down the aisle toward the rear seats while Brock eased his way forward to the cockpit. The door was open, and the pilot was snoring loudly. No cold nights spent outdoors for him.

Brock struck quickly, and the man sprawled to the floor with a metallic clatter. Frowning, Brock grabbed his shoulders to haul him out of the cockpit and realized with a spurt of distaste that the man was a cyborg. Swiftly he rolled the pilot over and searched him for a sleeve knife. It was the inevitable personal weapon of a Colonid. Finding one, Brock made a short incision behind the man's ear. Nothing. Wrinkling his nose at the hot unpleasant smell of human blood, he turned the pilot's head to the other side and made a second cut. Ah, there! He pried out the mental protector and probed ruthlessly into the unshielded mind, seeking piloting knowledge and accessory codes. Withdrawing with a slight shudder, Brock rolled the unconscious man into a locker and secured it shut. It would be more expedient to kill the man now that he had the information he needed, but Brock knew Ellisne would see the guilt in his eyes if he did so. Longing for the sleep there was no time for, Brock rubbed gritty eyes and reached out to secure the hatch lock.

Letting the Colonid mind overlay his, Brock fitted himself into the seat and activated the shuttle engines. They whined loudly to life, warming with a speed he was grateful for. There was the muffled sound of a shout and a pounding on the side of the shuttle, but by then Brock was already lifting off the ground and swinging the shuttle around. He pushed the throttle with the deft touch required to bring the mettlesome craft into an efficient launch without stalling. A headache was throbbing into life against his temples, but he ignored it. Overlay was the quickest way to learn a new skill, but it was never a pleasant experience.

He touched the intercom. "Pilot to passenger," he said with a grin, hearing Ellisne's startled gasp all the way to the front. "Strap yourself in and enjoy the ride."

"Brock!" she called.

"Yes, beloved?"

"They're climbing into the other shuttle. Do you think they're going to pursue—"

"Damn." He'd forgotten that. Swiftly he punched up an outside line. "Shuttle One to down craft," he said, rattling off the words in Imish. "Answering summons from cruiser. No emergency. Repeat. No emergency."

"Molaud!" barked a plainly relieved voice over the line. "What the hell? You about blasted us out of our skins."

Brock grinned, wishing he'd been able to do more than that. "Sorry," he said. "When the colonel says jump, I jump. *Alamam.*"

The other voice muttered something crude and broke contact. Brock laughed and let his body accept the thrust deeper

149

into the seat as he curved the shuttle up in a long graceful arc through the splendor of Amul's brief dawn.

"Brock?" called Ellisne. "What are we going to do now? We can't steal the cruiser, and we can't go all the way to Felca in a ground/space shuttle. What do you intend to do?"

Brock's smile faded and he stared unseeingly out past the pointed nose of the shuttle at the gold and pink-tinted clouds. "I wish I knew," he said softly.

ON BOARD THE *Im Naga*, Gahiani surveyed his bridge with sleepy eyes. The bridge crew had nothing to do but loll about and chatter to each other. Time hung heavily on their hands, and more than one glance went frequently to the ship's chronometer as the hours counted slowly down to the end of the shift. Gahiani was perhaps the worst clock watcher of all. He resented his ship being bottlenecked for this duty. After months of glorious, heroic fighting against Heldfleet, his crew deserved to go home to Kentra, to receive their medals and a triumph in their honor, and to enjoy a long-overdue leave. Instead, they sat here at the beck and call of an over-ambitious groundtroop colonel. The fact that she was security director for the governor of Baz I did not impress Gahiani. He had never met Nls Ton, but he knew that Ton's background was mediocre: military training at one of the minor academies instead of the prestigious Hagara al-Dad on Kentra and a family traditionally civil servants rather than of the warrior class. It was even rumored that Falmah-Al was Ton's lover. Gahiani sniffed to himself and examined the trim length of his fingernails. If that was the criteria on which Governor Ton chose his security directors, then Falmah-Al was out of her league. Gahiani's younger brother should have received that appointment.

"Captain," said the communications officer, breaking into his reverie. "Shuttlecraft is approaching. Pilot Molaud requests access to hangar bay. Correct approach code—"

"Acknowledged," said Gahiani, bored. He did not believe Falmah-Al was going to really find a goda. The things did not exist. They were old tales designed to frighten children. No

151

modern adherent of Im believed in them, despite an official stance otherwise.

"Opening hangar doors . . . Shuttle going in."

"Does the colonel want to talk to me when she comes aboard?" asked Gahiani with a close eye upon the chronometer. Two minutes until the end of his shift.

"Nothing's been said, sir."

"Good." Gahiani rose to his feet, and all bridge personnel snapped to attention at their stations. "Captain retiring from the bridge."

"*Alamam*," they responded in chorus.

The pair of hawk-faced Benshas standing duty on either side of the access well saluted as Gahiani stepped between them and dropped down the well on a swift cushion of air. It was an exhilarating descent that never failed to clear his brain. Counting off the levels under his breath, he saw the blue markings of Level 4 coming up and reached out with practiced ease to grab the rungs and curl himself up and into a horizontal well that spat him smoothly out on his feet into the corridor seconds later. Running a hand through his thick black hair, he stepped across the corridor and into the private haven of his quarters, stripping off his gloves and unbelting his tunic as soon as the door snapped shut behind him.

As befitting his rank, he had the largest quarters on the ship. They weren't spacious by any means, but the suite consisted of a sleeping cubicle, head, and sitting area with a desk and monitor control panel where he could offer reprimands, commendations, or have private discussions with his senior officers. On one wall hung crossed swords over the Collective's purple and amber banners, but the swords had been given to Gahiani's ancestor by Im's own hands and symbolized the long tradition of service by the Gahiani family. On the opposite wall hung the war axe of Gahiani's mother and a thick lock of long black hair bound with a leather cord which had been cut from her head when she married Gahiani's father. As soon as he had taken off his weapons and tunic, Gahiani crossed the room and swiftly kissed the lock of hair in obedient respect. Yawning, he dimmed the lights down to a comfortable glimmer and turned on low Bensha desert music as haunting and eerie as the people themselves. With relief he peeled off the armored vest that was only five millimeters thick and supposedly as comfortable as a second skin but instead was damnably hot, and stepped into the head to clean up.

When he emerged, minutes later, clad only in a short loose robe of white wool, skin tingling and hair still slightly damp, his mood had improved. He reached out to change the music to something more cheerful, and froze, eyes bulging as a pale ghostly shape shimmered before him. The close-clipped hairs on the back of his neck lifted, sending cold prickles across his scalp. His breath cut off. His mouth grew dry. His heart thudded violently into his ribs.

What in the dear name of Gazal was it?

Then the shimmering solidified and split into two shapes, and with a blink Gahiani recognized the Sedkethran prisoners.

"You!" he blurted out. It was a stupid thing to say. He was gawping. Where were his wits? He should be reaching for a weapon. Instead, he grabbed the open ends of his robe and tied it hastily together, using the action to cover a surreptitious sign of warding. He was a modern Imish; he believed in the reformed teachings. He was not a superstitious man, but although his intellect reminded him that the translucently pale couple with their narrow, almost human faces and grave eyes were simply aliens with unusual abilities of stepping through dimensional waves, his gut told him they were *marinnis*, demons of the air.

The male took one step toward him and stopped, drawing a disruptor and pointing it at Gahiani. His grey green eyes held the watchful stillness of a man accustomed to violence. The intricately swirled scar of a dire-lord stood out boldly upon one white cheek. Long-ingrained hatred stirred within Gahiani, burning away the startlement. He had not been this close to the Sedkethrans earlier when Falmah-Al had first brought them aboard his ship. He did not know how they had managed to get away from Falmah-Al down on the planet. But whatever they were up to now, they were not going to succeed!

He moved, but the dire-lord was quicker. A minute blast of deadly energy seared past Gahiani, scorching his arm so that he flinched to one side with a choked cry, and sliced off a corner of his desk with a faint hiss. The stench of charred synthetic fiberboard filled the air. Gahiani swallowed hard.

"What do you want?"

The dire-lord looked at him quite calmly. "Your ship."

For a moment the world froze. Gahiani fought down the

unwise urge to laugh. *This is madness*, he thought and could not quite curb his smile.

"Do you now? The two of you really think you can hijack a heavy cruiser. Do you know how many crewmembers there are? Do you know how many people it takes to simply operate a ship of this size? More than two."

The disruptor pointed at him did not waver. "I do not intend to operate this ship," said the dire-lord evenly. "Your crew will do so."

This time Gahiani did not hold back his laughter. "*Gazal!* You are mad—"

"No, but I have you in my sights," said the dire-lord. His eyes bored steadily into Gahiani's. "And you will give them their orders."

Gahiani stiffened. "Never! I am not your puppet!"

The disruptor lifted a fraction. "You can die."

"Yes, and if you kill me where will you be?" Drops of sweat beaded around Gahiani's mouth. *Sedkethrans do not kill*, said one corner of his mind. But his eyes kept staring at that dire-lord scar. He had heard about Held dire-lords. They killed. And very effectively too. "If I am dead, you have no plan at all. You would be wiser to surrender yourselves back into custody. This little escapade could be overlooked, providing you have not harmed Colonel Falmah-Al."

He started to lift his hand, but froze as the disruptor hummed to full charge.

"Brock," said the female, stirring nervously. "This is a stalemate. They aren't just going to deliver us to—"

"There are other ways to die than by disruptor," said the dire-lord. He ignored the female's outburst entirely and kept his gaze on Gahiani. "Do you know what I am, Captain?"

Gahiani's mouth dried until he could barely speak. "D-dire-lord."

"Very good." The Sedkethran bared his teeth in a way that looked very distant from a grin. "The Chaimu honorables are carnivores by tradition. Did you know that old-humans, such as yourself, used to be the quarry in arena games for the Gwilwans? The Chaimu are great lovers of tradition. Now and then they bring back old practices. It is also a tradition that when raw meat is to be served, it must be fresh, so fresh the throat is cut only seconds before an honorable dines. As a dire-lord it was my duty to cut throats for my suprin. Not with a knife, but with the teeth. Like so—"

154

As he spoke, he sprang at Gahiani with a quickness impossible to elude. Crying out, Gahiani tried to dodge, but powerful hands closed on his neck and arm, pinioning him in a strangling hold he could not escape although he struggled until his lungs threatened to burst. The dire-lord held him easily, and with slow deliberation bared his teeth once again.

"Infested dog, let me go!" cried Gahiani hoarsely.

Fingers as strong as pinchers closed on the vertebrae running up the back of his neck. The top of his head went numb and little black dots swirled in front of his bulging eyes as his head was pulled back, exposing his throat.

"*Gazal-ma!*" he whispered desperately. "Don't—"

He felt the pressure of teeth upon his jugular. Sweat was pouring off him now, running into his eyes, blinding him. Thoroughly terrified, he fought the urge to scream. He was a warrior of Im. He would die with dignity. But let it be quick. Oh, Great Im, let it be quick!

"Or," said the dire-lord abruptly, releasing him and pushing him back so that he staggered against the desk and nearly fell. "There are other ways. I believe you call my species ghosts. I could get inside of you and—"

"All right!" said Gahiani, breathing hard. He still clung to the desk, barely able to comprehend that he'd been spared. "Enough," he said, defeated. Shame and humiliation boiled through him, but at the moment he was too demoralized to care. "Enough. What do you want me to do, mar— What do you want me to do?" He had nearly said *marinni*. Rubbing an unsteady hand across his damp brow, he managed to straighten. *Marinnis* did not exist. This dire-lord was not a spirit. He was a creature, a thing as solid as anyone.

"Take the ship to these coordinates," said the dire-lord, extending a scrap of flimsy. "Tell your crew you are on maneuvers. Tell them anything you like, or nothing, if you command that much discipline. We'll launch the shuttlecraft from there."

"That's all?" Gahiani reluctantly took the flimsy and studied it. "A week to get there. I can't abandon the colonel and her people on the planet that long!"

The dire-lord lifted a brow. "Colonids are supposed to be tough survivalists. She will not come to harm."

"And what do I tell her when I return?" asked Gahiani, seething at the insulting term. *Call us Imish. We are Imish!*

"The truth. She is a great believer in truths, is she not?"

The dire-lord's grey green eyes hardened and he gestured at the intercom with his disruptor. "Start giving orders, Captain. Now."

Gahiani thought about the proud tradition of his family warriors. He thought about his duty and the shame of being defeated by a mere alien. He thought about the court-martial and the humiliating attempts to explain his actions. It was his duty to kill this alien, or at the very least to die himself in the attempt to resist such demands as these. His eyes shifted to the crossed swords on the wall, then returned to meet the steady gaze of the dire-lord. Were the dire-lord human, the shame of this moment would be less. It was not a humiliation to accept defeat at the hands of a human. Gahiani's mouth tightened. A dire-lord was by repute the greatest warrior of the entire Held. Human or not, he was a worthy opponent.

"It appears," said Gahiani slowly, trying not to acknowledge his relief at his own decision to do as he was told and live, "that I have no choice but to obey you."

The dire-lord blinked as though he had not quite expected such a rational response.

We are not all fanatics, thought Gahiani defensively and as he reached out a hand to the intercom he tried not to think about facing the wrath of Falmah-Al later.

"Bridge," he said crisply, lifting a not quite steady hand to wipe the sweat from his brow. "Execute a departure from orbit. We're going on special maneuvers into Quadrant One." Glancing at the flimsy in his hand, Gahiani read off the coordinates. "Make fastest speed. Captain out." And he snapped off the link before startled bridge personnel could voice any questions.

"Thank you," said the dire-lord.

Gahiani snorted, glancing at the female as she made a graceful gesture with slender hands. "This is futile, you know. The moment I leave my quarters to return to duty on the bridge, you will have no power over me. You dare not leave the safety of concealment here."

Annoyance sparked from the Sedkethran's eyes, and the respect which had momentarily shone in his face faded. "How short is the human memory," he said softly. "I warn you not to forget that we can strike from thin air if necessary. Do not test us, Captain."

And Gahiani, dry-mouthed once again, was left to watch as

the dire-lord contemptuously turned his back and led the female into the other room.

Four days later the shuttle emerged from the hangar bay of the *Im Naga* and darted off into the cold emptiness of unpopulated space. Gahiani watched its progress on the bridge viewscreen, well aware of his officers' curiosity as to exactly what was going on. Unauthorized maneuvers in Quadrant One, tangent activity during assigned duty under Col. Falmah-Al's temporary command, and the launching of a shuttlecraft with an unlogged pilot raised more than one questioning look. Gahiani sat with outward impassivity at his command post, but inside he writhed at each speculative glance cast his way by the first officer.

He knew what it all looked like; he knew very well.

Treason.

The very word made his blood run cold. Coerced assistance to the enemy fell under what was called Honorable Treason. There was no need to look up the legal codes. He had them memorized from his cadet days at the Hagara al-Dad. He knew the punishments for each offense as well.

To commit Honorable Treason meant obligatory discharge, statuatory fines, and denial of public office.

Dishonorable Treason was another matter. Punishment was summary execution, preferably at the location of offense, usually by fellow officers filing the charge.

The eyes of his first officer bored through his skull. Gahiani kept his own gaze rigidly on the viewscreen. Not by the merest flicker did he betray his discomfort from that steady stare. Hamin had no particular grudge against him, but Hamin never deviated from the strict line of duty. If he saw treason, he would act, swiftly and without mercy. Gahiani fought the urge to wipe his forehead. He did not even give way to the need to tap his fingertips on the arm of his chair. There was one chance to justify his actions into Honorable Treason, thus saving himself and his family from total disgrace. He waited, his strong captain's nerves standing him in good stead now as the shuttle moved away from the ship with infinite slowness.

The crew was standing by, awaiting his orders. Silence hung over the bridge, broken only by occasional in-ship communications chatter.

Gahiani watched the lengthening distance. The shuttle was increasing speed and turning now to take a course heading.

He stared at its squat lines, broadside now, his vision blurring slightly. There. He blinked. He swallowed twice to make sure his voice would come out steady and low.

"Gunnery."

"Sir!"

"Sight shuttlecraft."

Bewilderment flashed over the bridge. The gunnery officer was young, but well-trained. His hesitation was barely perceptible as he complied with the order.

"Target sighted."

"Lock on. Howsers two and four."

"Aft howsers locking on."

There were several eyes watching the captain now. Gahiani smiled very slightly, the smile his people knew well, the smile of a Gahiani warrior in battle. He squinted, slightly breathless from the anger that could no longer be restrained. The Sedkethran would pay for shaming him, for trying to use him! His hand clenched in his lap.

"Fire."

The viewscreen showed two green blips racing toward the shuttlecraft. Seconds later, the shuttle exploded in vivid color. Gahiani sat back in his chair with a satisfied grunt.

"Helm."

"Sir!"

"Lay in a return course to Dena Minor. Top speed."

As the ship heeled about, Hamin approached the captain. "An inexplicable little exercise, Captain."

"Yes." Gahiani looked at him coolly. He was safe now. Hamin had no grounds on which to suspect him. The relief was overwhelming. He need not avert his eyes from the lock of his mother's hair in shame when he returned to his quarters. "Don't worry, First. Falmah-Al will receive her explanations when we return."

It was a dismissal. Frowning slightly, Hamin rubbed the back of his ear.

"Have I the Captain's permission to personally inspect the hangar doors? Internal checks registered a slight malfunction on my board during shuttle departure."

"Anything serious?"

"No. But it should be checked."

Gahiani hesitated, uncertain whether Hamin was still suspicious and intended to look about the hangar deck for evidence. But the captain was unwilling to return to Falmah-Al's

158

wrath with sticking hangar doors. He knew she would want to come immediately aboard. Any delays would only fan her anger.

"Permission," he said, and was relieved when Hamin immediately left the bridge.

"What?" said Ellisne.

"Hush!" Quickly Brock placed a finger across her lips and pressed her back into the shadows of a bulkhead rib as a crewmember came hurtling down the well on a cushion of air. It was Hamin, the first officer. Brock grinned. His plan was working.

"He's heading toward the hangar."

"Are you still in control?" asked Ellisne worriedly.

Brock nodded. His mind followed Hamin's like a light leash. There had never been any question of trusting the captain. At the first opportunity, Brock had ambushed the first officer, deftly removed the mental protector with surgical instruments stolen from the ship's infirmary, and taken control of Hamin's mind. There was no malfunction of the hangar bay doors. But Hamin believed there was, just as in a few minutes Hamin would believe he had fixed the problem when in reality he would be assisting the departure of a second shuttle.

"Come," he said. "We'd better reach the hangar deck before he does."

Ellisne drew a deep breath, her face smudged with exhaustion, and *flicked* them to the cold cavernous expanse of the hangar. All illumination except sporadically placed safety lights was off, and the two remaining shuttles locked on their pads glowed a soft white in the gloom. Brock took Ellisne's hand as she swayed wearily against him and pulled her across the distance to the side of the nearest shuttle.

He was asking too much of her. Her strength was nearly spent. If he did not let her rest soon, her atrox might well be damaged. It was smaller than his and not designed for such frequent *flicking* of more than one person. He paused despite the desperate need to hurry and pressed his fingertips against the nerve points of her throat, sending some of his strength into her. She shivered and clutched gratefully at his hand. Her eyes opened with a slight flutter.

"Just a little longer, beloved," he whispered. "Then you may rest."

She nodded, and he turned away to release the hatch lock. The click and whir as it lowered echoed loudly in the silence around them. Brock swore in Chaimu and hastily pushed Ellisne up the steps. Hamin was coming. He heard the series of airlocks opening and closing. With a slight jump, Brock grasped the upper edge of the hatch and pulled himself inside, slamming his hand on the lock. Hydraulics hissed as the hatch slid shut and locked. Ellisne was standing in the entrance to the cockpit, eyes shut, drifting in and out of reality. For a moment Brock froze, unsure of what to do with her. She had had no sleep since they left Darjahl Imperial. There simply were no suspensor plates available for her use. It had caught up with her, and even the meditation techniques he had shown her so that she could rest without lapsing from this dimension were no longer sufficient.

"Ellisne!" he said sharply, aware on another level of Hamin crouching to open an access panel under the deck controls. "Ellisne! You must stay awake! I cannot support you and control Hamin at the same time. Ellisne! Stay awake just a little longer. We are not far from Felca. Try."

Her eyes opened and fell shut again. She was drifting seriously now. He could barely see her. "No resources left," she mumbled.

He had no choice but to risk everything. Swiftly, he reached out for her hand. His fingers passed through. Concentrating, he focused harder, dropping all control on Hamin, and managed to drift just enough to match her. He clutched her hand, his mind and strength shooting into her, drawing her back, sharing more than he himself could afford to give. She steadied just as he felt himself weaken dangerously. An unexpected pain in his chest made him pull back sharply. She swayed against him, although he could barely hold onto her. Then she pushed away and clung to the bulkhead, straightening her slender form.

"I'm all right, Brock," she said. "Can you get him back?"

"I don't know."

Stumbling into the cockpit, Brock dropped heavily into the seat and closed his eyes. Fighting off the drag of fatigue, he sent his mind leaping out to find Hamin's. The first officer was halfway out the airlock!

Come back.

This time, unlike before, there was resistance from Hamin as though he realized he had been invaded. Trembling from the effort, Brock grasped the sides of his seat and focused, slamming all his mentality against the other, whose resistance abruptly crumpled. There was no more time for finesse. He could no longer afford to be careful not to damage Hamin's mind. They had to escape before his strength gave out. Brock had given nearly everything to Ellisne. He wasn't sure he could go on.

But he had to go on. He had to last. If he didn't make it to Felca, no one anywhere would have a chance to stop Falmah-Al. Pushing away the need for sleep, the lack of sufficient food, and the weight of sheer exhaustion, he drove Hamin back to the controls, forcing him to alter circuitry so that hangar activity would not register on bridge instrumentation.

Now, he commanded as soon as Hamin's hands completed the task. Hamin responded, and pressurization warnings flashed across the dark expanse of the bay as the doors slowly opened.

Brock had the shuttle engines warming, and sat there willing the machines to hurry as the magnetic coil holding the shuttle turned the craft, which was then drawn down a magnetic line preparatory for the slingshot effect designed to launch the shuttle away from the ship without requiring utilization of precious shuttle fuel until the craft was underway. Brock sat tensely at the controls. The slightest suspicion from anyone on the bridge, and the doors would slam shut from direct override. A random scan aft by ship's sensors, and the shuttle would be detected and blown to bits as the decoy had been. This was a wild gamble, a reckless ploy with only the slightest chance of success. For, even if he did manage to escape, there might or might not be sufficient fuel to reach Felca. He did not trust his calculations. But he had to try.

His console blipped, bringing his attention back to the job at hand. "Brace yourself, Ellisne," he said, taking a firm grip on the controls.

With a rumble, the launch slung the shuttle out into space. The viewscreen filled with the gigantic image of the cruiser. His mouth dry, Brock hit maximum speed, and the shuttle vibrated with a shrill whine of protest. But she was well-built, this little craft, and his trust in the excellence of Colonid workmanship was justified. Reaching across the pit, Brock flicked on rear scanners in violation of the rule against an open viewscreen for a solitary pilot. His hands trembled slightly as he rechecked his course headings and nudged the shuttle by forty degrees to comply before switching to automatic and allowing the computer to take over. Even then he did not relax. Mentally he was counting, his nerves stretching tautly in anticipation of howser fire. If it came, it would be now.

He sensed the link between his mind and Hamin's crumbling. Brock broke it with a slight frown, aware that the first officer's mind had not been strong enough for such powerful domination, however temporary. Brock bared his teeth in the Chaimu way.

"Brock?" called Ellisne. "Is it working? Are we safe?"

"*Cuh*," grunted Brock, sagging back in his seat with relief as the range increased steadily between them and the *Im Naga*. "She's moving away. She hasn't sighted us. Great Meir above, she's going into implosion drive!"

"It worked!" cried Ellisne, coming into the cockpit to impulsively fling her arms around Brock from behind his seat. Her smooth cheek rested briefly against his temple. "They had only to look out to see us, but they are already gone."

Brock grinned. "This *is* Quadrant One. No doubt they were too nervous to stay here a moment more than necessary. They wouldn't want to run into Heldfleet and have to fight a pitched battle by themselves, especially when they are supposed to be standing by Falmah-Al."

"Do you really think Heldfleet has ships in this area?" she asked, smoothing his hair back from his forehead.

Brock sighed, allowing himself the luxury of relaxing beneath her gentle touch. "I hope so. The greatest concentration must be here. The inhabited planets in this quadrant are more numerous and better defended than Darjahl Imperial was. Colonid penetration into this quadrant has never been very successful."

"You and Rho tried sending out communications earlier without response. What if Heldfleet isn't here either?"

Her voice was troubled. Brock grasped her hand in reassurance.

"They have not all been destroyed," he said.

"Are you linked in any way?"

He nodded. "Not directly, but upon occasion I served as a conduit between the suprin and Esmir Eondal."

"Brock!" she gasped. "That is a dangerous thing—"

"Another Forbidden?" he asked teasingly, but she shook her head sternly at him. Her eyes were dark with a reprimand.

"Even for you, there are some things better left untried, beloved."

The amusement, small though it had been, abruptly died in his throat. He thought of the sacrifice to save the suprin, made too late, and exacting too great a cost physically. "Yes," he said quietly. His hand tightened upon hers. "Ellisne, if we do reach Felca, you know I must—"

His voice trailed off suddenly as he stared at the viewscreen. An unmistakable shimmer in the space fabric lay directly ahead in their path.

"Brock, what is it—"

"Abort! Abort!" blared the computer alarm. "Direct interception. Collision course."

Brock reached for the controls, but before he could retract from automatic, all functions abruptly shut down. Ellisne's fingers dug into his shoulders like claws; her bewilderment collided with his panic.

"What is it?"

"Ship," he said, punching vainly at unresponsive controls. "Coming out of implosion."

"The *Im Naga*?"

"I don't know." He slammed a fist onto the dead board. "Damn this thing! Why won't it respond?"

"Isn't it an automatic shut down to avoid collision?"

"Yes." He glanced at her, his mind frantically sorting through the information gleaned from the pilot Molaud for an answer. But his panic was blocking the overlay. He couldn't remember anything, and they were still sweeping headlong into the ship's path.

It materialized in front of them, so immense and so close the viewscreen could not compensate to bring all of it into focus.

"We aren't stopping," said Ellisne, suddenly comprehending.

"Inertia. And without power I can't move us out of the way. What stupid engineer designed this?" He threw himself half out of his seat and slammed a hand down on the communications board. "Dead. Everything's dead except the viewscreen."

"It's not the *Im Naga*," said Ellisne, her eyes locked on the viewscreen, now totally filled with the wedge-shaped ship bearing down on them. "Who?"

Distracted, Brock gave up his frantic efforts to reactivate power and gave the viewscreen his attention. His breath caught in his throat. "A wedge from a cluster ship!"

"You mean, one of ours!"

"It's turning," said Brock, his hands gripping the edge of his seat so hard they ached. "Yes, it's coming about, trying to avoid us. But there's no time. We're too close. We'll graze it."

"Brock—"

The flattened, slightly convex side of the ship wheeled across in front of them. Immense cluster ships were not designed for lightning speed or maneuverability, but the one hundred component wedges which formed each cluster ship were. There was nothing in the galaxy that could match them for quickness. But even so, Brock held his breath, certain there was not enough time.

Then he saw the bay yawning like an opened mouth in the side of the ship.

"*Luth muk shal!*" he shouted in Chaimu, leaping from his seat and nearly knocking Ellisne down in the crowded space. "It intercepted us this close on purpose. It knew our systems would shut down. It's trying to catch us. Great Meir—"

"Brock—"

He whirled and caught her by the arms, propelling her out of the cockpit and into the nearest seat in the passenger section. "Strap in. Quickly! Don't argue! If they succeed, it's going to be one rough stop."

She thrust his helping hands away. "Strap yourself in! I can *flick* to negate the force of a crash. You can't. Brock, stop fussing with me and take care of yourself—"

A loud crack drowned out the rest of her sentence, and suddenly the shuttle lurched violently as it was snared. Brock tumbled bodily over the top of the seat he was reaching for, then was slammed into the hard back of the seat as the shuttle's impetus reversed. Stunned by the impact, he threw out a hand, grasped something, and tried to lever himself up. But the g-forces were too strong. Ellisne's mind was shouting at his, but he was too dazed to respond. Around him welled a shrill noise, the scream of the shuttle's passage through air. It must be inside the wedge. And then he thought, *No! Not yet! We're still going too fast. They'll never stop us.*

He had seen this maneuver before, swift wedges darting about in deadly fights, swooping in to swallow enemy craft on the wing. He had stood on the observation deck overlooking the hangar, his entire body tensed in readiness to pluck the suprin away from such a dangerous place, his eyes locked in fascination as the quarry came screaming into the bay and struck the internal forcefield that acted as a gigantic catcher's net, stopping and absorbing the tremendous forces of impact. Sometimes enemy craft survived capture; other times they exploded. The occupants were sometimes intact and sometimes jelly.

Ellisne! Flick out! Flick out! We're going too fast. We aren't going to make it!

Hanging desperately onto the bolted base of the seat, his face ground into the carpeted deck that stank of dirt, smoke, and cleaner, Brock tried one last time to pull himself up and reach for the safety restraints. He could not see Ellisne. But he felt the tug of her will upon his and fought her off.

I won't leave you, Brock! If I can just reach you we will flick together.

You can't help me. Get out! He was almost sobbing aloud with despair at her stubbornness. All his life he had searched for someone to share with, someone willing to understand, to return freely the emotions he had taught himself to feel, who did not fear what he reached for or what he was. She must go. She must live.

Beloved—

Go! It was a cry from his soul. His mind seemed to swell, to burst as though by sheer willpower alone he thrust her away, making her obey him and *flick* to safety. For the first time in long, long days he felt his atrox, throbbing with life and not withered and useless in his chest. Hope leapt through him. Was it healed? Could he save himself as well?

But there was no chance to try, for just then the shuttle bucked, the nose flying up, and slammed belly first into the forcefield, flipping over on its back and crashing straight down to the bottom of the hangar bay. And all was still, and black, and silent.

ELLISNE *FLICKED* INTO the safety of the observation deck with
such force she slammed into a bulkhead and crumpled to the
floor. She sat there, dazed and unaware of her surroundings,
until the commotion of startled voices and hands reaching for
her snapped her back to reality. She was pulled to her feet by
a newan officer in the scarlet uniform of Heldfleet.

His eyes widened as they studied her. He glanced over his
shoulder. "A Sedkethran, Esmir! Great Meir above, where
did she come from?"

"From the shuttle obviously," replied the dry, leathery
voice of a Chaimu honorable, stepping into Ellisne's line of
vision. The esmir wore the stripes of his advanced rank in
glittering order on both sleeves. The pleated scarlet leather of
his tunic fanned out behind his scaled head, making it appear
larger than it really was.

Ellisne blinked, growing suddenly conscious of acute pain
across her forehead. She lifted a hand unsteadily to it and
touched cool moist blood, pale and sticky across her fingers.
Then she remembered.

"Brock!" she cried, wrenching free of the newan and
throwing herself at the glastel windows of the observation
area. Far down below her lay the shattered wreckage of the
shuttle, blackened and twisted. Men in baggy protective suits
climbed over it, covering it with thick chemical foam to
prevent fuel spills from igniting. Ellisne closed her eyes,
pressing her face against the cold surface of the window in
despair, and sought deep within herself for a link to him. Let

166

it be there. Oh, by the mercy of all that was ordered, let it still be there!

It was.

"He's still alive!" Whirling from the window, she started for the door, only to find her way blocked firmly by the newan officer.

"Just a minute there," he said sternly, frowning at her between the brows in the way of humans. "Some questions must be answered first."

She drew herself up with all the icy command of a Sedkethran healer. "My mate lies injured in that wreckage. Will you let him die while you ask questions?"

"You said Brock." The esmir shouldered his adjutant aside. "I know of only one man who bears that name. Is it the dire-lord?"

"Yes!" She saw the look of hope that flashed into the red eyes and let her urgency command her again. "Please, Esmir. Let me attend him."

The esmir signalled, and his adjutant sprang to open the door. "We shall all go to him," said the esmir, taking the lead. "This is most unexpected. Sedkethrans in an enemy shuttlecraft. The dire-lord found again. Luther!"

"Sir!"

"Prepare a communication to Cluster 807, informing them of these developments."

"Yes, sir!" Luther crashed his fist to his left shoulder. "Shall I also give orders to the bridge to resume pursuit of enemy cruiser?"

"No!" said Ellisne, breaking in on both to the surprise of herself as well as them. Association with Brock was tearing down all her careful training of what was mannerly and proper. Ashamed of her own unseemly boldness, yet determined, she faced the esmir squarely. "It is unimportant. We must go directly to Felca."

"Now see here, Healer—"

A look from the esmir quelled Luther. "This is a military vessel, not a passenger liner."

"It is the dire-lord's wish," she retorted with equal coldness, desperate to get to Brock. "We were on our way there when you intercepted us." When the esmir merely stared at her, she lifted a hand impatiently. "He is still under orders from the suprin—"

"*Luth muk shal!*" said the esmir in astonishment and

167

grabbed her arm with a force that nearly made her cry out. "He is alive? The suprin is alive?"

"No," she said, and turned away from the raw disappointment in his face to hurry down the spiralling metal steps to the bottom of the hangar. "Get away! Stop that!" she commanded the workers, who were still spraying foam everywhere. Stumbling a bit from walking too fast, she dabbed at her aching forehead with her sleeve, wiping more blood from her face, and clambered up on the wreckage only to stop in anguished indecision.

"Find him," she said. "You must find him."

"There's no pilot—" said one worker compassionately, but another broke in sternly:

"We have procedures here! All danger of fire must be eradicated before rescue operations can proceed."

"Get out of the way," said Ellisne angrily. Falling to her knees, she began tugging at the twisted pieces of metal, cutting her hands.

A barked command from the esmir, only now reaching the shuttle, sent the workers to her side. Moving her out of the way, they pried an opening into the wreckage. Powerful lamps shone inside, and they shook their heads.

"It looks as bad inside as out—"

"Did I ask for your opinion?" shouted the esmir with a roar that echoed through the hangar. "The dire-lord of the Held is in there. Alive. Get him out."

The workers moved with alacrity, clattering over the metal and grunting with their efforts to pry into the next section. Ellisne waited, holding her breath. She shut her eyes to concentrate on holding that slight link firmly. It was no longer certain. She was too tired. Her head was aching more and more. She could not keep her thoughts under the Disciplines. Was she merely imagining he was alive only because she wished it so much? Was she erring again as in her youth as a novice healer, when she had cared too greatly for her patients and had given too liberally of her inner resources? It had taken many sessions with the magstrusi to teach her less generosity. She knew now, thanks to Brock, that those sessions had put shackles on her. The magstrusi had twisted her gifts, molded them into small uses that could be controlled for purposes of the magstrusi. The hate she had also learned from Brock burned inside her. She would never make herself small again. But, oh, to think that she stood here safe and whole while Brock lay trapped somewhere beneath the wreckage!

She swayed. A hand grabbed her arm and steadied her.

"You need rest," said the esmir.

Surprised by his consideration, she smiled her gratitude briefly, then turned her gaze back to the work. "I cannot rest while he is in there. Oh, why did you do this to us? What harm were we? We weren't even armed!"

Luther stared at her as though she were mad. "You were in an enemy craft. Routine capture procedure—"

A shout from one of the workers cut him off. Ellisne would have rushed forward, but the esmir held her back.

"Wait until they are finished," he said.

But to wait and to watch was agony. She stood there, clasping her hands tightly together, her mind flying from rigid application of the Disciplines to worry and wild imaginings. He must not die. Losing him was too horrible to consider. Her breath strangled in her throat. All her Disciplines were lost, shattered inside her. This was what it meant to love, to open oneself to a vulnerability both precious and terrifying. *Beloved, please* . . .

Slowly, ever so slowly, Brock's limp form was lifted out. A gigantic Chaimu who appeared, apparently from the bridge, to speak to the esmir, was instead brushed aside and ordered to carry the dire-lord to the infirmary.

"Among these Colonids? The dire-lord?" The younger Chaimu stiffened.

"Yes!" snapped the esmir, with an angry flick of his hand across his brow ridges. "Dire-lord! Or do you decline the honor, Arkist Ivn?"

Ivn's brownish-red eyes moved hastily back to Brock, whose head was lolled back over a worker's arm. Smudged by black and tinged by an unhealthy grey, Brock's cheek nevertheless showed the distinctive swirled scar clearly. Ivn snapped to attention. "The honor is very great, Esmir," he said contritely and moved forward to take Brock's body in his strong arms.

"I must tend him," said Ellisne, but again she was held back.

The esmir scowled at her. "Keep your place, Healer."

And Ellisne had no choice but to follow the little procession out of the hangar and into the lift on their way to the ship's infirmary. Even there, they would not let her do more than watch as he was placed in a suspensor bed.

"But I am a healer!" she raged. "Why do you prevent me? Do you think I intend to harm him?"

The Chaimu physician took his cue from the esmir's hooded glance and sneered at her. "A healer? A mere healer? Sedkethran or not, certified or not, look at you. Bedraggled, exhausted, exhibiting manners no member of your race or profession would ever dare show. You are not fit to be entrusted with the care of Dire-lord Brock."

That stung deeply because it was true, yet the deeper instincts of a mate to guard and protect stiffened her. "And are you fit?" she retorted. "A medic, a potion maker. Do you intend to use drugs and knives?" She swung round to glare at the esmir. "If you are so concerned about the welfare of the dire-lord, then let me do my work!"

For a moment she faced the implacable glare of an angered honorable of considerable rank, someone whom in the past she would never have dared confront. Yet she did not care what breach she committed. She was so tired, so worried. Her very consciousness teetered on the edge of a dark deep chasm, yet she fought to keep her balance just as she fought to remain here at Brock's side.

"Or," she said with a sudden gasp, "are you enemies of the dire-lord? Are you a supporter of Nairin Tregher, who betrayed his father, the Held, and even Brock to the Imish? Are you determined to keep me from caring for Brock because you intend to kill him?"

"*Sug!*" roared the esmir, and she fell silent, her heart thumping at her own unforgivable insolence.

Her eyes dropped. "I crave the esmir's pardon." Then she lifted her gaze to meet his once again and sent the last barriers of Sedkethran privacy crashing by saying, "But Brock is my mate. We have shared all that there is of ourselves with each other."

It was an admission no proper Sedkethran ever made in public. A part of her flinched in horror, but she did not care. She would not let them brush her aside.

The esmir blinked and his old red eyes softened fractionally. "Nevertheless," he said gruffly. "You are in no condition to do anything. He isn't going to die. His injuries are not severe. And for you to attempt anything now would likely only weaken you both. Medic!"

The physician stepped forward to take Ellisne's arm and lead her away into a second, slightly smaller ward. He switched on a suspensor bed and stared at her with his teeth showing.

"When was the last time you slept, Healer?"

She returned his gaze, frowning, and reluctantly stopped fighting her own desperate needs for rest and care. "But you will wake me when he regains consciousness?"

The medic hesitated.

"Will you? Give me your word."

"He is in no danger. This concern is unnecessary."

She nearly screamed. Why couldn't he *understand*? She was so afraid that Brock would go on without her. And he mustn't. He had done so much, but he would need her help to face the magstrusi. Compromise was not a word he used, but a way must be found to appeal to the Elder Council. She could help. She must help.

"Promise me," she said, the world blurring about her. "The moment he awakens—"

"Very well," said the medic with a shrug. "Now get some rest."

A HELD CLUSTER ship was monstrous in size, a tremendous feat of engineering, concept, and design, requiring enormous quantities of fuel utilized through an internal fission drive that rumbled the entire structure slowly along at sublight speed. Intended for planetary defense, a cluster ship had no need for more sophisticated power. Its one hundred components possessed the quickness and agility necessary for blitz attacks, and throughout the galaxy there was no more stirring or frightening sight than to see one of the glittering silver behemoths abruptly shatter into fragments that flipped, rolled, and darted into lethal formations against the foe. Each wedge-shaped component was an independently powered and manned spacecraft, capable of spanning any distance on its own, brutally armed, and faster than any other, more conventional implosion-driven craft in Heldfleet. In the old, glory-filled days of the Held, there had been an entire fleet of cluster ships, one for each of the inner worlds and for several of the mid-worlds. Then, as the Colonids grew bolder and acquired more advanced technologies which enabled them to sprawl across the borders, the cluster ships were moved gradually to man the wartorn area of the fringe. Over the centuries, attrition, indifference, and astronomical costs had slowed the replacement of wedges so that disabled cluster ships were increasingly scrapped in order to supply sufficient wedges to others. The numbers had dwindled, but although now there were only a few majestic survivors of that proud fleet, they still stood out among the bottle-shaped destroyers, gritty little frigates and scoutships, and the heavy cruisers which had replaced them. And they still bore their identification numerals as a testament to better days of full supremacy over

Heldfleet. Now that the Colonids had the capability to shatter entire worlds, cluster ships were few indeed and carefully positioned in the quadrants which the Colonids had not completely secured.

Cluster 807, a vast multi-faceted figurehead to the motley flotilla of all that remained of Heldfleet, moved inexorably through space toward Darjahl Imperial at maximum sublight. The heavy cruisers, designed to sail gracefully in implosion drive, wallowed clumsily in Cluster 807's wake, the lesser craft in formation around them. It was the last concerted effort by Heldfleet to turn around the crushing defeat dealt the Held by the Colonids. Lacking a suprin, lacking sufficient manpower, ships, or hope, the old, battlescarred officers still commanding Heldfleet stood gathered on the upper bridge of Cluster 807, determined never to surrender as long as one Chaimu heart remained beating. They had assembled this final strike force through the grim days of crumbling defenses and vicious sweeps by Colonid forces. They had hidden their ships, found each other, and regrouped on nothing more than the refusal to go down before the barbaric old-humans. A briefly considered plan to rescue the nairin from a Colonid prison camp had faltered after spy reports came through of his treachery. After that, there had been no one to lead the expedition except old Esmir Eondal himself, and supreme command by a non-royal was unprecedented. Still, they had no one else . . . until now.

Greaved and corseleted in heavy charge armor, a straight Chaimu dagger belted on one hip, holstered strifer and communicator on the other, Brock stood in the shadows of the infirmary ward in silence, watching Ellisne sleep. She was no more than a pale glimmer of form, drifting in and out of dimensions, her long dark hair spread out about her head like a cloud as she floated gently up and down over the suspensors. He studied the fragile slope of her bones and the transparency of her skin, transfixed as ever by her beauty. There was a slight frown upon her brow as though her sleep were troubled.

Not by me, I hope, beloved.

He stretched out a hand to smooth the frown away, the touch of his fingers light so as not to awaken her.

My gentle one. I drove you as I would a warrior. You hadn't the strength. Forgive me, beloved.

"Dire-lord!" The whisper, hoarse and insistent, came from the doorway.

Recalling the impatient officers gathered outside waiting for him, Brock reluctantly drew his hand back from the coolness of her flesh and left the ward.

At once, as he faced their fierce, eager eyes, the old habits of rank fell like a mantle across his shoulders. He was back in his rightful place among warriors, a counsellor of war, a shield of protection to the throne, a dire-lord. He pulled himself erect under the weight of the charge armor and held his head higher as though already he smelled the blood and fire of battle. Restored by rest and proper food, he scarcely noticed the ache of his bruises or the persistent throb in his leg as he limped into their midst.

Arkist Ivn saluted briskly, and the others followed suit. "We are ready to escort you to the esmir."

Picking up his helmet from the bunk and tucking it correctly beneath his left arm, Brock was far too aware of their jubilant hope and eagerness. *Do not put your faith in me*, he thought with a sigh and forced himself to respond with a crisp nod.

"I am ready," he said.

They snapped into formation, three on either side of Brock, with Ivn taking the lead, and marched along a seemingly endless corridor to a lift, which went up and up and up forever. Ivn barked a command as the lift doors opened, and the escort saluted as one as Brock slowly stepped off into the upper bridge of the cluster ship.

For a moment his presence failed him as he took in the watchful eyes, the grim faces, the glittering insignias of high rank. These twelve were the upper echelon of Held military force. These were the old warriors, scarred survivors of a thousand conflicts, representing the best strategic minds alive. Brock's eyes flicked to each face, recognizing them all: Eondal, bearing the weight of immense age, his fierce heart unsoftened by the toll of time; Rumarc, who began his career as a pilot and advanced to the command of the entire destroyer fleet; Igrit Sigx, a Varlax as tall as a giant with a blue mustache that would have trailed the floor had he uncoiled it; Cunsk, wily head of Intel Five with a legion of spies networked throughout the galaxy; and eight others, all renowned, all wearing medals awarded by the suprin.

It was the first time Brock had ever stepped onto an upper

174

bridge on his own, without following at the suprin's back. He suffered a strange attack of embarrassment or shame, as though he had forgotten his place and entered where he was not allowed. *I am only a Sedkethran renegade*, he thought. *How can I take a place here?*

The esmir stepped forward as Brock stood rooted there, and his old knees creaked as he slowly knelt down and bowed his scaled head.

"Dire-lord Brock," he said, forcing a gruff voice into tones of deepest respect. "We of Heldfleet honor your safe return."

"Bon . . . *chuh*!" snapped a voice, and the twelve crashed out a salute.

Brock returned it, his vision blurred with emotion. For a moment his throat was too choked to speak. He bowed his head gravely.

"Dire-lord," said Rumarc, his voice shrill and clear unlike most Chaimu. "We have but one question to ask concerning the death of the suprin in the last battle of Darjahl Imperial."

Brock looked at him. "Ask."

"Was the suprin alone in his last moments?"

Ah . . . the question that encompassed so many, including the matter of rightful succession, the secrets of state, the honor due a dying suprin, and religious proprieties.

Do I dare reach again for the throne? Brock asked himself. The upper bridge was overheated, meeting the Chaimu level of temperature comfort but not his own. Their eyes bored into him as they waited for his answer. The scent of scale oil used by so many honorables as protection against the drying effects of recycled air cloyed his nostrils. For a moment he felt crushed and small and tired. Perhaps he had left the safety of the infirmary too soon. But hiding from responsibility did not take it away.

He could feel the smooth warmth of the goda band encircling his wrist beneath the tight sleeve of his corselet, and as though they had been spoken only a moment ago, he could hear again in his mind the last words of Utdi. The little band of rebels hiding in the tunnels beneath Impryn had chosen not to honor the suprin's choice. Would these men of power and rank likewise refuse? And if, by chance, they did turn aside from tradition and accept him, was he ready? Could a crippled Sedkethran truly be a suprin? Was he truly the one the Writings warned of, the one the magstrusi feared? As though

175

conjured up by the thought of his old teachers, something foreign intruded upon his mental shields, nudging them.

"Dire-lord?" prompted Rumarc cautiously. "Was the suprin alone in his last moments?"

"He was not alone," said Brock.

"Ah." The esmir lumbered stiffly to his feet and bared his teeth. "Did the nairin join him?"

"No. I alone remained with Utdi. I gave him the Rites of Eternity."

There was a stir among the twelve and several explosive, if low, Chaimu oaths. The esmir's red eyes narrowed upon Brock.

"Is that all?"

For answer, Brock pulled off his gauntlet and lifted his left arm. The corybdium metal of the goda band flashed dark green upon his wrist. Even Eondal flinched.

"I wear it," said Brock, his eyes stabbing to each man as they stared wide-eyed and mesmerized at him. "By Utdi's order. I was chosen by Utdi to succeed to the Superior Life, and with his own mouth did he condemn the treachery of his son."

Silence gripped the upper bridge, then Eondal croaked in a whisper, "The ceremonial dagger?"

"Taken from me by Tregher just before he gave me to the Colonids for interrogation."

"Then it is lost."

"I fear so."

Did they believe him? Brock wondered. They seemed stunned, their expressions heavy and guarded as their eyes shifted to each other. Again he felt that mental nudge as though something strove to tap his mind, and in sudden anger he whirled and limped furiously to the communications console. Without asking permission, he punched open a line to the lower bridge.

"Dire-lord speaking," he said curtly. "Our current position?"

"Course heading steady, proceeding standard by one toward target, present bearing twelve mark seven."

"Distance from the Praxos System?"

There was a slight pause as his question was relayed to the appropriate officer and back again. "Two point four parsecs."

"Thank you. Dire-lord out."

Brock turned away from the console, his thoughts whirling. Close enough! More than close enough. They knew. The

176

magstrusi had already detected his presence as well as his purpose. They were already trying to keep him away.

Have you forgotten? he wondered angrily. *I am stronger now than when I left all those years ago. You will not stop me in this way.*

"Dire-lord?" asked the esmir. "Is something wrong?"

Brock shook away his thoughts and turned back to the matter at hand. "Do you believe me?" he asked.

They seemed shocked by so direct a question, and even Eondal blinked.

"It is," he said slowly, "without precedent. A dire-lord is under oath to serve the will of the suprin until death."

"And sometimes after," said Brock grimly. "Come, Honorables! I am not trying to claim the throne. At the moment there is not one—"

"As long as we stand, the Held stands!" shouted Cunsk furiously. "We seek your leadership for this fight, Dire-lord, nothing more."

Brock drew a deep breath and pulled his gauntlet back on. "My fight is elsewhere."

"Explain!"

"You would serve me as a dire-lord, but as nothing further," said Brock with a wry smile. "Interesting."

"No one serves a dire-lord!" snapped Rumarc with a snort. "You—"

"Quibbling!" roared the esmir loudly enough to rattle the ceiling panels. "Would you spend the rest of the day arguing over rank order in the manner of protocol archivists? *Cuh!* Think, Honorables! Use the brains Meir gave you. The dire-lord has not joined us to follow our orders. He still serves Suprin Utdi. He has just said so. Are you deaf?"

"Is it serving Utdi to proclaim himself the new suprin?" challenged the Varlax.

"And who would you have instead, Igrit?" retorted Eondal with a sneer. "Tregher the black nairin? That *liviling bfrat* who cost us three-quarters of our fleet by selling our battle plans to the Colonids? You, Cunsk—" a clawed finger jabbed at the chief of Intel—"have proof of it."

"None of us intend to bend knee to Tregher," said Cunsk.

"What then?" roared Eondal. "Mabruk was destroyed. We breathed the ashes of our children. There is no more of my line, or of yours, Rumarc, or of yours, Cunsk, or of any of yours! Our genetic banks are gone forever! When we die, there are no more of us. And what becomes of the Held without the Chaimu?''

"Nothing. It is finished," said Igrit, blinking flat yellow eyes and tugging at the string which held his mustache coiled.

"You live in the past. As a Varlax, you should know better." Eondal flicked a hand across his nose ridges in exasperation. "We ceased being the Chaimu Empire centuries ago. We are Held now. If we are to survive these accursed humans, we must shake off the stranglehold of mindless tradition. Did Utdi not make his choice? Did it not show wisdom?"

"Or desperation," muttered Cunsk, causing Brock to look at him sharply.

"And what does it matter?"

"It matters a great deal!" said Rumarc. His eyes flicked to Brock and then back to Eondal. "Your flaw has always been impatience. You don't trouble to think out the consequences, Esmir. If Brock becomes suprin, he founds a new dynasty. Great Meir! He is Sedkethran—"

"*Cuh!* That old argument. The dire-lord has proved himself a warrior many times over. He has fought with the best of us. He—"

"I understand what you are saying, Rumarc," said Brock, taking the argument away from Eondal. "I am an exception to my race. And you fear a dynasty of nonviolent suprins."

"Precisely."

The esmir's face seemed to collapse. He heaved a gusty sigh and turned away, his massive head drooping. "I am too old to live another generation," he said hoarsely. "What is to become of us without leaders?"

"I suggest that unless we deal with the direct problem at hand, the question of future leadership will not matter," said Brock, regaining their attention. "The suprin did not give me the goda band out of tradition. He gave it to me to be used."

"*Luth muk shal!*" The esmir's oath rose above the others'. "What are you saying? It is not to be done! Even in our darkest hour we have not considered actually using the godas."

"Then it is time you did," said Brock grimly, aware that he could hold the truth back no longer. "Colonel Falmah-Al of the Imish forces has Goda Secondary."

"*What*?"

"No!"

"Impossible!"

"Even now, her technicians are working to learn how to activate it." Brock's gaze swept their incredulous faces. "You have all seen examples of Imish technology. It will not take them long. When your wedge captured me, Esmir, I was on my way to Felca, to activate Goda Prime."

A great hush fell over the upper bridge. They stood there huddled, afraid to look at each other, afraid to look at Brock.

Then Rumarc shook himself with a grunt. "You are mad," he said flatly. "Completely, hopelessly insane. You disappear for weeks when the suprin dies, then you suddenly arrive among us in a Colonid vessel, claiming the throne for yourself and announcing that you are going to destroy your own world. I say you are mad. Totally mad. Or you are spying for the Colonids. Why else appear now, when we are on our way to attack them?"

There were sharp murmurs at this.

"Don't be an old fool!" shouted Brock furiously. His gaze swept all of them and he wondered, why do I bother to help them? Why do I keep trying? I have given up my ability to slip through time. I have given up my home world. I have lost a friend. Why not leave them here in their fruitless plan of attack and take myself and Ellisne to a safe, abandoned corner of the galaxy?

The pressure on his mental shields suddenly returned, harder, like a punch to his mind. He swayed slightly, but did nothing beyond conserve his energy to maintain his shields.

I want it all. I want the Held in my hand.

The intensity of that desire burned through him like a banked fire suddenly uncovered. His memories flashed back to that day in the arena, when he had stood blood-splattered and breathless, knowing triumphantly that the suprin could choose no other but him as dire-lord. Even then the flame of ambition had been alive. He had stood there, panting lightly with the blood-smeared dagger slippery in his hand, and watched the suprin leave his throne to make the announcement. It was his first sight of Suprin Utdi, but even now Brock could not recall details of face or attire. When he looked at Utdi that first time, he saw only the living symbol of the Held itself. And he had burned to be in Utdi's place. Loving Utdi as a father, protecting Utdi, serving Utdi, had in many ways been only a form of cherishing the Held. Utdi, Meir keep him, had known this, and it was why Brock now wore the goda band.

The magstrusi of Felca had seen his ambition from the moment of Change, when he had left the crystal Hall of Harmonies and walked out into the frosty air to enter his assigned barracks and a new way of life. The magstrusi had feared his abilities, his ambitions, and his resistance to control. And what they could not control, they shattered.

Not me. Not this one.

"Did the dire-lord hear my question?" asked Cunsk coldly.

Brock turned to face him, lifting his brows. "No."

"I asked you how Falmah-Al came into possession of Goda Secondary."

If I take the throne, I must fight for it, Brock thought. *They will never simply give it to me.*

"Dire-lord?"

"He is thinking up lies!" said Rumarc angrily.

Eondal stiffened, watching Brock closely. "Careful, Rumarc!"

"Why are you so frightened of the truth?" asked Brock quietly. He had no intention of attacking the old honorable. "If I tell you that I led Falmah-Al to the control room of Goda Secondary, would you be at ease?"

"There! He admits his guilt!" Rumarc shook a finger. "He has gone over to the other side!"

"Be silent," snapped Cunsk. His eyes, hooded beneath thick brow bones, watched Brock intently. Brock knew he was concentrating on voice patterns and respiratory release, trying to gauge the truth in the manner of a good interrogator. "He said he led her there—"

"Precisely!"

"It is a statement of action. He does not explain motivation—"

"Greed, of course. They have—"

Brock threw back in his head with a harsh laugh. "What could the Colonids offer a dire-lord except a knife in the spine?"

"*Cuh*," said Eondal in approval, standing back from the feint and ripost of words as though he were watching a game in the arena.

Brock's eyes swung to Cunsk, whose judgment, he knew, would be ultimately what Eondal sought. It was to Cunsk alone now that he spoke:

"I led her there because she followed me, staying out of detection range. And when she captured our ship, my pilot Rho told her the location of the goda."

"Your man. Your responsibility," muttered Rumarc darkly.

Brock ignored him. "I showed her how to find the control room because she convinced me she wanted only to deactivate the godas permanently. The Colonids are as frightened of them as we are."

"But she dealt falsely."

"Yes." Anger came through Brock's voice as he saw again the agony frozen on Rho's narrow face as the Slathese crumpled to the floor. "The controls are dead. Time has been too much for them. But her technicians are working now to reactivate the weapon. They may have already succeeded. They are clever."

"A cluster ship against a goda," said Eondal slowly. The words seemed to hang in the air. "No chance whatsoever."

"That's why I must go to Felca without delay," said Brock. "Only a goda can fight a goda. It's the only way to stop her."

"No!" shouted Rumarc. "It is a trick! He will surrender Goda Prime to them also, and then they will have two godas!"

"Even if they have one, we are lost," said Cunsk impatiently, turning on him. "Be silent."

Rumarc reached for his knife. "I will not be ordered about like some mere lackey, spymaster! State your hour—"

"There will be no duelling!" roared the esmir, raising his fists. "We are officers under action. Keep your place, Rumarc, or face court-martial by the Fets."

Abashed silence fell over the upper bridge, and Rumarc's hand fell away from his weapon. Satisfied, Eondal glanced at Brock. "You must go to Felca."

"Yes, Esmir."

"If you activate the goda and move it, all atmosphere will be ripped away. The population will die." Eondal cocked his head. "As a Sedkethran, how will you face the responsibilities for those deaths?"

Brock had been waiting for this question. Drawing a deep breath, he said: "They need not die."

"Explain."

"Felca is not the source planet of my race. It is not a planet at all. It is a constructed goda, strategically placed near the center of the empire for maximum defense and then populated. Think about the peculiar abilities of Sedkethrans. Their strengths as empathic healers. *Flicking* between time. Sedkethrans were designed by the ancient Chaimu engineers just as godas were designed."

181

"*What?*"

"Be silent!"

"We are, so to speak, the mop-up crew for a goda battle. Who better than a race of healers able to avoid injury simply by stepping out of the dimension?"

Brock waited, watching them digest the idea. Eondal began nodding his massive head.

"The old legends. I remember. I remember bits. The old songs about Sedkethran warriors from a distant star. How loudly we sang those as youths, laughing all the while. We thought they were jokes, parodies. Sedkethrans are so stuffy, so formal, so damned peaceable! But behind each legend hangs a strand of truth, eh, Dire-lord?"

"Tell us more!" commanded one of the other officers.

Brock withdrew behind a mask of formality. "Legends are for leisure. I do not have it, honorables. I must go to Felca." He did not want to admit that he knew little more than what he had told them. He had gleaned a few things from stolen glimpses at the Forbidden Writings; the rest was speculation.

A babble of discussion broke out, quelled at once by the esmir.

"But what about the Sedkethrans?" he asked Brock. "Do they know this?"

"Most of them? No."

"Then, will they believe you?"

"There is safety inside the goda. But it is the magstrusi whom I must convince." *Whom I must fight and defeat,* thought Brock grimly. *Before I defeat Falmah-Al.*

"When do you go?"

"Now. I request a ship."

"It is yours," said the esmir.

Brock shifted the helmet under his elbow. His head was high. His heart was thumping faster beneath his atrox at the thought of returning to Felca at last. *I saw these things long ago during those cold nights upon the glacier when I searched the stars across the sky. I saw them and they troubled me, but I did not understand them then. Beware, my old teachers.*

"There is something else?"

Brock nodded. "The healer Ellisne. Guard her safety in your keeping. Do not let her follow me."

"As you wish. Fare well, Dire-lord, in your battle," said Eondal, giving him a salute.

Brock returned it crisply. "Fare well in yours." Wheeling

182

about, he strode from the upper bridge, his escort in formation as before, as befitting his rank. Ten minutes later, he stood on the narrow command deck of a wedge, watching from the viewscreen as it broke from the cluster ship and sliced away in a long arc to avoid the rest of the flotilla, aiming at maximum speed for Felca.

On the upper bridge of the cluster ship, the esmir also watched a viewscreen. Cunsk stood at his side.

"You realize, Esmir," he said softly, "that when Brock controls a goda he will control the Held?"

The esmir bared his teeth. "If Meir favors us, Brock will control the entire galaxy."

"He will never dare use the weapon. Surely he will only bluff with it."

Eondal rolled an eye sideways to look at him. "Worried, Cunsk?"

"Aren't you?"

"Should I be?" Eondal left the question as bait, wondering just how much Cunsk knew.

"I have seen the old operations manuals. And— I have clearance, Esmir!"

"Yes," said Eondal mildly. "But if you intend to explain precisely to me what will happen if the godas attack each other, I do not want to hear."

"It will be the end!" Cunsk's voice rose, and he hastily coughed. "Of everything! There will start a chain reaction of negative energy which—"

"I have said I do not want to hear it," said the esmir more sharply. "If a leader is ignorant of all the ramifications, he cannot be afraid. I will not go into my last battle afraid, Cunsk."

"We should all be afraid," said the chief of Intel Five darkly. "We should find a way to stop them."

Eondal fixed him with an old red eye. "How?" he asked and turned away.

MOBA GLACIER HAD ground its way closer to the sea during the years Brock had been gone. It towered over Clinic One, a city nestling along the narrow curve of beach. The glacier was a sleeping giant growling and thundering inside itself, grey-green with age but not diminished. Brock stepped off the landing pod, squinting with an immediate flinch against the bitter lash of wind off the glacier. All these years he had missed the cold in the over-heated chambers of the Chaimu, and now he found himself wishing it was not quite so chilly. Muscles tensed, he gathered his fur-lined cloak more tightly around the charge armor he wore, much to the startled disapproval of the port official, and turned to raise his fist at the shuttle. With a whine of its engines it lifted off into the sky, disappearing quickly inside low, grey clouds.

It was mid-afternoon, the hour of meditation. As soon as the roar of the shuttle died away, an oppressive quiet engulfed Brock as he stood there, sniffing the cold damp air and gazing seaward. The water was mostly slush in the protected curve of the bay, with ice floes dotting its surface. A school of gremin were sporting out near the first breaker, surfacing with quick blows of spray and darting about with shrill cries. Overhead, a cannox wheeled through the air, plump-white against the metal-grey sky, its webbed feet a brilliant orange.

"Weapons are not permitted beyond this point," said the port official sternly when Brock turned to leave the gated area of the landing pod. He spoke with the soft, rounded vowels of the east, but his voice was implacable; his eyes were flat with discipline.

Brock met that gaze as though it were not staring right through him. "I carry my weapons anywhere," he said with equal flatness.

He did not have to identify himself. There was not a Sedkethran alive who did not know the shame that one of their race was a dire-lord. And it was as a member of the Held that Brock stood here now. The port official was bound by negotiated agreement to defer to any ranking Heldman.

Brock waited a second longer, then his head lifted. "Let me pass."

The port official lowered his head and pressed a button, releasing the gate. As Brock strode through, however, the man whispered, "*Promadi!*"

Brock's step faltered only fractionally at the insult, then he continued as though he had not heard.

He rented an airsled sealed with a clear glastel bubble, the kind commonly used for public transportation by the infirm or by those who were too old to *flick* with accuracy. It chuff-chuffed softly along the deserted streets lined with smoothly stuccoed dwellings or high walls delineating private gardens. No windows faced out onto the streets. Architectural lines were curved, never sharp angles. Colors were soft: the earth tones of beige and gold and pale mauve interspersed here and there with the official grey stone of government buildings rising in short, conical towers. The air was spitting tiny ice pellets now. They rattled off the glastel bubble, and he saw them bouncing upon the pavement. Occasionally the air shimmered in brief waves, and he knew that someone was *flicking* somewhere, meeting a friend, taking care of an errand, performing a duty. Brock frowned, longing to see someone out walking about, although such a thing was rare, especially at this time of the day. He had tried to prepare himself for his return, but just the same he was struck by the bleakness of it all. Even if he saw someone, they would turn aside from the *promadi*. It is *not* a homecoming, he told himself firmly, but still felt drawn with loneliness. He wished he had brought Ellisne, but it was too dangerous for her and the life she carried. *My child*, he thought proudly, lifted by new emotions. *Our child. Our sharing.*

The sled passed a sprawling compound on the outskirts of the town. The rooftops of row after row of utilitarian barracks showed above the wall. The muscles in Brock's stomach tightened, and he increased speed, refusing to stare, yet finding his eyes drawn to it all the same as he wondered if there were any young boys or girls trapped inside those walls who felt hatred, confinement, stiflement. How many talented young minds were the magstrusi crushing today beneath the Disciplines?

The pressure against his mind was constant now, like a persistent headache. He was alone. He carried nothing beyond standard weapons. It would be a simple matter to stop him. But Sedkethrans were a nonviolent race. Such a solution would never occur to them.

The street ended abruptly, and there were no more buildings. Ahead of him were only stubby cliffs riddled with caves, and inhabited by thousands of waterfowl screeching, fighting over nests, and stealing eggs. The face of the cliffs was strewn with nest materials fluttering messily in the lash of the wind. Sleet was collecting on the ground in white pockets. The wind buffeted the sled as he turned it toward the glacier. He was ashamed of purposely delaying a confrontation with the magstrusi. There was so little time. What if the controls of this goda were also dead? Who would he find to reactivate them? He should be turning back to the training compound, not sightseeing. The natural life on this planet, scant as it was, was doomed. He was afraid of the urge to stretch out the few remaining hours; he was afraid of his own compassion. Hatred was safer.

But just the same he kept going straight for the glacier. Minutes later he was upon it, the sled hovering with slow puffs of air that created swirls and eddies in the dry layer of snow dusting the surface of the ice. He craned back his neck, looking straight up at the sky through the bubble as he had looked straight up during those clandestine nights spent out here as a boy. Then, tangled and confused inside by longings and hot feelings of rebellion, he had stared in fascination at the jewelled spray of stars against a velvet sky. And somehow he had sensed that the stars were his destiny. Then, he had not known how they could be. He was only a boy, his back smarting from the sting of his latest whipping, his mind numbed from the endless litanies of memorization, his future already determined; he was destined to be an orderly in one of the numerous clinics. He had been determined too erratic to be a healer. He showed no aptitude for engineering services.

Abruptly his hand slammed down on the controls, and the sled landed. Cutting the engine, he flung himself outside on the ice, bracing against the wind that nearly whipped him double and sent his cloak billowing out around him. The sleet cut his face and made him gasp. Squinting against it, he held up a hand to shield his eyes.

I am back from the stars! he shouted, communing with the glacier as it growled and snapped beneath his feet. The wind shrieked in his ears, numbing his body with cold. He held onto the sled to balance himself. *You were right, ice. My destiny was waiting for me. And now it is time for yours.*

There was nothing more to delay for. With a sigh, he pulled himself back under the shelter of the bubble and started the sled up again. He wanted to go to the Cave of Harmony, but that was impossible. It was accessible only by *flicking*. Frowning, he turned the sled back toward town. For the first time in years he wondered about his parents, but he could not look for them. He did not know what they looked like. He did not know if they were still alive. *For that ignorance, Magstrus Olbin, I hate you.* He suddenly wanted to see the dwelling in which he had been born, but he did not know where that was either. Perhaps he had been born in another town. The memories were too dim, too uncertain, repressed at the time of Change, and not resilient enough now to be brought back. He thought of sprawling, noisy Chaimu households filled with extended families, exotic treasures, loud music, laughing children, and the complex scents of cooking food. Each time a new child arrived from Mabruk, very small, very wide-eyed, very shy, there was a celebration with days of feasting, and telling wild stories, and giving toasts, all the friends of the family invited, sometimes from other worlds, and extravagant gifts showered upon everyone by the proud parents in honor of the child's official naming. How different from stark, perfectly ordered Sedkethran households, where children were still born from their mother's womb but never loved or feasted or showered with gifts.

How do the Imish raise their children? he wondered, then brushed the thought aside. He was coming to the gate of the training compound.

For a moment as he halted the sled and leaned out to speak to the porter, staring at him with a stony face inside the glastel booth, Brock felt a release from the mental pressure. The headache faded. His breath hissed out in relief, only to choke as the pain slammed back with doubled strength. Brock flinched, reeling back slightly, and caught himself with both hands against the pilot's brace. For an instant he knew nothing but that inexorable pressure, crushing him so that he could not see or hear or breathe. He could not withstand it; surely it was too great even for his powers to resist.

Just as suddenly it was gone, that immense strength draining away like an ice puddle evaporating under the weak sun, and Brock sagged against the pilot's brace. Dazedly he managed to lift his head and focus his vision. They must have brought everything they had against him, he thought, and it had not been enough. They couldn't crush him!

His confidence rushed back. A bit unsteadily he straightened himself and looked out at the porter once again.

"I have come to see the elder magstrus," he said.

The porter's flat eyes stared right through him without any variant in expression, and he replied, not to a *promadi,* but to the Held dire-lord, "You are expected."

Brock glanced across the compound, where children were exercising naked in the brutal lash of wind-driven sleet, and saw a long, pillared loggia running along the flank of the building but no doors. Shame at his deficiency caught him in the throat. His hands clenched hard at his sides, and he had to fight himself before he could ask: "How do I enter?"

This time there might have been a flicker of surprise in the flat eyes, but it was no more than a fleeting shadow. Of course, thought Brock with a bitterness he could not control, a dire-lord would know nothing about *flicking*.

The porter replied, pointing, and Brock climbed out of the sled, leaving it at the gate. The instructors ignored him as he strode the length of the compound, his charge armor making him seem bigger than he actually was and his cloak billowing to increase his size yet more. But the children faltered, their eyes growing round with wonder as they stared.

I am their first warrior, he thought, masking his limp beneath an extra swagger. Better than that, I am their first Sedkethran warrior. *Look, little ones, and see what you should be.*

"*Auel!*" bawled the instructor, the gutteral notes of that command sending resurgent memories through Brock. The children jumped obediently to resume their exercises, and his boots crunched on across the ice-coated gravel.

He found the door unlocked and ducked into the shelter of

the building. Glad to be out of the icy bite of the wind at last, he sighed and brushed the granules from his face. He was standing in a small vestibule with plain plaster walls and a tiled floor. A hallway curved ahead of him, and he followed it, his senses alert for whatever might lie in wait.

At least the intolerable pressure on his mind had ceased after that last attack. In its place remained only the light, polite tapping of a request for a mind link. He bared his teeth grimly as he moved quick-footed and silently along the corridor. He had no intention of giving them the slightest access into his mind.

And then he was there, standing in the round chamber of the elder council. It was dimly lit by a skylight in the ceiling. The walls stood shrouded in shadow. As Brock entered, he felt a chill that had nothing to do with temperature levels. *We are enemies*, he thought. *There can be no compromise*.

He walked to the center of the room and stood motionless for a long time. There was no need to announce himself. The magstrusi knew he was here. They would respond when they were ready. But as the waiting lengthened, he turned his head to one side and then to the other with a frown. There was not time for their games. How close was Falmah-Al to success? Had her technicians already unlocked the goda's secrets? Was it already on the move down a relentless path of terror?

As an acolyte, he had entered this place cautiously, drawn by insatiable curiosity to peek at the Writings forbidden to his sight. Now his head came up angrily. In two strides he reached the stone altar in which the Writings lay sealed. His forefinger jabbed the button. With a faint whir, the altar opened to reveal the scrolls in their protective cases. Drawing off his gauntlets, Brock seized a scroll and tipped it out of its case. He read swiftly, his mind automatically unlocking the coded phrases that had once taken so long to decipher. How easy, how simple they were now!

He scanned enough of the first scroll's contents to be sure it did not contain what he sought. Tipping it back into its case, he seized the next and opened it. Still nothing about the entrance to the goda control room. He reached for the third. . .

"Stop!"

A lightning bolt of pure white energy crackled through the air, jolting his wrist so that he dropped the scroll and jerked back his hand. His entire arm tingled fiercely, but he scarcely

189

felt the discomfort through the rage which blazed up through him. By Meir above, he had vowed they would never whip him again!

As he turned, he activated his charge armor, and its protective hum was a familiar sound in his ears as the forcefield encased him in a golden aura of safety.

"Olbin!" he shouted.

But the magstrus did not reply.

Frowning, Brock bent to pick up the scroll he had dropped. Again the whip of energy crackled, this time across his shoulders. His charge armor spat furiously, neutralizing the blow. Baring his teeth, Brock opened the scroll. Another whip lashed out, trying to knock the scroll from his hand. Lifting his arm, Brock deflected the blow and went on reading with rising excitement.

This was it! He stared at the symbols, mentally rearranging them into a map. The entrance was here! Right in this room!

A forked tongue of energy split the delicate parchment, which blackened and curled at the edges. Brock hastily blew out the sparks.

"Fools!" he shouted. "Would you destroy your own precious Writings?"

"Better to destroy them than to let your eyes defile them, *promadi*!"

It was Olbin's voice, disembodied, booming at him from the darkness concealing the vaulted ceiling.

Brock had wondered, during the flight from the cluster ship, what he would say to his old teacher during this confrontation. Now that the moment was at long last here, the words seemed to dry up in his throat. The arguments were unimportant. Revenge, boasting, flaunting his powers . . . what would any of them serve? He had more important things to do here. Laying the scorched scroll aside, he picked up the last one and opened it.

"No!"

This time the whip was accurate and focused. The ancient scroll case shattered in Brock's hand.

"Go!" ordered Olbin. "Leave this chamber, defiler! Leave this world!"

Dusting the shards from his hands, Brock shrugged and put his shoulder to the altar, heaving to move it aside. It was very heavy, and budged only a few inches with a grating of stone upon the tiled floor. But he saw the edge of a door set into the floor and quickly summoned his strength for a second try.

The mental attack came without warning, hammering his mind savagely so that he fell to his knees with a grunt of pain. Beneath the agony of that intense pressure, which seemed to make his entire skull explode, anger turned cold and bitter in his stomach. He would not let their prejudiced stupidity give Falmah-Al the victory!

"*Cuh*!" With a grunt, he hurled their attack back at them, focusing his own mind on Olbin's in an effort to crush it. His atrox hummed in his chest; he felt a surge of power. They could not beat him. He was stronger. He could feel them crumbling beneath the onslaught of his mind. Shouting aloud, he raised his fists in the Chaimu sign of victory, aware of nothing except his own strength, his hatred of them like a fire that would not be quenched, and his nearness to success. Just a little more, and the magstrusi would be finished forever. . .

A healer's pin—long, thin, and precise—plunged into his neck, piercing nerves that stiffened him in agonized, rigid paralysis. Equally abruptly, his mind was pierced by the astonished thought: *My charge armor should have protected me!*

"Fallacy," said Olbin, breaking off his attack as Brock's faded. "You have forgotten your own people's abilities. It is a simple matter to *flick* a solid object through an energy field."

By rolling his eyes, Brock could barely glimpse a robed figure holding him spitted and helpless. Anger at his own false pride choked him. He had been so stupid!

"You have me, Olbin. Get on with it."

"Is death the only pattern your mind has learned? A pathetic lesson, surely. We cannot crush you. That, you have already discovered."

"I shall go down through that trap door," said Brock, "unless you stop me."

"We have stopped you."

"And will you go on holding me here forever like an insect on a pin?" Brock's body beneath his neck was numb. Permanent paralysis? It would be so easy. A slight twist of thumb and forefinger. . . .

"Agreed. We are temporarily at a stalemate," said Olbin. "But not for long. Healer Megsin, take our prisoner to the waiting area. There must be a debate called by the elder council to determine the best manner of trial.''

''No!'' said Brock, well aware that such a trial could run for weeks. There wasn't time. ''Olbin, you must listen to me! The Imish have a goda. The only way we can—''

''Silence! You will not speak further blasphemies!''

''Hear me! Olbin, you—''

The healer jabbed the pin deeper into Brock's neck. There was a sudden flare of white-hot pain, and then he knew nothing at all.

HE AWAKENED LATER sore but clear-headed and was surprised to find himself in a simple cubicle of the type assigned to novice healers during their training. The bare plaster walls were pale mauve and devoid of decoration. There was exactly enough room for the suspensor plates of the bed and a woven-cloth chair between the walls. Brock's armor was gone. He wore only his padded undertunic and trousers. Frowning, for he had expected to be placed in one of the seldom-used detention cells of ungstan carbonix, Brock sat up, curling his legs beneath him as he bobbed gently up and down on the suspensor field. He reached out to switch it off, but before he could do so, the door slid silently open as though the person outside had been waiting for him to stir.

A slight young man, wearing the brown and white surplice of a novice healer, entered with an air of deference Brock did not expect to be given to a *promadi*. Behind him came another healer, an older, stocky man with a silver cast to his dark hair. The cubicle suddenly seemed far too small.

"Please do not attempt to get up," said the healer. His voice was deep and modulated on all tones to be soothing. "I am Silves, senior healer on the staff at Clinic One. This is my best pupil."

Bewildered by the courtesy, Brock found himself inclining his head in a formal gesture of acknowledgment. What trickery were they attempting?

"Your physical condition is a most fascinating one, quite a rarity, in fact, which I would like my pupil to examine.

193

Normally this occurs only in the advanced stages of aging, and even then it is not—"

Brock's eyebrows knotted together in sudden understanding. Silves was referring to his damaged atrox. It was an unspeakable invasion of privacy.

"I am not a specimen for your lecture notes!" he shouted, his vehemence startling both men. "Get out!"

Silves made a conciliating gesture. "But surely you realize that an injury of this magnitude cannot be reversed if it is not attended to in time. To ignore the problem, to refuse treatment is—"

"Until I ask for treatment you can not offer it. Do you think just because I am a *promadi* and a prisoner you are not bound by the honored rule of courtesy?"

"But wait!" said Silves contritely, holding out his hands while the novice seemed to shrink with embarrassment. "Our first law is to heal. You do not drift in your sleep. You are not able to *flick*. You are crippled, perhaps needlessly. The fact that you are to undergo trial does not deny you access to treatment."

The healer's voice rang with sincerity, and Brock was caught by a tide of intense longing to be whole once more. If only something could be done! He tried to detect any hint of Influence in the healer's voice without success. By Sedkethran law any prisoner had access to treatment, just as Silves said, but to be treated meant lowering personal shields, exposing one's innermost self to any probe. He would be vulnerable, too vulnerable.

"No," he said. "You may tell Magstrus Olbin that my mission is more important than my health."

The novice gasped, but Silves pulled up his head as though he were listening to something far away. His eyes, so alight with concern and compassion a moment ago, turned flat and dull. He blinked once and his gaze lowered to Brock's face.

"It is offered, then, as part of a bargain."

"What? A new atrox in exchange for what?"

"Leaving Felca."

"Is that all?"

"Should there be more?"

Brock shook his head, regretfully aware of the moral questions and knowing he must not falter. He must not let personal gain or compassion for a doomed planet sway him from the larger question.

Silves's face creased into lines of shock and fear as though Olbin was finally telling him what Brock had come there to do. "Please," he whispered. "What kind of monster can destroy his own world?"

I cannot answer you! thought Brock desperately, afraid to meet that anguished gaze.

"We have devoted our lives, our culture to peace and health," said Silves. "We have striven to offer the entire galaxy the benefits of our research. Why do you want to put an end to the good we do? What is so twisted, so evil within you that you have lost all compassion—"

"I am not trying to destroy the Sedkethrans. I am trying to save them. Yes, save them from their own stagnation, from their own cowardice. When the Chaimu built the godas—"

"Error!" said the voice of Magstrus Pare, breaking in.

Silves and his pupil exchanged startled glances and hastily departed.

In their place appeared a tall, spare figure and one shorter and withered. Magstrus Olbin and Magstrus Pare, so faded and indistinct as they reached out from the depths of another dimension Brock could barely see them at all. But their voices, indicators of still-powerful wills and intellects, boomed out strongly.

"Error," said Pare again. "The Chaimu built nothing of this magnitude. We—"

He broke off at an angry hiss from Olbin, and Brock grinned.

"Yes, yes, sit there baring your teeth like your bloodthirsty masters all you like," snapped Olbin. "You think you have tricked us into telling you the despicable secrets of Sedkethran pre-history, but you—"

"Not pre-history," interrupted Brock. "Pre-stagnation. Of course. All those legends about the fierce Sedkethran Auxiliary are true. We were a powerful military force, highly advanced, cultured, innovative. And then we built Goda Prime."

"A barbaric piece of conceit. A horrible weapon that should never have been created. Its very existence is a crime. And the Chaimu compounded it by copying out two more godas." Olbin's voice shook. "We shall never finish paying for what we did. Never!"

"And so it was guilt and an overwrought conscience that changed us," said Brock, feeling his way. "The Forbiddens, the severe training, the repressions. We were made to live on this barren planet, to populate it so that its disguise remained complete. We were made to deny emotion, to concentrate on our healing abilities exclusively as self-induced reparation."

"Yes, you impudent abomination!" Pare's image wavered, then grew more distinct. "*Yes!* The council agreed to it. We had to do it! So long ago . . . we were young, full of our own cleverness, conceited, and appalled by what we had finally reached for. Too much, too much! It was the only way."

"It was not the only way," said Brock through his teeth.

"And now you want to undo centuries of careful training and breeding," said Olbin. "Can you not for once put aside your petty concerns and realize that this is for the greater good of Felca?"

"Felca is nothing but Goda Prime!" shouted Brock. "A weapon! It is not a planet. It is not our home! And my petty concerns, as you call them, are the Sedkethran people who have been cruelly oppressed by a foolish mistake and who live in chains! Chains of the mind. Chains of the soul. What right have you to commit this crime, which is far, far worse than the creation of the godas ever was?"

"He must die, Olbin. Don't you see that now?" said Pare furiously. "From the first, from the hour of his birth, I warned you of this, but you held out. You wanted to preserve his abilities. See where they have brought us! He reaches for the greatest Forbidden of all."

"You have always feared me," said Brock slowly when Olbin remained silent. "That's why you treated me so harshly."

"You were punished because you would not obey!"

"No, because you knew I would some day come back and change everything here." Brock turned off the suspensor and stood up, facing them as they wavered and shimmered before him, indistinct ghosts, holding back their inevitable decay by the strength of their own wills. "I serve the Held as my early ancestors did, proudly and with honor. Whether the godas should have ever been created is one matter. The fact that they were kept and not destroyed shows greater culpability. Goda Secondary is in the hands of Falmah-Al of the Imish forces. She intends to use it. She cannot be stopped unless I activate Goda Prime. If there was another way I would have used it."

"But you cannot undo centuries of—"

"Can't I? Warn the people, Olbin. Tell them to take shelter

beneath the surface. The interior of the goda will be shielded sufficiently to protect all of us.''

"No. We are irrevocably committed to peace. We abhor violence in all its forms. You will stand trial, and you will be executed for breaking our highest laws with your blasphemy and treason. And for the corruption of Healer Ellisne, who has not returned with you.''

Brock's head lifted proudly. ''She will bear my child. Even if I cannot free any other Sedkethran from your chains, she is free. And the child will be free. Our race will return to what it was meant to be. And nothing you can do will alter that.''

"You fool!''

Olbin's whip crackled fiercely, slamming Brock back against the wall. Lifting his hands he tried to protect his head and face as the whips snapped out again and again, mercilessly breaking across his body, jerking it back and forth until he fell dizzily, gasping and blind with pain, to his knees.

"There will be no trial!''

"There will be no debate!''

"You will die!''

"You will die!''

The whips drove each word home, flaying him raw, leaving him numb and then shooting fresh hot pain through him. He gritted his teeth, refusing to cry out, refusing to give them the satisfaction of seeing his fear that they might kill him now on the spot. He held on as long as he could, dragging himself up after every blow, but at last the world spun into greyness and he fell thankfully into it.

Consciousness was seeping back slowly when a muffled explosion tilted the entire world and brought him completely awake. Bits of plaster and dust rained down upon him, choking his nostrils. The floor was rough and cold beneath his cheek. He opened his eyes and found he could see out of only one. The other was gummed shut with blood. He lifted his head, but immediately gasped, freezing until the fiery agony slowly faded back to a bearable level. Then he tried again, more cautiously this time, and managed to get his hands beneath his chest. After that it was a matter of gradual levering until at last he sat upright, trembling and holding his breath. There was no movement that did not cause pain. His tunic was in tatters, streaked with blood. He wiped at his face with his sleeve until his eye was cleared, and then, when he thought he could stand without collapsing, he got slowly to his feet. Another explosion, closer this time, threw him flat beneath half the ceiling.

Stunned, he waited until plaster stopped falling, then cautiously crawled out, stumbling and disoriented. Colonids, he thought vaguely, holding onto a wall that seemed suddenly crooked. That was the explosion dispersal pattern of Colonid drop bombs. He must warn the suprin . . . no.

Coughing in the dust, Brock tried to clear the confusion in his brain. Not the suprin. The suprin was dead. He wiped his face with his sleeve, clearing the blood from his eye. This wasn't Impryn; this was Clinic One . . . on . . . on Felca. Colonids *here*? He jerked upright.

The door was locked. He beat his fists upon it in frustration, then ducked with his arms over his head as another bomb rattled the world with a deafening blast. This one was close enough to knock the breath from Brock with its concussion. One of the walls crumbled, the falling chunks bruising him worse than any beating, and the door shrieked as its metal was twisted and pocked by flying debris from the other side. As soon as things stopped falling, Brock squinted through the fog of dust and scrambled through the opening, determined to get out of there before another bomb landed square on top of him. Coughing and weaving, he staggered through the debris-strewn corridor, unsure of where he was or of how to get out. Somewhere in the distance were the cries and moans of people in pain.

Fools! he thought savagely, climbing over a fallen section of ceiling blocking most of the corridor. Overhead, he could see straight through to a cloudy sky. *Did they really think the Colonids would respect their neutrality?*

"Help! Please help!"

The soft cry came from directly ahead. Brock squinted, trying to see through the gloom and dust, and slid, clattering loudly, down the pile of debris to the figure half buried at the bottom of it.

"Silves."

The healer clutched his hand gratefully. "My leg . . . caught."

"Easy. Watch your head while I try to pull some of this away." Brock began tugging at plaster flakes, shifting at the pile until he uncovered a splintered length of roof beam which held Silves pinned. Setting his feet, Brock strained to lift it, and felt fresh fire awaken across his back and shoulders from the whip cuts. "Pull yourself out. Quickly!"

Silves barely managed to drag himself clear before the beam slipped from Brock's hands and crashed down. Gasping for breath, Brock fought off a wave of dizziness and squatted beside Silves. His fingers ran along the injured leg, probing until the healer gasped.

"Broken," said Silves in a thin voice.

Brock lifted an arm to wipe the blood from his face and gingerly explored the depth of the cut on his forehead. No wonder he was so light-headed. Ripping a sleeve off his tunic, he twisted the length of cloth and bound it about his head. Then he touched Silves's shoulder.

"Which way out?" Another explosion, not as close as the last, drowned out his words and he had to repeat the question.

Silves pointed in the direction Brock had been going. "Closest exit. My student was with me when . . ."

Brock glanced at the mound of debris and shook his head. "I'm sorry, Healer. Can you stand? Take my hand. I'll support you."

"Not yet. I must rest. Must collect myself, my Disciplines."

"You can collect them while we're moving. It isn't safe to stay here."

"I don't understand." Silves looked up at him blankly.

Brock loosed an impatient Chaimu curse. "The Colonids are bombing us—"

"No! We have no quarrel with them! We are—"

"Neutral?" asked Brock angrily. "Don't be a fool. They recognize no such distinction. They have come to make you slaves. Now get up and come on!"

"I'm too weak. I'll slow you down."

Brock grabbed his arm and pulled him upright, feeling the healer drift with pain as he came to his feet. Brock put his shoulder under the healer's arm and steadied him.

"Now," he said grimly. "We get out of here."

Outside of the building, Brock propped an ashen-faced Silves against the wall to rest and anxiously scanned the sky for Colonid attack craft. There they were, wheeling over the bay in lazy circles and then screaming in.

"Down!" shouted Brock, grabbing Silves and throwing them both flat.

A series of loud pops like the exaggerated sound of bones breaking paralleled the streets of Clinic One.

Silves lifted his head in surprise. "Not bombs. What—"

"Nust gas cylinders," said Brock. "The bombs come from their ground crawlers. Those will be moving in as soon as the gas takes effect."

"Horrible! We have done nothing to them. Why should they attack us in this barbaric way?"

"Because they are barbarians," said Brock, pulling him up. "Come on. We've got to reach the magstrusi chamber."

They hobbled across a narrow courtyard, Brock's heart pounding madly at being exposed in the open. Someone shouted, and two figures in brown healer's robes came running toward them.

"Healer Silves! You are alive! We thought everyone in that side of the complex had been killed."

Brock broke in before Silves could collect his breath to answer. "Have you a report on the exact extent of damage? Is it a coordinated strike at all clinics and settlements on Felca, or just here? Have the food supplies been destroyed, and is the water contaminated yet? What about planetary communications systems? Are those intact?"

They stared at him in bewilderment. He clenched his fists, longing for a handful of good seasoned warriors under his command.

"Answer him!" commanded Silves with a sharpness that startled them yet further. "Where are your wits?"

"But . . . forgive me, Healer Silves, but he is the *promadi* ordered for execution."

"Nonsense," snapped Silves. "The Colonids have marked us for execution. Brock is the only Held warrior we have to help us save ourselves."

It was Brock's turn to stare at him in surprise. "Is it possible?" he whispered.

"I believe in survival," said Silves. His eyes fell from Brock's, then met them again. "I have always believed in peace, but peace must be upheld on all sides. This—" he pointed as an attack craft screamed overhead, making them all flinch—"is unjustifed. Give your orders, Dire-lord. I will follow them."

"But the magstrusi have forbidden—"

"What?" demanded Brock fiercely, turning on the novices. "Have they forbidden life? Have they forbidden you survival?"

The two youths shrank back. "Of—of course not."

"Then where are they? Where are the magstrusi now when you need their leadership?" Brock snorted. "Stop wasting time. The communications center is the most important. You, stay with Healer Silves. *Flick* him below the planet's surface, where there is safety."

"But we are not allowed in the lower caves—"

"Stop arguing. You, come with me," said Brock. "You can show me how to find communications."

Briefly he set his hand on Silves's shoulder, then he grabbed one of the boys and hustled him on across the courtyard. "*Flick* us there."

The youth goggled at him. "But you are Sedkethran."

"Yes, and my atrox no longer functions," snapped Brock, ready to leave this useless guide and go on his own. "Now, will you—"

A flat crack overhead, and the noxious stench of nust gas sent him leaping at the boy, rolling with him on the ground to avoid the yellow cloud drifting down. "Lethal gas!" he said, clamping a hand over the boy's mouth and holding his own breath. To his intense relief, the boy asked no more questions and *flicked* them out of danger.

They reappeared in a cratered street strewn with bodies and *flicked* again, arriving at the communications center in two more stages. The young healer pushed Brock toward the equipment and sank to the floor, pale with exhaustion. Brock sprang to check power levels. Not yet cut off. Good. He experimented with switches until he found the long-range transmitter and boosted it to maximum range and power.

"People of Felca!" he said, aware that as soon as he started his transmission he would have only seconds before a bomb came his way. Ruthlessly, he put the Influence voice patterns of Magstrus Olbin in his speech: "Your only chance of survival is to *flick* to safety beneath the planet's surface. Repeat. *Flick* to the lower caves."

A building whine warned him. He whirled, seizing the boy. "*Flick* us out of here! Anywhere! Now!"

With the boy's groan in his ears, Brock felt them waver unsteadily in and out, then they were gone, escaping the concussion of a blast by a split-second. They reappeared outside in an alley that reeked with nust gas. The boy sank to his knees, clutching his chest.

"I can't go on!" he cried.

"Run then," said Brock, grabbing his arm and pulling him

into a scrambling run that took advantage of every inch of cover. *Disciplines*, thought Brock, ignoring the ache in his lungs and the trembling exhaustion in his legs. He dragged the boy, who grew slower and slower and finally stopped altogether.

"No farther," he gasped, shaking his head. "No."

Somewhere nearby a woman was screaming. Brock smelled fire, and smoke had begun to fill the sky. It was growing dark, but he knew the attack would not stop until the Colonids decided their victims were ready to crawl eagerly to surrender.

Surrender. Brock snorted at the word. How could the Sedkethrans surrender when they had forgotten how to fight?

He could not stay with the boy. He had to get to the chamber of the magstrusi, where the entrance to the goda control room was.

Brock gave the boy a little shake. "Take care of yourself. Get to safety as soon as you can."

And he ran on, shouting at everyone he saw to *flick* below. Some nodded; others stared at him in bewilderment. He passed a burning inferno that had once been a patient ward and saw workers desperately trying to pull the helpless victims from the flames.

As the bombing stopped, trailer sleds came rumbling overhead to blare out commands in one of the Held dialects, ordering assembly and surrender.

You will not win, Colonid dogs! thought Brock, his breath sawing in his lungs as he pushed himself on. *I will not let you!*

It was dark when he finally staggered into the training compound. All the children were gathered outside in small huddles, silent, herded by their instructors, foolishly waiting in good order for the slaughter.

"What are you doing out here?" Almost too breathless to speak, Brock still managed to roar out the words.

Two instructors faced him, slender rods in their hands, determined in their own naive way to defend their charges. "The magstrusi told us to comply with the Imish demands."

"A thousand damnations upon the magstrusi!" shouted Brock. "Go back in the buildings."

"The buildings are unsafe."

"Then *flick* the children below ground to the caves. The lower caves."

"Forbidden—"

Brock's fist struck the man to the ground. "Do not speak that word again! The Colonids will kill you, all of you, unless you do what I say." He turned on the other instructor, a reed-slender woman with short-cropped hair.

At once she stepped back, holding the long rod before her like a weapon. "You are as bad as those who seek to destroy us."

"Be logical," said Brock, watching her stiffen at the insult. "You have a choice. Stand out here and be slaughtered at the Colonids' convenience, or go below to safety."

"The magstrusi have given us their instructions."

Beside her the other instructor climbed slowly to his feet, holding a hand to his jaw. "They will not harm children—"

"Don't be a fool," snapped Brock, at the end of his patience. "They have bombed the patient wards indiscriminately. They blew Mabruk out of existence without warning. They do not know the meaning of compassion. To them, we are the enemy—"

A trailer sled rumbled directly over them, drowning out his words. A blinding spotlight stabbed down, illuminating the compound in stark white light.

"You see?" said the woman. "The violence is over. We have demonstrated our willingness to—"

"No!" cried Brock, seeing the pivoting motion of slammer guns aiming at them from the sled's undercarriage. "Run! All of you!"

Whirling, he grabbed two of the nearest children and propelled them ahead of him, dodging behind a pillar of the loggia as the slammer guns began spewing death across the compound. The screams pierced Brock. He closed his eyes, shaking with anguish as he clutched the two young bodies close to his, feeling their terror merge with his anger and frustration. Some children came *flicking* into the loggia, sobbing as they dived into the shadows. Others shrieked as they were cut down.

Brock shook himself into action. "Quickly!" he shouted, hearing the sled's engine throttle down as it circled. "We can't stay here. Keep low!" he said as the spotlight swept into the loggia, freezing them like small helpless animals blinded by a hunter's torch. "*Flick* into the building. Go to the magstrusi chamber. Hurry!"

The slammer guns tore into the stucco walls, cutting one young girl into pieces. The others flicked, vanishing into thin air. Except for the two still hanging onto Brock. He looked down at them in startlement and met wide, terror-stricken eyes.

"Go!" he said. "There's no time to be frightened."

The little girl buried her face against his hip and trembled against him. The boy flinched as the slammer guns all but shattered the pillar they were hiding behind.

"She can't *flick*, magstrus!" he said desperately. "She's sick. She isn't strong enough. I can't leave her."

"Get to safety," said Brock. "I'll bring her."

The boy hesitated, torn. "She is my sister," he gasped out, plainly terrified to make such an admission. "We are twins."

It was Forbidden for siblings to retain their bond for each other, but twins always resisted repression. Brock gently touched the boy's head, then crouched, holding both tightly in his arms, as a section of the pillar was blasted away over their heads.

"I'll protect your sister with my life," he said.

The boy's startled eyes flew to his and widened at what they read in Brock's face. Then he nodded and touched his sister's arm. "Hurry, Hannia."

He *flicked*, leaving Brock to scoop Hannia up in his arms and dodge to the next pillar just as the one they had been hiding behind exploded to a mere stub. And it became a twisted, scrambling run of target practice. First one to shoot down the little man gets the gunnery prize, thought Brock grimly. He dived headfirst into the shadowy end of the loggia, and rolled like a ball, holding his body around Hannia. He could go no farther without breaking into the open. Gulping in a breath while the sled lifted and circled, seeking a better angle to reach him, Brock shifted his weight and felt the drainage grate beneath his feet rattle loosely.

At once he leapt off it and dropped Hannia in order to seize the grate with both hands. He ripped it up, feeling a muscle pull in his back as the grate resisted at first. Flinging the grate aside, he got the child by the arm and dragged her down into the hole with him, aware he was being too rough and not having enough time to be more gentle. The slammer guns thudded angrily at the spot where they had just been, chipping stone into the hole in a fierce splatter that cut flesh mercilessly. Hannia screamed, and Brock pushed her ahead of him into the tile drainpipe.

"Crawl," he said. "As fast as you can."

"It's so dark!"

But in spite of that whimper, she was accustomed to following training instructions, and she began to scuttle along the pipe on her hands and knees. For Brock it was a close fit. Flat on his stomach, with his shoulders painfully compressed, he struggled to slither along behind her, hoping the pipe did not narrow up ahead. If he got stuck, it would be a long horrible death of starvation. That is, providing the Colonids didn't decide to pump nust gas down the pipe instead.

LT. IZAK WAS FIDGETING nervously as he took his place on the transender platform, but Nls Ton paid him no heed. The governor gazed a minute longer at the awesome sight of the goda filling the spaceport viewscreen. A smile crossed his face that he did not trouble to conceal. Why shouldn't he show his pleasure? This was the day of his greatest triumph. Falmah-Al had brought him a goda, the prize of all prizes, an operational, deadly, invincible goda. With this to his credit, he was certain to be recalled immediately to Kentra for rewards and promotion, perhaps even to the wearing of the medallion of Im!

Rubbing his hands together briskly, he bounced up onto the platform beside Izak and gave the transcender operator a nod. Seconds later, he was standing open-mouthed in the gloomy control room buried deep beneath the surface of the goda. The design was unobtrusive, functional, and alien. The walls curved where he did not expect them to. The lighting was too dim for comfort. The air was chilly and smelled stale.

He did not care. He did not mind any of it. Forgetting that until today he had been furious with Falmah-Al for having allowed the dire-lord to escape, he smiled at the colonel and her deputy as they approached and saluted him smartly. They wore dress uniforms, crisp and polished right down to their gunbelts. Returning the salute with sloppy indifference, Ton gazed straight into Falmah-Al's intense eyes. They were glowing like black obsidian that had been fired, and he found himself caught by old memories. She had been beautiful in her youth, her body as muscular and sinewed as a boy's, yet wholly female, her need to please greater than her ambitions. Yes, he remembered his Kezi, his delightful *houri* of the night. And now, after all these years of argument and enmity when she had plotted against him and stood in his service like a poisoned thorn of distrust, she had brought him the ultimate gift. With the goda in his possession, he had supreme power. He decided to overlook her spying upon his personal affairs, her incredible blunders, and her unauthorized attack upon the planet Felca.

"Kezi, my dear," he said, dispensing with formality. "Fairest huntress, raw meat to your table a hundred times over!"

That peculiar light flamed more brightly in her eyes at the compliment, but she merely inclined her head and signalled to her deputy.

"Would the governor be pleased to have a tour?" asked Lt. Tirza.

"The governor would," responded Lt. Izak.

The crew of technicians were largely non-military, looking rumpled and ill-at-ease. Ton's few questions were answered with a degree of vagueness that brought his brows sharply together.

"What is wrong with these people? Don't they know what they are doing?"

"Not entirely," said Falmah-Al as the two deputies stepped back to let them speak in private. "We have basic operations figured out. The rest is less certain."

Ton lost his breath. "Dangerous!"

"Why?" Falmah-Al eyed him coolly. "There is enough power here for anyone. Why worry about the rest?"

"Indeed." Relaxing, Ton laughed. "I am most pleased. You realize what this means for my career?"

Her glance sideways was sharp. "Let us discuss your career in my quarters."

Her voice was soft, almost pleasing. Ton drew himself up and expansively decided to reward her in a personal way.

Leaving the deputies behind, they exited the control room and walked through a rough-hewn passageway into a series of small chambers carved from the rock. This area was well-heated and comfortable in a spartan way. Ton lifted his brows as he glanced around, noticing the lack of personal possessions beyond a pack lying casually in the corner. The bunk looked hard and narrow; he found himself wishing for his luxurious suite in Impryn.

"Well, Kezi," he said huskily, touching her thin cheek. The skin was stretched tautly over her bones, making her face all angles. He preferred a plumper profile, but what did it matter? It was a small enough exchange for what she had given him. Besides, he could see the hunger in her dark eyes, smouldering from beneath lowered lids as she pressed her cheek against his hand and stepped closer.

"It's been a long time, Nls," she whispered. "You left me to follow your dreams when we could have shared them equally."

"Don't stir up old arguments." He buried his face in her hair, inhaling its faint scent of herbs. His hands slid across her shoulders and down her back. "Thank you, Kezi. I knew that no matter how far apart we might grow, you would always help me advance—"

The knife plunged deep into his abdomen like a shaft of ice. Stunned, for a moment he could not breathe; he could not comprehend what had happened. Then he gazed down into her flaming eyes and saw the full malevolence of her hatred.

"Help you!" she spat, patches of scarlet burning on her cheekbones. "Why should I? You've used me and despised me and discarded me as you pleased, and now it's my turn."

"But—" The coldness in his belly spread out in a sudden ripple of weakness. He sank to his knees, his eyes staring at the blood seeping between his fingers, at the blood blazing crimson across the blade of the knife in her fist. "But you brought me here to give me the goda—"

"I give you nothing! I brought you here, Ton, to show you what you will never have! Ultimate, supreme power. It's mine! I am going to take this goda to Kentra, and I am going to wear the medallion of Im. Not you! I am going to rule this entire galaxy. And you, Ton the Butcher, are going to die."

"No—"

"Yes, die. Unmourned, unloved, and despised." Lifting her foot, she gave him a shove so that he toppled over.

Something seemed to part inside him, and the last thing he heard was her laughter, harsh and mocking, above him.

Falmah-Al bent down and wiped her knife blade clean upon his sleeve. His sightless eyes stared at her boot toe.

"You fool," she said, and without a backward glance returned to the control room.

Tirza was waiting alertly and as soon as Falmah-Al appeared, the deputy pulled her disruptor on Lt. Izak.

"Governor Ton is dead," said Falmah-Al, and before shock could do more than flash across Izak's face, she added, "You can join my army or die with him. Make your choice!"

His narrow eyes shifted from face to face. Then he stiffened to attention and said, "I choose to join your army, Colonel."

Her lip curled with contempt. She had never trusted this worm, and he had just proven her suspicions correct. "Traitor!" she said. "There is only one army, that of Im! Kill him, Tirza."

"*No*—"

There was a brief burst from the disruptor and then silence. The unpleasant stench of burned flesh curled through the air. Lt. Tirza stepped back, holstering her disruptor. She signalled two of the guards standing on duty. "Clear it from the bridge," she said.

"Colonel!"

Falmah-Al glanced toward the technician monitoring the scanners.

"Relay coming in now from Baz long-range sensors, linking to ours. A fleet of Held ships is approaching the system."

The thrill of the hunt sprang through Falmah-Al. She stepped to the man's post. "How many?"

"Undetermined as yet. Distance is too great." He hunched over his instruments, concentrating. "But the size of the blip indicates a substantial number."

"Their last attempt at retaliation," she murmured. "Fools! Wait until they see what we have to shove down their throats."

Tirza frowned. "But, Colonel. I thought we were returning directly to Kentra—"

"With this opportunity to crush the Held once and for all right in our laps?" Falmah-Al laughed. "We'll wipe Heldfleet from existence as though it never was!"

Chief technician Egel turned pale. "Colonel," he said, rising to his feet. "Surely you do not intend to actually fire the weapons."

"But of course," she retorted coldly, displeased by his cowardice. "One does not enter a battle unless one intends to win it."

"But when they see us, they'll surrender," said Egel. "Surely they will surrender."

"I don't care whether they do or not. I intend to test this weapon. And it might as well be on a moving target."

"But the entropy reaction. We aren't sure just what will occur—"

Falmah-Al's eyes narrowed dangerously. Her hand moved to the weapon at her side.

"Return to your post!" barked Tirza, and Egel sank down in his chair like a heap of limp clothing.

A tense silence hung over the control room. Falmah-Al's gaze swept the frozen faces.

"Helm," she said tersely. "Plot an intercept course."

And in silence she was obeyed.

Holding hands, Brock and little Hannia stumbled into the round chamber of the magstrusi. To his relief it was still intact and had not been bombed. To his surprise it was filled, not just with children but also with instructors and healers.

"Hannia!"

"Dunen!" She released Brock's hand and ran forward to the embrace of her brother. "Dunen, I was so scared."

He hugged her tightly, his young eyes lifting past her thin shoulder to thank Brock. "Hush. You're safe now."

"No," said Brock, coughing. His throat was raw from the smoke and gas he'd inhaled. As soon as he caught his breath, he said, "We're not safe until we are below ground in the lower caves."

"But surely we need not penetrate so far—" began someone, only to falter under Brock's weary look of impatience.

"It is the magstrusi who should decide," said another. "Let us call the elder council."

"There isn't time." Brock shoved his way through their ranks to the altar. It still set askew, half-revealing the trap door. "Hannia and I are only minutes ahead of pursuit."

There were fearful stirrings. In the corner, a female healer was rocking a child in her arms. The child stared fixedly at nothing; its body was rigid with shock. Others were whimpering as healers tried to tend their wounds. There was no sound worse than that of children in pain, thought Brock.

"We must go below," he said, his voice as sharp as the whip of a magstrus. "Now. There is no time to argue."

"But—"

"There is nowhere else to go."

"He is right," said an old instructor who had trained Brock

years ago. "They have come to slaughter us. They intend us no mercy. Let us follow the dire-lord."

"Wait!" commanded a stern voice from above them.

With a sinking heart, Brock tilted up his head to stare at the dim outline of Magstrus Olbin.

"Do you so quickly forsake the Writings?" demanded the magstrus to the silent crowd. "Do you so quickly turn aside from the way of peace and serene order?"

"How does the way of peace help us now?" demanded Brock sharply. "We have no weapons. No defense against the butchers outside."

"If we obey their instructions, they will not harm us. My children, do not let this *promadi* carry you away into his own evil. Return to—"

"Where?" broke in Brock furiously. "Return outside? Is that what you are telling these children to do?"

"Yes."

Seething, Brock seized a blood-stained child and held him up. "You would rather see the entire destruction of our race than admit that we were the original inventors of the goda weapons. That we were the greatest warriors in the galaxy. That we were admired and valued by the Chaimu as allies."

Someone gasped, but he was beyond caution. Twice before he had stood forth and asked for followers and both times he had been rejected. If the Sedkethrans chose now to obey the magstrusi and die, he might as well let himself be slaughtered with them. There would be nothing left to strive for.

"You speak blasphemies!" shouted Olbin. "You shall die for it, *promadi*—"

"No!" shouted a healer, a plump matronly woman with grey streaked through her hair. She reached up and took the injured child from Brock's arms.

"What is this?" demanded Olbin, his form shimmering to greater distinction. "Do you join in this disobedience, Healer Sarilai? Do you wish to be proclaimed *promadise*?"

"If it is disobedience to reject your order to die without reason other than the pleasure of Imish barbarians, then we disobey," she said calmly. Only Brock saw her hand tremble at her side. "If it is disobedience to follow Dire-lord Brock and live, then I choose to disobey. Call me what you wish, teacher. I have eyes, and I have intellect. I see that an exile has risked death to return here to save us, and I honor that."

"He is falsehood! He is danger!"

"No," she said, and her words fell like stones in the pool of silence around her. "Perhaps he is truth, and you are not. Perhaps you are the deception."

"Blasphemer!" A whip crackled out from the air, making several children cry out in fear, but although Brock quickly stepped in front of Sarilai, the whip did not strike.

"I also follow the dire-lord!" shouted an instructor.

"And I!"

"And I!"

Like a tide, they surged forward to stand with Brock, their faces hot with anger as they faced the shimmering forms of the elder council.

"Fools!" said Magstrus Pare, his voice so faint it could barely be heard. "How will you survive without us?"

"As we did before you," said Brock.

And the magstrusi faded away.

"Hurry," said Brock, not bothering to hide his relief. Swiftly he marked off the children into small groups, assigning a group to each adult who had the responsibility of *flicking* the children down. It was a long distance; the children could not *flick* that far on their own. One and two at a time they began vanishing, quiet now and calmer, standing patiently for their turn. Brock kept everyone going as adults *flicked* back and forth, making sure they went in relays so that there was a moment of rest for each one.

Renar, the old instructor, stood beside Brock. The skin was stretched tightly over his skull; his body was whip thin, dried up like ancient leather and equally tough. "We should be in better training," he muttered. "We are not equal to this task."

Brock was listening for the footsteps that he knew must come at any minute. "Hurry," he said to a young woman who paused with a hand to her eyes. "You must keep trying. Hurry."

There were only a few children left now. Hannia and her brother had been among the first ones taken. Brock glanced at Renar, who had treated him no more harshly or kindly than anyone else during his days in the barracks.

"You had better go down, old man. It is a long distance."

"Where you intend to go, yes."

Brock glanced at him sharply.

"Of course I can guess what you have in mind," said Renar with an unreadable smile. His old eyes were dim and

212

hooded. "The magstrusi told us as soon as you arrived. How far you reach. But then we often had to repress the desire for leadership within you."

"I do only what I must," said Brock. His keen hearing, amplified by mental scanning, caught the approaching cadence of booted feet ringing out upon stone. His heart leapt. "They're coming! Quickly!"

There were only two children left. They were scooped away. Brock turned to Renar. "Now what is to be done? There is no one to help you—"

Renar laughed softly and grasped Brock's arm. "You were always impetuous. It was another fault we could not repress in you. Who is to take *you* if I do not? Come."

And they *flicked* just as a round of disruptor fire spat across the room.

The grey mist of non-dimension seemed to wind in an eternal spiral, down and down without end. Brock closed his eyes in the sweet coolness, his grasp on Renar firm, sharing in the old man's strength and giving of his own. And then, as though it had taken no longer than the space of a heartbeat, there was that tiny jolt as they passed back through the thin dimensional membrane. They were in the caves.

Brock stared in wonder, astounded not so much by the size of the cavern as by the city which had been constructed inside it. The architecture was Sedkethran, rounded and graceful, but there was more whimsey in the small spires and fluted columns adorning the buildings. He sniffed the air and despite a faintly metallic smell of dust, he detected nothing stale about it. He looked overhead at the vault of stone but could not find the source of the soft, clear light illuminating the cavern. Brock blinked. *We did this*, he thought. *My people. My ancestors. My blood. Nothing the Chaimu have ever achieved surpasses this*. A strong rush of pride caught him in the throat.

And the city was not empty. People *flicked* here and there, examining it, pausing in the barren avenues, peering into windows that actually faced out onto the streets. Brock's eyes widened as he tried to count how many people stood quietly at the edge of the city. A thousand? Two thousand? More? One by one their heads were turning toward Brock as he and Renar stepped forward. Soon they were all staring.

"Dire-lord!" It was Silves who came pushing his way through the crowd. His leg was already repaired. He limped only slightly. His greeting was warm as he paused before Brock. "I am pleased to see you safe and with us at last. The city is most intriguing, isn't it? Have you been here before?"

Brock shook his head, his eyes straying past Silves's shoulder to stare at the spires again. "They came," he whispered, his voice still choked. "How many people came?"

"We estimate five thousand from Clinic One. There has been contact from others. It seems your worldwide message got through. Approximately fifty thousand altogether are now beneath the planet's surface."

"Fifty thousand . . . . out of forty million."

"The Imish have killed twice that many." Silves looked grim for a moment, then he touched Brock's arm. "Come. You look as though you could use some attention to those hurts."

Exhaustion swept over Brock. Wearily he forced it back yet again. How long had he been pulling on his innermost reserves? It seemed an eternity since he had stepped off the wedge. But if he sat back and rested now, and Falmah-Al unleashed her goda. . . .

"Some food, yes," he said, pulling away. "The rest must wait. Will you *flick* me lower? To the control room?"

Silves frowned, distaste and horror reappearing in his grey eyes. "You remain committed to that course?"

"Yes." Brock met his gaze firmly. "It is not enough to pull ourselves inside this sphere, never to venture out again. That is a form of cowardice equal to what we have been living all these centuries on the surface."

"But surely you understand!" said Silves. "Surely you see our position. As the race of complete nonviolence, how can we tell the rest of civilization that we are the inventors of the goda weapon? Does such an admission not undo all that we have accomplished?"

"We accomplish nothing until we openly admit who and what we are, to ourselves as well as to others," said Brock. "We must take responsibility for this. Even if it means we must use it."

"But—"

"If we created the godas, can we stand back and let the Colonids have one? You have seen today what they will do with ordinary weapons—"

"Yes, I have seen." Silves frowned, clenching his fists.

"Very well. I shall not argue further. You know what is best to do, Dire-lord."

"Will you *flick* me to the control room?" asked Brock.

Silves glanced away. "Will you tell these others what you intend to do?"

"No. It will take time for them to adjust to a new way of life, to new—or should I say old—concepts. Some will never adjust. We do not have time for councils and discussions. A democracy, Silves, does not run a war efficiently."

Silves frowned for a long moment, then slowly nodded. He held out his hand. "I shall *flick* you lower."

THE JOLT INTO reality was abrupt. Total blackness engulfed them. Crowded next to Brock, Silves drew in an unsteady breath. ''I can go no farther. Ungstan carbonix!''

Brock sniffed the air. It was very thin, very cold. The mass of earth above them was crushing. The pressure of trying to breathe and move at such a tremendous depth felt like a wall. He stood motionless in the darkness, trying to take his bearings from the eddy of air around their faces to the rocks enclosing them. Soft, almost silent little currents. He extended a hand in one direction and touched nothing. Rotating to his right, he reached out again. His fingers brushed stone, dry and sharp cut. Rotating again, he touched nothing. Again, and he jerked his hand back from the slightly porous surface of living metal.

''What is it?'' demanded Silves, moving closer so that their shoulders touched. Brock could hear his breathing quicken. ''What did you touch?''

''The door. Wait.'' Frowning, Brock drew upon the suprin's instructions as he had before in the depths of Amul. Beside him Silves ceased to breathe at all, and in the resulting absolute silence, Brock spoke the sequence code.

The door slid open slowly, smoothly, and as it opened a dim glow of light gradually brightened, giving their eyes a chance to adjust with it. Air as cold and sterile as that above on the glaciers curled into Brock's nostrils. He stepped into the control room, his eyes widening with wonder as he glanced about. Soft whirs and purposeful clicks could be heard on

every side as instrumentation panels awoke to life and began
pulsing beneath dust covers that slid automatically into recesses in the control banks. The rough-hewn walls of stone
which had surrounded the control room of Goda Secondary
were concealed here behind gleaming panels of polished metal
and acoustical absorption material. Soft carpet deadened
their footfalls. Anatomically styled chairs fitted with complicated life support and communication linkages waited at each
station. In the center rose a cylindrical booth of clear glastel.
It contained a backless seat, 180 degrees' worth of instrumentation, and a headset suspended from the top. Nothing seemed
old. Nothing seemed disfunctional. It was as though there had
never been a standby of five centuries.

An emotion he could not describe swelled through Brock.
"Goda Prime," he whispered reverently.

Across the room, Silves turned his head. "What did you
say?"

It broke the spell. Brock abruptly turned away from the
cylinder. "I'm going to contact the esmir. That is, if I can
find communications."

"This?" asked Silves, pointing. "No, this perhaps?"

"Yes." His head cocked to one side, Brock examined it
critically, matching what he saw to the overlays of the suprin's
memories and the Colonid pilot Molaud's knowledge.

"It is all incomprehensible," Silves said. "I know so
much about caring for the sick, and nothing about machines.
How incredible to think we once had such technology and so
completely turned away from it. Can this thing truly destroy
the galaxy?"

"Yes."

Silves rubbed a hand across his face. "What does any
individual, any race need with so much power?"

Brock began flicking toggles, tentatively then with increasing confidence as a frequency band lit and boosted the standard hailing signal to overshoot the Colonid forces currently
decimating the surface of Felca.

He met the healer's troubled frown. "To live, a person
needs food, shelter, and the means of obtaining both. You
might as well ask why were we given minds and abilities? I
know only that repression is wrong. If you are presented with
the problem of an unusual disease, Silves, and you invent a
new way of curing it which unfortunately no one else believes

217

will work, do you throw the idea and the method away? Or do you try it?"

Silves's eyes flickered. "It would be very difficult not to at least test the theory."

"Of course. An idea, once thought of, exists and becomes part of the collective consciousness. Once born, it is not easily removed—"

"Basic wisdom corollary," said Silves nodding. "I see your application. But—"

"Extend it. Is it logical to throw away a workable theory simply because it does not presently fit into what we wish to use? How does one throw it away? It exists, and someone somewhere will find it and use it. If we have a talent or a special ability, are we not responsible for using it? Is it not wrong to never utilize it?"

Silves drew back. "You border on Forbiddens."

Brock nodded with an ironical twist to his mouth, and the healer winced as he realized what he had said.

"You see how illogical this is?" pressed Brock. "Why have an ability if it was not intended to be used?"

"What if it was intended to test our ability not to use it?"

A sharp beep distracted Brock from the discussion. He whirled back to the communications panel. Warrior training told him to use coded Battlespeak, and he opened with the most recent Heldfleet code he knew, uncomfortably aware that the Colonids had probably cracked it weeks ago.

"Goda Prime to Cluster 807. Come in please."

"This is Cluster 807," came the response cautiously after a ten-second distance lag. "Repeat identification."

"Dire-lord Brock commanding Goda Prime. This transmission is for Esmir Eondal only. Repeat. Private transmission."

"Stand by."

Brock waited, consciously forcing himself not to fidget with impatience.

"Do you follow the orders of this esmir?" asked Silves in bewilderment.

"No. But I need information before I pull us from orbit. There is—"

"Dire-lord!"

It was Eondal's gruff voice, crackling across space with an urgency that alerted Brock.

"I am here, Esmir. Operation successful. Goda Prime is in my hands."

"We intercepted Colonid messages indicating an attack on Felca."

"Correct. But there are survivors—"

"How many?"

"We estimate fifty thousand."

Even over the ten-second lag, Brock heard a small gasp behind the esmir's voice. His heart leapt.

"Ellisne?"

"Yes? Brock? Oh, Brock! Are you well?"

"Yes, beloved. We are coming."

"I heard." Her voice held all the tones of relief, anxiety, and pride. "Thank you for saving so many. I know it cannot have been anything but difficult. I wish I could be at your side. You—"

"Dire-lord!" Eondal's voice broke in harshly. "How fast can that goda move?"

Bewildered by the sudden change of subject, Brock frowned. "I'm not sure. Why? Have you reports that Falmah-Al has managed to move Goda Secondary?"

"Reports? Meir above, man! My scanners just picked up the accursed thing on long range. Beyond Darjahl Imperial and approaching quickly. We'll—"

"Change course, Esmir!" said Brock in alarm. "You can't face her with Heldfleet."

"I can't hide Heldfleet either. If we've picked her up, she's bound to have spotted us."

Brock frowned, coldness spreading through him. *Ellisne!* he thought in anguish. "Evade. Run. Do whatever you must, Esmir, but don't stand off in direct battle. Don't destroy yourselves just for the glory of the Held."

"Don't worry," said the esmir drily. "We'll do our best to wait for you. But hurry! We haven't much—"

An angry burr of interference cut across his sentence. Certain Colonid scanners had picked up the transmissions, Brock cut communications and cursed aloud.

"Surely they can surrender if they must," began Silves, but Brock stopped him with a scornful laugh. Inside he felt sick. What if he couldn't get there in time? And he had left Ellisne with Eondal to keep her safe. Great Meir!

"You don't know Falmah-Al, Healer," he said. "She'll blast Heldfleet to dust before they can even ask for terms."

"Can you operate the goda alone?"

Brock followed the healer's glance about at the station

chairs. "Perhaps, but it is doubtful." His eyes strayed to the cylinder. Unease caught in his throat. "That is central station. Where I must be." As he spoke, he tapped the goda band on his wrist. "I will need your help, Silves. And that of your brightest, most flexible staff. Novices or full healers, it doesn't matter. And if you know any engineers—"

"Yes," said Silves, nodding. "I shall call them now."

He turned away, lifting a hand to his temple, and Brock reluctantly stepped up to the cylinder and stuck his head inside. He had seen similar devices before, especially on ancient Chaimu craft. The pilot linked directly with the ship, his mind amplified through the headset to enable it to merge with operational computers. But it required years of training and a certain mental pattern. Otherwise linkage could blow a man's mind apart.

"What is this?" asked Silves, coming up behind him.

Startled, Brock withdrew his head and turned. Eight people stood in the control room, staring about in astonishment mingling with curiosity.

"What is it?" asked Silves, brushing past Brock to poke in his head. "It looks like a symbiotic access point similar to those we use in our psychotherapeutic unit." He drew in his breath with a hiss, sounding almost Chaimu. "If you're going to use *that*, then you must have your atrox repaired. Without it, you won't be able to amplify sufficiently, and you won't be able to drift in order to minimize the stress factors. The drain will be tremendous."

Brock swallowed. He'd been afraid of that. "How long will it take to repair my atrox? If it can be repaired at all?"

Silves frowned, suddenly looking remote and professional. "If you will permit . . ."

He pressed his palm against Brock's chest, where the ripped tunic was stiff with dried blood and black from dirt and smoke. "Severe damage." He made it an accusation. "Extended neglect. However, some natural healing is indicated. Yes, it can be repaired."

Brock sighed, an unconscious weight suddenly dropping away. "I thought it was beyond hope. How long?"

"Multiple applications would be the best approach. However, the quickest treatment would require several hours and there would have to be at least a day or two before anything more strenuous than drifting was attempted."

Brock was already shaking his head before the healer finished. "No. There isn't time. We must leave orbit now."

Silves frowned. "But you haven't a chance without—"

"That doesn't matter," said Brock grimly, pulling away. "It must be done. Let's get started."

"But, wait!" Silves blocked his path. "At least during the journey there permit me to begin applications."

"I must be conscious at all times," said Brock. "I can't depend—"

"We are in this together now," said Silves sternly. "You must trust us, as we are being called upon to trust you. Let me try."

"All right." Brock nodded. "At the first opportunity. Believe me, Silves, I am not anxious to step into that booth unless I have a chance of coming out again."

"Can we leave orbit without you being in there?"

Brock frowned. "No. But direct linkage won't—shouldn't be necessary." Not giving himself time for more doubts, he swung into the booth and fitted himself in the seat.

"Healer Silves, what do we do?" asked one of the novices diffidently.

Both Brock and Silves looked at her. "Take a seat, each of you," said Brock. "I'm sure the computers are programmed for the contingency of an inexperienced crew. Accept those communications linkages and follow any instructions you are given."

"You make it sound so simple, Dire-lord," said Silves drily, and Brock grinned.

He waited until they were all in place, then, holding his breath, he laid his left forearm in the groove across the top of the instrumentation and fitted the goda band into its notch. A smooth shudder ran through the control room. Complicated patterns of light flashed over indicators, and tactical boards opened. A viewscreen activated, bringing in an enormous panorama of space and the next tiny planet of the Praxos system. Brock gasped at the magnification power. There was a rumble, felt rather than heard, and the neighboring planet suddenly jumped at them. Someone in the control room cried out. Brock thought of the atmosphere shearing away and wondered how much of the planetary surface was being torn off. A vision of dying Sedkethrans shook him like a dark spear into the mind. Guilt overwhelmed him, making him clench his free fist. Indeed his hands were bloody.

221

"Brock!" called Silves, breaking through his wrenching thoughts. "What coordinates?"

Hastily Brock pulled his wits together. He would think about dying Colonids instead. At least he had the satisfaction of knowing the entire force sent to destroy Felca was now destroyed itself. Giving Silves the coordinates, he added, "Maximum speed, Silves."

"Yes. You were right, Dire-lord. I have only to tell the computers what we want."

Brock nodded. So easy. They were on their way. He hoped they would be in time.

"Dire-lord."

The soft voice woke Brock. He straightened immediately, annoyed at himself for dozing off.

"Goda Secondary is on our screen."

Brock stared up at the vast viewscreen, his eyes darting from the appalling carnage of burning and disabled hulks hanging crookedly in space to the dim outline of Darjahl Imperial lying beyond. "Heldfleet," he whispered. "*No . . .*"

A wedge swooped by, its once sleek sides scored black from the battering it had taken. Brock took hope. One survivor. How many others?

Silves was shaking his head regretfully. They all sat slumped in their chairs, diminished in Sedkethran horror at senseless violence. Brock's gaze narrowed. He had lost them. Temporarily or permanently, he was not sure. Closing his eyes, he sought that inner tie to Ellisne that told him she was still miraculously alive.

"*Cuh perser mon,*" he said grimly to himself. It was the prayer all Held warriors spoke before going into the arena. And as he said it, the screen turned and he saw Goda Secondary looming at him.

It was a daunting sight. Lumpy and mishapen, with vast parts of its disguising surface sheared away down to the metal structure, it hung out there like a taunt.

"Brock—"

Ignoring Silves, Brock reached up and pulled down the headset to fit it over his temples. He flinched at the pain of initial contact, then steeled himself against the discomfort, forcing himself to make the adjustment, to separate his mind rigidly into compartments capable of assimilating the rapid-fire chatter of computer lines. Silves had given him two brief applications. He felt stronger than he had for a long time, but he could not help but wonder as he settled himself deeper in the seat how long his atrox could hold out against the demands he would shortly be making upon it.

He opened an outside line to the other goda. Falmah-Al answered at once, as though she had been expecting his call.

"At last, Dire-lord!" she said, her voice ringing out harshly. "You have interrupted my sport, but no matter. I shall finish with Heldfleet later."

"No, there will be no later for you, Colonel," said Brock, tensing himself. The interior of the booth was hot and stuffy. He could barely breathe. "Your bloodbath is over."

"And you destroyed the force I sent against Felca." Her dark eyes, mad and lusting for vengeance, blazed at him from the viewscreen. "Millen was my best fighter. I did not think you had the stomach for such a move, Dire-lord, but you will pay for the lives of my men."

"The fact that I am a Sedkethran has frequently made opponents underestimate me. Now, Colonel, let us call an end to this. We each have a goda. Will we destroy each other? Or will we recognize a new balance of power and make agreement—"

"I knew you would cry for peace!" she shouted. "You poor pale fool, why should I strike a bargain with you? At last I have my chance to rule the Collective, to rule even the galaxy if I so choose. You try to bluff. I am amazed that you dared bring your goda from its orbit. How many millions did you kill? Are their souls crying upon your conscience, ghost? You'll never fire on me. Two godas locked in battle? When we finished there would be nothing left. You know that. You are powerless."

Brock's mouth set itself. His mind was already leaping, firing orders at the computers, bringing up low-register weaponry equivalent to the howsers a conventional heavy battlecruiser carried.

TARGET MATCHED, responded the gunnery computer.

Fire! ordered Brock, and felt the backlash as two precise pinbeams stabbed at Goda Secondary.

"Dire-lord, *no!*" shouted Silves, twisting around in his seat.

Falmah-Al's face abruptly faded from the screen in a burst of static, to be replaced by a long view of her goda. Ignoring Silves, who was now pounding on the glastel of the booth and still shouting at him to disconnect himself, Brock watched through narrowed eyes as chunks of the goda surface split off, boiling dust and rubble into space.

COMMUNICATIONS DESTROYED, reported internal computers.

Raise shields, ordered Brock. *Maneuver. Z minus forty-thousand myls. Gunnery. Realign target sights.*

Silves was still beating on the booth with both fists and trying vainly to open it. But Brock knew the booth would remain sealed as long as he was connected to the headset. His gaze flickered briefly to the healer, and his concentration wavered for a fraction. Pain shot through his temples. He winced, then drove it away, regaining complete concentration.

SECONDARY RETURNING FIRE, said the computers.

"Crew," said Brock into the mike. "Brace for impact." He did not even see Silves turn and run back to his chair. Brock's attention was focused totally upon his own job. He swiveled on his seat, his hands flying over controls in response to instructions coming in over the headset. The entire control room rocked, shuddering with enough force to slam Brock's abdomen against the edge of his instrument board. He lost his breath for a moment and wheezed desperately, then was jerked backwards in the recoil. Pain jabbed through his skull as he again failed to maintain concentration. The computer linkages seemed to be searing trails through his mind, and he fought to catch up, still winded. His atrox, trying from automatic reflex to drift and *flick* in sequence in order to maintain perfect linkup, began to throb as it had not done since he first injured it.

There came a second, harder shudder as Falmah-Al fired again. She was ignoring low-registry weapons. He wondered if her technician Egel even knew how to access them.

Boost shields, he told the computers, and the control room lights dimmed as power supplies were swiftly rearranged. What was happening to the Sedkethrans who had taken refuge in the cave? But Brock had scant time to wonder about them as he upgraded weapon power.

RECOMMEND MAXIMUM FORCE, said gunnery computer.

Denied! He ordered more maneuvers, still seeking the correct angle to split open Goda Secondary. There must be a seam axis. If he could hit it precisely with the low-registers, there would be no need to engage the dreaded—

WARNING! WARNING! NEGATIVE ENERGY ENGAGED. ABORT SHIELDS. ABORT SHIELDS.

A claxon blared insistently over the control room, and Silves and the others were exchanging frightened, bewildered glances.

They were all dead, thought Brock. The entire galaxy was finished. His free hand clenched. Damn Falmah-Al! She was insane! Didn't she know what she was doing?

ABORT SHIELDS! ABORT! ABORT! ABORT!

Brought back to what he was supposed to be doing, Brock gave the command, momentarily bewildered by such insistence on dropping their shields, then suddenly understanding. The computers were flashing information back and forth so rapidly now he could not keep up. He heard himself scream in agony, and his body arched in a reflex he could not overcome. Goda Prime turned slowly on her axis, swinging up closer to her sister.

Closer, he commanded, fighting his body to keep it still. There was no escape. There could be no escape. Already space was tearing, the delicate balances of matter and energy failing as the blast from Goda Secondary spread out, diffusing quickly, rippling out wider and wider like the concentric circles of water disturbed by a pebble. *Closer!* ordered Brock, desperate to stop as much of that diffusion as he could. Goda Secondary loomed larger and larger on the viewscreen. They were on a collision course.

"Brock!" screamed Silves. "What are you doing? Brock! Remove the goda band! It's your only chance to stop this! Brock, we're going to crash! *Brock—*"

But Brock was too busy coordinating the pulsing out of controlled bursts of negative energy, blotting as much of Falmah-Al's spread as possible.

CONTAINMENT. MAXIMUM FORCE RECOMMENDED, said the computers.

This time Brock listened. The control room shook visibly as rumbling vibrations betrayed the stress of such tight proxmity between the two godas. She had tried maximum force once, determined to destroy everything just to defeat him. She would try it again.

Target, he said. *Maximum containment.*

Goda Prime. Not just the first goda built, but also the strongest. The goda provided with a failsafe mechanism to contain the ultimate mistake. The trick lay in timing. He must buffer negative energy with negative, matching them equally without the slightest degree of error, in order to recreate positive energy in the blast. He hovered intently, alert to the slightest pulse in his monitors, ignoring screaming nerve endings and the roaring in his ears. His heart was thundering in distress beneath an atrox that was raw agony. He paid none of it any heed. His mind was completely chambered now from the rest of his body, focused down upon those monitors, ready to interpret and act as soon as Goda Secondary struck again.

Would Falmah-Al recognize that she was defeated? Would she acknowledge stalemate? Would she turn away from insanity?

Secondary fired, pouring out everything she possessed in her power banks. It was massive, fast, consuming. Even as he ordered the match, Brock felt the lag in his reaction time. The computers made the match, but it was too late. Secondary's blast was ahead of Prime's, outracing it, unraveling time, unraveling space, unraveling existence. Everything was falling out of sync, vibrating madly, fading.

Boost! he screamed to his computers. *Maximum gain*!

Compensation suddenly leaped with a surge in what remained in Prime's own power banks. He stayed with the monitors, his own brain shredding inside his skull until he was only dimly aware of the ripple slowing, slowing, stopping, reversing, speeding.

Stop! he ordered, desperately hanging on. *Contain*!

And the ripple of overcompensation from his own goda died back, stabilizing as the two godas moved slowly apart, widening the stability of the area, pulling the tearing fabric of existence carefully back into place. With containment established, there was one last thing to do.

ABSORPTION RECOMMENDED, said the computers.

Brock was not sure how many times that recommendation was repeated before his mind grasped it. His body had ceased to exist. He was suspended entirely between two points of reference: the goda band on his wrist and the headset. Hang on. He must hang on.

Absorption commence, he said, and there was immediately an alteration in the steady roar filling the control room. Goda Prime began to gently sap the power banks of Secondary, compensating containment as needed until at last, at long, long last, Goda Secondary hung less than twelve hundred kilomyls away as an emptied body. The explosion came fifteen seconds later, spinning Goda Prime back like a gigantic ball held safely behind its restored shields.

STANDING DOWN FROM BATTLE SEQUENCE, droned the computer, kicking on automatic.

The clamp holding the goda band firmly in its niche released, and the agony searing through Brock's skull abruptly ceased. The silence replacing the linkage was almost as bad. Brock slowly moved clear of the headset. His eyes were wide and unfocused. He felt drained and cold . . . he had never been this cold before. The door of the glastel booth slid automatically open, letting fresh air inside. He could not draw it into his lungs.

"Brock! You did it! I don't know how, but you did it!" Silves was shouting, crowding at the booth with the others.

Brock frowned, trying to comprehend the words, but they were only sounds blaring at him. He pulled his arm from the niche, and it fell limply to his side. Then he was moving forward, effortlessly, without his own volition, and it was not until he toppled out of the booth into cold endless darkness that he thought, *I have carried out my suprin's orders. I am now free to die.*

He awoke slowly to the splash of sunshine upon his face. There was the luscious, heavy scent of maryh blooms upon the air blowing in through an open window. Outside, he could hear the burbling splash of a fountain and voices, male and female, chattering in low murmurs of sound. Beside him, Ellisne was humming a melody in soft counterpoint to the droning of an insect blundering in and out through the window. Opening his eyes, Brock turned his head slightly to watch her. She was always nearby when he awoke, her womanly form swelling with the life growing inside her, her hands busy with the intricate stitchery she was working. *Beloved.*

Her eyes lifted from her work to meet his gaze, and at once became luminous with her love. "Good morning, beloved. How was your rest?"

For answer he started to rise off the suspensor bed, but with a quick, graceful gesture she stopped him.

"Wait. Silves is eager to examine you—"

"Again?" Brock loosed a mock groan and lifted a hand to

227

rub the sleep from his eyes. "He told me yesterday I was well. Why can't these healers make up their minds?"

She laughed, bending over him to give him a quick caress at his throat. "Because caring for the Held's next suprin makes them nervous. And Eondal insisted they be here."

"Wait." He grasped her hand, holding her when she would have gone out. "It's the great day at last, Ellisne. You are not sharing your thoughts. Why? Do you still have doubts?"

Her eyes clouded slightly. "There will always be doubts, beloved. We have spoken of this before. I cannot erase my training as completely as you have done."

"Ellisne—"

"There are so many changes, Brock! Too many, coming upon us too quickly. It is a life I do not understand. The responsibilities. The rituals. The power. I cannot keep up. Perhaps I shame you."

"Never." He watched her eyes, seeking what was really troubling her. "You knew my ambitions from the moment of our first contact. And you are adapting beautifully."

She turned her face away. "I think of our child. What will his life be like?"

"His path will be harder than mine," said Brock, thinking eagerly of the approaching birth. "He will have to prove so much. Are you frightened for him, Ellisne?"

"For all of us." Her eyes, grave and dark, turned to Brock's. "I watched the battle there beside the esmir. The exploding ships, the howser fire, the violence of it seemed as nothing compared to the *hate* burning in every heart. It was everywhere, all around me, this lust to kill. I—" She shuddered.

So this was what was troubling her. Or at least part of it. Brock sighed. "Now you have seen war. Not just through my memories, but for yourself."

"How can you endure it?" she asked. "How do you deal with the guilt afterwards?"

"The only way is to fight according to your honor and your conscience and when it is over, to try and forget—"

"Forget?" she said sharply. "Is it right, to push such things away?"

"What is the point of this, Ellisne?" he demanded. The peace of the morning had faded. He was suddenly afraid of her remoteness. Had he lost her? Why had she brooded upon these questions? Why had she waited so long to ask them?

Why had she hidden her doubts from him? He had thought his world secured at last. Now it seemed to be crumbling again.

"Have you changed your mind about us? Only a remnant of our race has survived. Can't you forgive me for what I have done? Can't you understand?"

His anguish came through his voice. Ellisne turned around as though she had been struck and rushed to his arms.

"No, Brock! Oh, no, no! You misunderstand. I have said it all wrong. I am so foolish. No, beloved, I blame you for nothing. I saw it all. Don't you see? I saw that evil colonel deliberately choose destruction. She unleashed forces no one should command. I saw the end of existence itself. And you stopped it. I am no scientist. I do not understand how you did it or how such a terrible process could be reversed, but you did not let it succeed. You were right all the time, even when none of the rest of us could see the true threat. And, Brock, even if we had never shared, even if I had not *known* you, I would have recognized all that you are in that moment when you risked destroying yourself to stop her. Oh, Brock . . ." Her voice faltered as he embraced her tightly and she clung to him as though she would never let him go. "You were so hurt, so nearly gone even Silves despaired for a time of bringing you back."

"But I am well now," said Brock, touching the nerve points along her throat in a gentle caress. "I had the very best healers in the galaxy. And now the Held has a chance again."

He was reassured. She was just suffering a nervous reaction to all that had happened. She had been so strong, so cheerful during his convalescence. It was natural that she must break down sometime.

"You still don't see, do you?" Abruptly she pulled away and stood twisting long strands of her hair in her hands. "You have forgotten all about the multiple time streams and that future vision I saw with you."

He rose to his feet with a frown. "Ellisne! That isn't going to happen. You aren't going to—"

"Won't I?" she asked, her face haunted. "Won't I? Your Fet assassins will not be standing between us to protect you."

"Ellisne, no—"

"But it's just as we saw that night in Impryn! Every day I have watched the prepartions, and my fear has been a spreading sickness. The rituals, the ceremonies, your decision about the scar, even the color of my gown. It's all the same. That leaves only the knife for my sleeve and a command secretly planted by the magstrusi. Oh, Brock, I am so frightened—''

"Hush, beloved. Hush. You aren't going to kill me. Don't . . ." He caught her close, holding her when she would have broken away. "The time streams foretell nothing except possibilities. And the possibility you fear isn't going to happen. You stepped away from that future long ago when we first shared on the stolen scoutship.''

"Are you sure?" Her voice was muffled into his shoulder. He could feel her heartbeat thudding with his. "Are you really sure?"

"Yes." He tilted up her chin, forcing her to meet his gaze. "Completely sure. I will continue to make enemies throughout my life. But you, beloved, will never be among them. You told me once to listen to the deeper instincts. What do yours tell you now?''

"That . . . that I could never harm you, not for any reason!" she cried, the despair in her eyes clearing away. "Brock, I have been so foolish, so worried.''

"Well, do not worry any more. And, Ellisne," he said firmly. "I know it will take a long time to erase your training. Any time you are troubled, talk to me about it, and I will help you. Don't brood and worry by yourself. That is the way of error.''

A smile lit her face. She sighed as he rested his cheek upon the top of her head, inhaling her warm fragrance.

"While I have you, Brock, I am safe," she murmured.

"Good. Let's *flick* away and—''

"Brock!" she said with a jerk of dismay. "The healers! The esmir! I forgot all about them. They have been waiting for hours—''

"Let them wait longer. I'd rather you examined me.''

"This is no time for mischief," she said sternly, but a glow suffused her face with delicate color. "If you put them off, they may change their minds about making you suprin.''

"Ah." Brock obediently dropped his arms.

She left the room, taking some of its brightness with her, and a moment later Silves and one of his novices entered with formal gestures of greeting. Behind them Brock saw one of the scarlet-cloaked Fet assassins standing in the doorway. Brock's smile faded, and a little shiver of anticipation ran through him.

"The day is yours," said Silves, using a traditional courtesy, but he smiled warmly as he spoke.

Brock sighed as he sat down, bobbing gently on the suspensors. "Another examination? You promised yesterday was the last one."

"Yes, and that was before I knew the extent of today's investiture ceremonies. If you permit?"

Brock nodded and closed his eyes while Silves's cool, skilled hands merged with his flesh. There was a strong flow of strength into Brock, and then Silves stepped back with a slight bow. His eyes smiled approval down at Brock. But beyond a healer's satisfaction with a recovered patient lay something more; they had become close friends in these past days.

"I rejoice in your achievement," he said quietly, filling Brock with a surge of pride.

Brock rose to his feet. "Thank you, my friend."

"Enough dawdling in there, Healer!" barked a gruff, familiar voice. Esmir Eondal came striding in with two richly garbed honorables at his heels, executed an impatient sketch of a bow to Brock that consisted primarily of lifting his palm to his chin and then flicking it across his nose ridges. "It is time for the robing. Have you eaten?"

"No." Brock exchanged a private smile with Silves. The old esmir seemed the most nervous of any of them.

"Good. We'll get started then. With your leave, Healer?"

"Oh. Of course." Hastily Silves and his novice departed, squeezing past the Fet assassin standing guard.

I'll have to choose a dire-lord of my own soon, thought Brock in startlement.

"No time for Sedkethran daydreaming," said Eondal, hissing impatiently. He grunted, and servants began filing in with the imperial garments folded on their arms. The honorables took these one by one from the servants, handing them to the esmir, who in turn handed them to Brock to put on.

There were undergarments of the finest Drakian flaxlin, so pure it was still stiff. Over these went loose trousers and a tunic of imperial green. He stamped on soft boots of Gwilwan leather, trying not to think of the imperial privilege which permitted him to wear the skins of the royal mad ones. He was the first non-Chaimu suprin in the history of the Held, but the Chaimu traditions still remained and would likely cling for a long time. The goda band fitted beneath the narrow cuff of his tunic. His right wrist was encircled by a heavy gold bracelet studded with rare purple gwirleyes. Their beauty was breathtaking; they masked powerful anti-assassination devices. Brock bowed his head while the esmir fastened the broad collar of striated gold, platinum, and corybdium plates linked together in multi-colored patterns across his chest and shoulders. The weight was unexpectedly heavy. He straightened to accept a belt around his waist. The ceremonial dagger lost to Tregher had been replaced by another blade of bard crystal that sang on a different, possibly purer note when swung through the air. And over all of this went a floor-length surcoat of brilliant purple, stiff with metallic thread intricately embroidered.

As Eondal's gnarled old hands smoothed the surcoat over Brock's shoulders, his impatience fell away and the slightly fierce expression in his red eyes softened. He stepped back and this time bowed fully and most respectfully to Brock.

It was time. Brock stood a moment, communing with himself, Disciplining away undue pride and vanity. It would not be easy to keep the shaken Held together, much less resurrect it to its former glory. There was much to be done. He would have no leisure to recline on a throne and bask in his power. *Suprins before me*, he thought humbly, *keep me wise*.

Then, head held high, he left the room and, flanked by his contingent of Fet assassins in their masks and scarlet cloaks, he walked down the simple staircase outside the plain quarters where he had been staying with Ellisne on the esmir's country estate. The fountained courtyard had been cleared. Heat from the blazing sun struck him like a blow. He breathed deeply of the flower-perfumed air as he strode across the courtyard and into the more ostentatious buildings of the villa proper. Ahead in the distance he could hear the fanfare of horns heralding his approach. There was the buzzing murmur of the crowd which stilled abruptly as the warriors standing guard at the double doors snapped to attention with a resounding clash of their pikes.

Eyes slightly dazzled from the brilliant sunshine outside, Brock entered the cool interior of the vaulted ancestorial hall of Eondal's family. The hush over the packed room was profound as he walked through the bowing honorables and other ranking members of the Held. Ahead, beyond the central dais where the brazier and its heating brands waited, stood Ellisne, dazzling in a small pool of sunlight shining in from a window overhead. She wore a long straight gown of white embroidered with gold, and she was transparent in that pellucid light, her eyes glowing like the flames he must soon face.

The Fets around Brock peeled away smartly to stand at attention at the base of the dais. Upon it stood the chief assassin, just as years ago he had stood waiting for Brock's appointment as dire-lord. That blue swirled scar which Brock had worn proudly for so long was still a mark of servitude. As suprin, he could not bear such a mark. Silves had argued long and hard for the honor of removing it, but Brock had refused.

"It will be struck through with a single stroke," he said. "A strike against servitude, to remind the people of the Held how close they came to slavery under the Colonids."

And Eondal's red eyes had glowed as he considered the idea, finally inclining his massive old head in approval.

The esmir emerged from the crowd as Brock took his place on the dais, standing uncomfortably close to the hot brazier. A slight tremor passed through him, but he held it down. He had been brave before. He would be brave again. There were far greater responsibilities to face in the future.

Resplendent in full-dress uniform, the esmir began a series of low-pitched grunts. It was the signal for the proceedings to commence. Priests of Meir chanted softly in the background, unseen but clearly heard. Incense rose into the air.

"Today we raise a new dynasty," said Eondal gruffly, his powerful old voice booming out over the litany. "Today we serve a new suprin, one who comes to rule us not from the right of blood but from the right of combat. By the oldest laws of the Held it is an honorable progression. Does any question it?"

The silence remained unbroken. Brock saw a slight ripple of tension loosen in the esmir's erect shoulders.

"Then we so proclaim Suprin Brock."

Stepping to one side, he nodded at the chief assassin. Brock faced the masked Fet, steeling himself beneath the sternest of Disciplines. From the other side of the room he felt Ellisne's mindtouch offering strength. As before, there must not be the slightest flinch to blur the mark. The chief assassin lifted a hissing brand, its tip glowing white hot. Brock closed his eyes as it came steadily closer. He could smell the heated metal. His nostrils quivered slightly, then he stilled even that slight movement.

The moment of pain was sharp, blinding, and over.

"Suprin," said the blurred voice of the chief assassin, artfully muffled behind the mask to defy identification.

Brock opened his eyes, easing out his breath. The pain was already fading. It had not been as bad as the original scar.

He smiled one-sidedly and grasped the slim golden sceptre handed to him by a priest. His other hand reached out to Ellisne, who came shyly to stand beside him as the brazier was cleared quickly off the dais.

"Bon . . . *chuh*!" snapped an officer of the honor guard, and the warriors crashed out a salute.

"Long reign to Brock!"

Outside, a battery of dispersal cannon fired round after round, and Brock lifted his fist high into the air, his eyes glowing with the dream he had carried for so long. The goda band flashed green and smooth upon his wrist.

"The Held forever!" he shouted.

And the cheering swelled into a mighty roar of victory.